The Man Who Guarded the Bomb

Arab American Writing

Other titles in Arab American Writing

The Man Who Guarded the Bomb

Stories

Gregory Orfalea

Syracuse University Press

For a listing of books published and distributed by Syracuse University Press,
visit our Web site at SyracuseUniversityPress.syr.edu.

ISBN: 978-0-8156-0977-3

Library of Congress Cataloging-in-Publication Data
Orfalea, Gregory, 1949–
The man who guarded the bomb : stories / Gregory Orfalea. — 1st ed.
p. cm. — (Arab American writing)
ISBN 978-0-8156-0977-3 (cloth : alk. paper)
1. Arab Americans—Fiction. I. Title.
PS3565.R427M36 2010
813'.54—dc22   2010003226

Manufactured in the United States of America

For my brother Mark

who created a place where stories (and great food) thrive

and for Matthew, Andrew, and Luke

who required a story a night "with your mouth" (not rushed or glib, but with wonder, lest the teller risk them staying awake), and who, when told their father was leaving his job, had the perfect sense to say, "But I thought he was a writer."

Born and raised in Los Angeles, **Gregory Orfalea** took degrees from Georgetown University and the University of Alaska. He directed the Writing Program at Pitzer College of the Claremont Colleges, and currently teaches Middle Eastern and Eurasian émigré literature at Georgetown University.

Orfalea's 2009 memoir, *Angeleno Days,* treats his growing-up years in Southern California. The author of two acclaimed histories, *The Arab Americans: A History* and *Messengers of the Lost Battalion,* Orfalea has also published two books of poetry and completed two novels. His work has been widely anthologized. Currently researching a book about the founding of California by Junipero Serra, he divides his time between Washington, D.C., and Los Angeles. His wife and he have three sons.

Has the rain a father?
—Job 39:38

Contents

Acknowledgments

The author wishes to thank the editors of the following journals and anthologies in which earlier versions of these stories first appeared: *Triquarterly* ("The Chandelier"); *2Plus2* ("The Life of a Nail"); *The Guadalupe Review* ("Fabiola"); *Mizna* ("Brother of Figs" and "Vivi in Hell"). "A Perfect Stranger" is to appear in *Folio*.

"The Chandelier" has also appeared in *Fiction of the Eighties: A Decade of Stories from "Triquarterly"* (Triquarterly Books, 1990); *Multicultural Voices*, edited by Rita Dove (Scott Foresman, 1994); *Imagining America: Stories of the Promised Land* (Persea Books, 2002); and *Viewfinder*, edited by Dr. Christine Gottstein-Strobl (Lengenscheidt [Germany], 2009). "Victory Boulevard" appears in *Arab and Latino-American Literature*, edited by Nathalie Handal (forthcoming).

The Man Who Guarded the Bomb

A Portrait of the Artist
in Disneyland's Shadow

To fall in love at twelve—or sixty—is a dangerous thing. Anything in between should not be taken too seriously.

But to fall in love in a place transformed to a dream-on-earth may be asking for it. Add to this, the girl I picked out of the school yard happened to be going with my best friend. She was stuck on him, but in a windfall that made me ready to hang myself on a meat hook in prayerful thanks, he went nuts for the blind girl on my block, who was crazy about me. Well. More reasons than one to pick up the stylus and etch "SOS" on rock that some future archaeologist might identify as the impulse to write.

Before I introduce the young lady at the hub of this ruckus, and the gang that surrounded the terrible ardor, let me part the dust. Or orange branches, which no longer exist because of the Magic Kingdom.

Anaheim for me does not mean Disneyland, though I watched with wonder the Matterhorn rise, foam boulder by foam boulder, above the orange groves. It does not mean Knott's Berry Farm, though my nostrils quickened at the smell of boysenberries more than gunpowder. There were no Angels then, but there were lower-case angels called friends who disappeared as sure as youth, without a hint of departure. It was not a place to visit or vacation or order your imagination like a coloring book. Anaheim was not generic anything, but specific, as childhood is a collection of specifics that make up the indelible life. It was my home, my hot hermitage, the place I first knew I was going to write until I dropped because the world was too beautiful and sad. The world was leaving or changing almost as soon as you welcomed it. I knew early on if I didn't write or imagine, something—or everything—would die. Not the least Deborah Nodnok.

How was I to know that I would become Disneyland's rival on earth and in heaven? At least the heaven of the Matterhorn.

To me, Anaheim means black widows in new garages, carpets of snails feasting on tender grass, everyone young, even the old people, and great storehouses of sunlight drawn from even into the night, so that night was only an afterthought of day. I hardly remember the night in Anaheim. Was I always awake? Anaheim in our housing tract of Lincoln Park was a childhood in an era when the nation was still a child. Call it a child whose knees are being skinned with a hospital over the horizon. But child still, brash and open, sparkling in eye, spry of knee, clothed by sun and home where even concrete seemed soft.

No one in Anaheim in that early season hired landscapers to tell them how to configure their small plots of earth. Each household did it itself, as if given by the developer a little canvas to experiment with and draw green. Artists of the land, growers of children and walkways, veterans of a world war where each day was a terrible invention. My father drove our blue-and-white '59 Ford wagon to and from the nursery for peat or plants or pink scalloped concrete, and we could see from the Santa Ana Freeway the only mountain in Orange County slowly erect itself over the land.

"The Matterhorn, Dad!" I whispered loudly.

"We'll beat it. You watch. We'll have our yard in place before they top that thing with snow." Dad barked at me to get more Bandini and upend the manure out of the wheelbarrow onto tender dichondra he had just seeded. Then he turned it all together with the eight-pronged rake. How I loved that stink! From it all would grow.

One late-August day that summer the Alps came to Orange County, I was out front watering the boxwood hedges, inhaling the earth under the odorless, button-leafed dichondra when I noticed a chubby girl with chalk-white skin standing still on our sidewalk. Her ear was cocked.

"Are you a boy?"

"Excuse me?"

"Are you a boy? You seem to water like a boy."

"Well, how does a boy water?"

"Boys water loud."

My spigot was directed at short range, and I suddenly realized I was squirting the peat moss off the soil.

"And how do men water?"

"Men water far and soft, like the beginning of Beethoven's Sixth."

The girl pulled on the straps of a yellow halter attached to short pants. Her thighs oozed out of the stretched fabric. She did not seem Californian, though her hair was blonde, dull blonde in a tight bun. There was not a hint of sun on her skin. She was silent a while, her gray eyes moving, aimed at the sky, the sidewalk, then me, briefly, before the street.

"Look," she said. "I'm blind. I've run away."

"From where?"

"Across the street. That's my house."

I'd noticed a man dumping his stink of manure onto bare ground and a tall, large woman with big eyes and mouth wearing a turban directing where he should dump it. I'd noticed a blonde kid younger than I with a butch haircut. But I'd never seen this girl before.

"My name is Jimmie Lou."

She stuck out her hand as if she were to shake our front yard. I dropped the hose, walked over to her, and took this hand. It was sweaty. Her breath smelled of creamed corn.

"How long are you running away for?"

"Oh, I don't know. As long as I can. Does a half hour sound too long?"

"No. That sounds okay."

"You don't mind if I sit on the sidewalk and listen to you water?"

"No harm, I guess."

"I don't suppose you have a chair nearby."

"In the garage . . ."

"No, no, please forget what I said. I like the sidewalk. Keep working. By the way, how old are you?"

"Twelve."

"You speak older. But you water young. I'm fourteen. That means I'm more mature. Does that bother you?"

A Portrait of the Artist in Disneyland's Shadow   ＊   3

I shrugged my shoulders.

"Pardon me. I couldn't see that."

"Sorry. Somebody has to be fourteen, I guess. Somebody has to be twelve, too."

"I find you rather on the philosophic side. That's very nice. What is your name?"

"Frank. Frank Matter."

"Matter? You do!" She gave a little cluck. I didn't respond, just flicked my nozzle.

"I like to use the word 'rather,'" she said. "The English do that. I think the English are really the best writers, don't you? I've been reading Louisa May Alcott. Isn't she English? I sure hope so, because I love the way she uses the word 'rather.' And 'daresay.' And 'truly.' It just adds more life."

I was puzzled. "How do you read?"

"Braille. I read by my fingers."

I heard somewhere about this Braille, but I had never seen it.

"How does it work?"

Jimmie Lou described the embossed dots on a sheet of paper that gave her her rich world of words, but before she could finish, a yell from across the street fluttered the young jacarandas: "JIMMIE LOU! WHAT ARE YOU DOING?"

"Coming, Mother! That's another thing I like about Louisa May Alcott, Frank. There's a certain, how do you say it, *balance* about the English that one has to admire. Don't you feel so? And isn't it excellent the way they use 'one'? 'One' instead of 'I.' Don't you think there is something more cir-cumsubstantial in being one than being I?" She stood up, dusting off her white hams and backside. "I prefer 'Francis' over 'Frank.' Francis, thank you. This has been a most enjoyable running away."

Her mother met her halfway across the street.

"Jimmie Lou, REALLY. You know you're not supposed to cross the street alone."

"Oh, Mother, no worry. I've made a new friend."

"Jimmie Lou, you're going to get run over."

The mother seized her daughter, who smiled in her disorientation, a smile I felt was meant for me.

"My word, Jimmie Lou, that boy is . . . a boy! What are you doing?"

"Oh, Mother, Francis is rather smart beyond his years."

"I don't care if he's Albert Einstein. You could get run over." She gave me a cross look after alighting in their driveway. I raised my nozzle.

Next door to Jimmie Lou were the Jacobses, an older, mild couple, Jewish immigrants from England, who had had a late-in-life small son named Dick. I promptly nicknamed him "Jo-cabs." Dickie Jo-cabs was a frenetic runt who had a New York accent, making me wonder in the logic of childhood if he were adopted.

My other friend was Tommie Blaw, who lived on my side of Nutmeg Street, three homes to the south—that is, inching toward Disneyland, the magnetic pole of our compass. His family had come to Orange County a year before mine, one of the first on Nutmeg, from Terre Haute, Indiana. Like the Jacobses, they were older; one got the feeling that, in addition to the young couples, Lincoln Park drew families that had gone bust in midlife or were trying, in quiet, sunny desperation, to start anew. The Blaws were an odd twosome. Mr. Blaw drank. He sat in the gloom of the small living room, the shades drawn, sipping his beer, bathed in the blue light of his blonde television. (Televisions in those days were blonde, brunette, or redhead—today they are only black or gray.) Mr. Blaw did not appear to work. Yet he seemed a product of work, or ground up by it. I think now he must have worked the blast furnaces of Terre Haute and perhaps was on disability and took to the suds. Mrs. Blaw had nonstop smiles and movement, as if her husband's scowls were a fuel.

"Look." Dickie Jo-cabs was showing us how to mutilate baseball cards by laying them down on the street and slamming on our bicycle brakes right over them. When he shredded my hero, Sandy Koufax, over the manhole cover ("Serves him right for leaving Brooklyn"), I was so angry I put Gil McDougall, Whitey Ford, and Mickey Mantle in a row and destroyed them. Jo-cabs was livid; he charged my bike, knocked me off, and we proceeded to blacken each other's eyes.

At the beginning of seventh grade, Dickie Jacobs leading the way, we quietly stopped our bikes in the narrow cement corridor in back of some doctors' offices. No kickstands, Dickie signaled. We leaned the bikes against the cinder-block wall and ducked below a window. Slowly,

Tommie, Dickie, and I surfaced our eyes like periscopes into the office of Dr. Ira Fleishenheimer, who, with his blonde nurse, was peering into the mouth of an old man whose shock of white hair was cocked backward. Blood flecked on a white handlebar mustache. He was crying. The siphoning hose hummed.

"Oh, Zigrit, zis is not good," said the dentist. "Too much blut. Precious blut. It is time for za zecond Novocain. Za first has been uzeless."

Before long we were treated to the sight of Nurse Sigrit climbing into the lap of the patient who cried out softly as she administered the second Novocain, half naked. Dr. Fleishenheimer, who kept yelling from deeper in the office, "Zo! Zo!", spied us and rushed out, screaming, "You! You perverts!"

The next day we mutilated a record number of baseball cards; even managers Walter Alston and Casey Stengel got it. Thus began my throbbing sense of what Dickie Jo-cabs called "the ba-doing-doing" and how it was related to girls. No one in my family had told me the facts of life, though I vaguely recalled my father speaking of planting the seed. It was lost in the dichondra and snails. But soon stirring in my skinny, little brown body in untold ways was the body and soul of a girl.

I'm not even sure I knew I had a soul before Deborah, forget the body. I was told that I had a soul, and that sin could blacken it. My image of a soul was a white sheet wrapping my heart like butcher paper. On this sheet would be splattered each week the indelible ink of disobediences, unkindnesses, and seeing Nurse Sigrit screw the guy in the dental chair with her gelatinous body. I had been to confession to the priest at our Anaheim parish, Father Masterson, an average of once a month and could hear him sighing at my offenses. (Nitwit confessions clearly wore him out, though at the time I thought myself the lowest of the low.) Father Masterson came alive when I mentioned the charms of second Novocain.

"You did what?" he breathed through the purple weave of the screen. His shadow sat up.

"I . . . committed adultery. Once."

"How old are you, young man?"

"I am twelve."

"Are you sure you know what you are saying?"

"Yes I am, Father. I did something bad."

"Can you . . . describe how you committed adultery?"

"Well, I, I, she took her clothes off."

"She? She did?"

"Yes, Father. And took the *menanee* and . . . oh, Father, I can't speak."

"That's all right. Get your breath, boy. Let's get this picture a little clearer. You say some woman took your what?"

"*Menanee.*"

"Is that what you use to go whizzle?"

"Yes."

"So, she took your whizzle and . . ."

"No, no, Father, not *my* whizzle."

"Well, whose whizzle are we talking about?"

"The man in the chair."

"You committed adultery with a woman who was in a chair with another man."

"Yes, Father, that is exactly what I did."

"Well, my son," I could hear the good father chuckling to himself, "you live a very illustrious life."

I touched my forehead. It was hot.

"Before I give you your penance, let me ask you one other thing."

"Certainly, Father."

"It is no sin for your mother and father to exercise their marriage vows."

"Say again, Father?"

"Do you know that it is not *wrong* the way you came into this world?"

"That's good to know, Father."

"And that that man and woman you saw being very excited in that chair . . ."

"That's true, Father, they were very excited."

"Were the same pair who brought you into this world?"

"You mean—"

"That's what I mean. Your mother and father were engaging in conjugal love. There's nothing wrong with conjugal love. It is a gift from the Almighty."

"But my mother and father weren't—"

"Now say your penance. Your only sin is against modesty, my friend. It isn't adultery, or mortal sin. It is a venial sin at most."

"I see, Father."

"Make sure you say one rosary of the Joyful Mysteries and think of all the joyful things God has given us on this earth."

"Like the second Novocain?"

"What was that?"

"Oh, nothing, Father. It's too hard to explain."

"Joyful Mysteries now."

"Yes, Father."

"Say your Act of Contrition."

It was during my penance for having broken the Sixth Commandment, as I knelt at the altar of St. Boniface Church mumbling the first Joyful Mystery about Mary being visited by an angel who tells her that she is about to give birth to God, that I beheld Deborah Nodnok up close for the first time. She was bathed in the blue light coming through the stained-glass window of the Virgin at the Cross. It was the new girl in my seventh-grade class whom my best friend at St. Boniface, Pug Wilson, had pointed out. She existed somewhere in the hinterlands of the girls' class, but here kneeling near the confessional I had just exited, she was alone.

Deborah had thick black hair that arched up from her scalp and fell on her shoulders. Her skin was white as Sierra snow, and her lips full, as if they'd been stung by a bee or about to say something, but couldn't. As this fitted perfectly with my own disposition, I imagined we were in silent conversation every time I saw her. I was enamored. Her eyes were glacier blue, an interior blue that thousands of years of ice make, now coaxed out by a California sun coming through the blue of Mary's robe. She implored God, it seemed. Then bent a dark fountain of hair to her clasped hands.

It amazed me that this beauty could have sinned. What could possibly be torturing her? Suddenly, she looked up and saw me holding my Joyful Mysteries. Hot iron dropped in my gullet. My cheeks bumped with blood. I could not *not* look at her. She smiled briefly, looked beyond me at the red light gone off at the confessional, meaning someone was about to come out. It was Pug Wilson. He blushed like a salmon, holding the door for Deborah, before heading toward my pew.

"What are you in for?" he whispered, kneeling too close.

"You mean my sin?"

"No. Your penance."

"A rosary of the Joyful Mysteries."

"That beats me. I have to do two rosaries of the Sorrowful Mysteries." He pulled out his wooden rosary and propped up a nervous smile.

There was now no question but that Pug Wilson was leading a more interesting life than I. And it wasn't long before he confessed to me the source of his sin.

"She gave me her tongue."

"Come again?"

"She, she stuck her tongue in my mouth, and I stuck my tongue in her mouth, and boy, was it good."

"Who are you talking about?"

"Her." He nodded across the school yard, lifting his milk carton. He had opened the wrong side of the carton, completely mangling it. Milk dribbled down his chin.

"You mean Deborah Nodnok?"

"Oh, yes, that's exactly it. But don't tell anyone! Please, Frank! It's hard enough staring at myself in the mirror. Because you know what it is."

He was not asking a question. He assumed I knew what it was. I said I didn't know what it was, but I wanted to know. What was it?

"Father Masterson told me if you kiss someone with the intention of getting aroused, you have committed mortal sin. And I did."

"What do you mean? What happens when you—"

"French it? I'll tell you. You start really sweating. And then your heart is pounding in your chest like a, like a—"

"Jackhammer."

"Yeah, that's good. A jackhammer. And then. You blow your wad."

"Your what?"

"I can't say it again." Pug repressed a smile. He had a naturally tan face and nice white teeth and a butch haircut that always had a touch of wax at the forehead, like a blessing. He was a happy-go-lucky fellow, a little on the chubby side, but a gamer on the sports field.

I soon discovered that Pug was talking about ejaculation, which I immediately confused with indulgences, that somewhat pecuniary system whereby a sinner could subtract from forced labor in the afterlife. A Catholic version of reduced sentence for good behavior. There were all kinds of ways to stack up these freebie days in the great beyond, days when you might be cowering in a dark corner of Purgatory, a place, we were told, where the flames licked as hot and hard as Hell whose only relief was that they were, indeed, temporary, and the soul, well scrubbed by the fire of all impure thoughts—failures to take out the trash, curse words, and other minutia of the venial—would be sprung through the trapdoor to Heaven.

Indulgences were various and variously had. For example, you could get one hundred days off your time for one ejaculation of the rosary on Good Friday. There were certain holy cards of saints, which, when prayed to, got you five, ten, fifteen dozen days off your sentence. I recall Saint Boniface, the patron saint of our parish in Anaheim, wielded a hefty half year for simply reading the prayer on his holy card. You can bet your ba-doing-doing that that card was in more favor for boys jacking off than a rookie Maury Wills. Saint Boniface cards were gold, pure and simple.

As one might surmise, there was a certain circularity to all this. It didn't take too much adding of two plus two to know that, armed with a drawer of holy cards of key saints and other illuminati, such as the pope, one might sin with impunity, or at least sin venially. There really weren't many ways, outside of French kissing, that you could commit a mortal sin at twelve in my time. You might pile up the indulgences for a cozy night, as it were. No sinning on the horizon? No sweat. Gather up a few hundred days out of jail by praying to Saint Stephen, the first martyr. Then go out and party.

There was one catch to all this. No one was quite sure for how long any sin would put you in the sky slammer. For example, how long, truly, would a white lie land you in that mournful mezzanine? (Or was it the basement? The place of Purgatory was never clear. It was simply between Heaven and Hell. In fact, the more you thought about it, Purgatory sounded pretty much like Earth, give or take a few thousand years. I won't even speculate on Limbo, that sad upper-deck miscellany that included unborn children, the insane, Ubangi tribesman, Eskimos, and other unfortunates who had not heard the Word, or couldn't.) No one was entirely sure of the weight of any given sin—intentionality was important, gravity was important, though what was grave and what not was never spelled out. There was no price tag for punching out your cousin that said, "Six years in Purgatory." Thus, you were always playing a guessing game with indulgences.

And that was why the pope's blessing was the Big One. Indulgence Numero Uno. In fact, it appears to be the only indulgence left in the church, someone having gotten wise to the holy card system, perhaps feeling that there were no accountants in Heaven or on Earth who could keep track of it.

It came to pass that I spotted a Pius the Twelfth holy card in a crack in the St. Boniface playground macadam while we were listening to the final game of the bitter 1962 Dodgers–Giants playoff game. Ice plant growing from the crack of a pepper tree's roots partially hid the card. I pocketed it quietly just after Pug burst out crying when in the last inning the Dodgers' Stan Williams walked in Jimmy Davenport, the go-ahead and ultimately winning run, essentially throwing the seven-month season away in less than a minute. The moans of the crowd at Chavez Ravine crackled through the transistor, but Pug spotted me taking my ransom from God for this horrible reversal. He dried his eyes and asked if he could have the Pius. I told him no. It was my find. Then he begged me like a dog in the kennel, knowing of its industrial vacuum-cleaner prayer.

"Please, Frank, I've gone over the edge. I'm in serious mortal sin with Debbie."

It hurt to hear him drop her last name. That in itself told me he was pretty close to planting the seed.

"I'll think about it," I brushed him off, my eyes burning. There was no way to relieve myself now of my addiction to the sight of Deborah Nodnok. I would wait for her after school, shooting baskets in the small court over which a sickly palm hung. When she would emerge in the line of girls—by sixth grade they had separated us, the skirts here, the pants there—I would fix on her as she emerged from the dark corridors of St. Boniface: the dimples in her cheeks, the knowing, intimate smile she would give to one of her friends, the Alaskan-husky blue of her eyes drilling me as I stood at the free-throw line. What was it about her combination of light and dark? Her ebony hair contrasted so strongly with the parchment skin that I must have sensed the angel and devil of Bobby Vee's song right there on the lunch benches.

I began to flail about for emotional pontoons to the object of my affection. Certainly, I could not use Pug Wilson. I had to woo her away from him. But how? I fell on the idea of family—Deborah Nodnok had ten sisters and brothers. Perhaps I could shake out a sibling and fill him with the brilliance of my mind, the accuracy of my set shot, my solid instincts with the soil—capture an ally deep in the camp of the probably hostile Nodnoks.

Deborah's brother Dwayne suddenly appeared on the basketball court after school. He was one grade younger than I, but he had the same black Irish look—black hair, a milk of skin with a few freckles tossed on the nose, and penetrating blue eyes. He was handsome. The whole Nodnok tribe must be in line for a movie career is the way I saw it. I assumed them Irish—almost everyone was, except for a scrap Italian, Mexican, or Arab such as myself. The last name was a stumper, though, and I think now they may have been Czech or Polish. I pumped Dwayne with every tidbit I could cough up in the five minutes before he, Deb, and the younger Nodnoks ran into the family Volkswagen van to go home: "Fine shot, Dwayne. Frozen rope. That's what Chick Hearn calls a swish. Did you know, Dwayne, that Frank Selvy is the only guard in history to score one hundred points in college basketball? Don't know who Frank Selvy is? Why, Dwayne, he's the weak-side guard on the Lakers. Feeds Jerry West. You know, don't you, that there's no star without a feeder. There's no West without Selvy. Look what he gave up to make West a big shot—one hundred–point production at Furman. Don't know what Furman is? It's college, Dwayne, a great college located in upper Manitoba. Manitoba is a province of Canada. Hey, great shot, Dwayne. Did you know that without the moon you couldn't swim at the beach? I wonder if your sister knows the importance of the moon. Your sister, dumb? Don't think so, Dwayne. She's a very bright individual. How do I know? Well, let's just say that's for me to know and you to find out."

I was a veritable Disneyland of information when it came to trying to contact Deborah Nodnok across the abyss of the school yard. I had a natural inclination to exaggerate, to leap forward in my imagination, to uncork verbal roller coasters and wild rides that could snare my prey—for a higher good, of course, one I hardly had the words for. Was I, in a sense, vying with Disneyland?

Then it happened. The first wet dream. It came as Deborah Nodnok approached in my sleep, not taking off anything, as Nurse Sigrit had done, but asking me to help her with her coat. The Santa Anas were blowing. The brush of her lustrous hair against my face and her turning to look at me with husky love. I awoke wet, throwing my pajamas in the reed-woven hamper. That night my mother wanted to know if I was okay. She said my father wanted to talk to me. He took me on a walk out in the little outdoor alcove off the mudroom that he and I had fashioned for Mother, a grotto of a statue of the Blessed Virgin standing on a brick platform. He suggested we say an "Our Father" together in front of Mary. After that, we went out back, sitting at the redwood picnic table facing the redwood weave two feet above the redwood back fence Lincoln Park had given us, all for more privacy. Privacy had begun its ascension in American life, and there was no sense that redwood was endangered.

"Do you think you wet your pants last night?" my father asked in a direct, intimate way that inspired trust.

"I don't know," I said warily. "How did you know that I might have?"

"Your PJs."

"Uh-uh."

"Was it exciting just before you found yourself with wet pants?"

"Yes."

"Well, you didn't wet your pants."

"Well, what did I do?"

"You ejaculated."

This is where my mind fogged over, as we were told the prayers said to gain indulgences were ejaculations. In other words, five ejaculations of the Joyful Mysteries. I was too stunned to fight it, but rather accepted at face value this conflation of the Sacred and the Profane. The story of sexual intercourse that my father then spun only added to my amazement. It was a story full of pauses that involved a man planting a seed in the furrow of his wife and the both of them becoming "as at peace as you get in this world." That seemed like something worth doing.

"Didn't you remember me telling you this when you were ten?"

I confessed that I had completely forgotten everything but the seed. I think now I probably wiped out the actions as being adult folklore, too fantastic to be believed.

"Maybe because I didn't tell you how he planted it." Rubbing his forehead, he plowed through a disquisition on the spade of the piece, as it were, using the Arabic *menanee*.

"So what happened last night, Franky, was what we call a 'wet dream.' You probably got excited by a girl in your dream as you would if you were going to mate her and you let the seed come out of your body. You know there are two to three hundred million seed in your semen?"

I asked him if I had committed a mortal sin, and he said no, because you're not in control of your body and you can't commit a sin unless you intend to. That made the old stones settle.

"Do you have a crush on a girl?"

"Yes."

"Do you want to tell me about her?"

"Oh, no. No. Except that she is beautiful."

"I'm sure." He mussed my hair, smiled, and said it was time for dinner, and not to worry, the body couldn't store up two to three hundred million seeds at one time and wet dreams were a way of getting rid of the overflow. That seemed fair enough. He left out what I vaguely sensed growing with Pug Wilson and Deborah Nodnok, namely, something very powerful between wet dreams and conjugal love, a vast gray area of desire that the priests and nuns understood no better than anyone, and sometimes a lot worse.

Jimmie Lou listened to me watering one day and said, "You're going to dig a hole in the ground." I guess she had caught me daydreaming, spraying the nozzle too thin at one place. Always amazed me how she could tell this without seeing, but at this time I figured her ears must be the size of a bat's.

"Are you in love?" she asked.

I said nothing, but opened the spray wider and covered the dichondra, darkening the green.

"It's nothing to be ashamed of. I would rather think that it is a mark of maturity. I can't imagine Dickie Jacobs and Tommie Blaw being in love. Such an emotion is beyond them. But you. You have a big heart."

"How can you tell that, Jimmie Lou?"

"Well, for one thing, you are always out here every day after school watering or turning the soil or trimming the hedges."

"But it's something I'm supposed to do. What's that got to do with my heart?"

"Oh, everything! Everything!" she cried and walked wildly into the street back to her house before her mother could ball her out. I was shocked.

After dinner, Jimmie Lou's mother called on the phone and asked if I would read to her daughter from *Emma*. I agreed. After about an hour, I said, "I think we better stop now, Jimmie Lou. It's getting late, and I have to take out the trash."

"Oh, Francis," Jimmie Lou's voice quavered, "I can't bear it. Please, just give me the first sentence of chapter 12. It's all coming to a head now. Just give me a glimpse, please." She was sitting on her bed as I read from the rocking chair, and she bent forward and swatted my leg.

"Forgive me, I didn't mean it to be so hard," she said, hiding her face.

"No problem, Jimmie Lou. Here's the first sentence: 'Till now that she was threatened with its loss, Emma had never known how much of her happiness depended on being *first* with Mr. Knightley, first in interest and affection.'"

Jimmie Lou practically fell off the bed. I helped her get her bearings. She asked me to fetch a Kleenex from her dresser, and she blew hard in it, wiping tears from her eyes, begging me not to tell her mother, asking me to forgive her, pleading with me not to worry, that she wouldn't do this again, and hoping that I would come back soon to finish chapter 12.

"I promise, Jimmie Lou."

Then she hugged me, something she had never done before, and she said in a husky, distraught voice, "Deborah Nodnok has no idea of the man you are!"

One Saturday, Pug Wilson was dropped off at my house by his mother—he lived some hike from Lincoln Park, even closer to Disneyland (he claimed to go to sleep at night hearing the whistle of the faux nineteenth-century train as it endlessly circled the Magic Kingdom). While we were tossing the football in the streets, Jimmie Lou made one of her alluring cracks: "I can tell you have big, soft hands." Pug was smitten on the spot. Soon he was inside her house, listening to her ream off with the tips of her fingers the ending to *A Tale of Two Cities*. It was quite a sight watching old Pug Wilson, usually randy at the world, now bawling like a baby caught in a rat trap as Jimmie Lou intoned Sidney Carton's soliloquy at the guillotine, "'It is a far, far better thing that I do, than I have ever done; it is a far, far better rest that I go to, than I have ever known.'"

"Don't you think it's time to get back to the street, Pug?" I growled.

"Okay, okay. It's one heckuva story, though."

"You bet."

"Don't you think she has a neat voice?"

"I suppose."

Then he whispered, "She also has a nice set."

This struck me silent, as I had never thought of Jimmie Lou's body. It was a pudgy body, and her endowment up top never really mattered to me one way or the other. But it wasn't the first visit I was to get from Pug on the weekends, and nearly every time he had an excuse to visit Jimmie Lou. He even brought her flowers one day. She seemed delighted, jumping around like a pudgy pogo stick. As I brooded, halting in my next read of *Emma*, Jimmie Lou hooked my collar, her eyes rotating in their sockets, and said, "Oh, Francis, don't be jealous. No one could ever take your place. Pug is a cad, that is quite evident, even to the blind."

One day in the lunch yard at St. Boniface, drinking my milk carton down with a slow savor as it was a hot spring day, I spied Deb Nodnok lacing her hand nervously into Pug's. Pug looked away. He didn't appear very touched, and I thought: What a waste of affection. She may as well have held hands with a clock. I rubbed my fingers nervously and shooed off someone who wanted to play tip-ins. In fact, I heaved the basketball so hard it hit one of our nuns in her habit. She turned and glared. I ran to the end of the school yard, hooking the chain-link fence, and stared out on Lincoln Boulevard, wondering how far I might be able to get before anyone would miss me.

That afternoon Tommie Blaw said, "Let's throw dirt clods." We headed to the end of Nutmeg Street where there was the vacant lot before the path to Anaheim Bowl.

"This is a good hideout," Tommie said, slamming himself against a hillock made by a tractor, excess earth from Lincoln Park. I picked another hillock in our tradition, and soon we were lacing each other with dirt clods, the substitute for snowballs in a land of no snow.

"Hey, take cover!" Tommie Blaw hissed, looking out at the street as if a common enemy approached.

It was my little sister Vivi, about eight, bouncing a rubber ball, adjusting her glasses. She had an early astigmatism that pulled one eye to the corner and forced her to use thick glasses at an early age, the only child in her class bespectacled. She was a dark-complected girl with ginger in her. She liked to cartwheel before the family on holidays. But somehow she had been muted by the glasses, and her bouncing of the little ball represented to me a silent sort of comeback.

Cruelty has a way with comebacks.

"Wait till you see the whites of her eyes," Tommie whispered, leaning behind his hillock, dirt clods lined near his shoulder like minié balls for cannon. I quickly rearmed, sinking my hands into the sorry earth, seeing in my mind's eye Deborah Nodnok's hand enter Pug Wilson's, wanting to slam my brakes over Pug's face.

"Open fire!" Tommie yelled.

Dirt clods rained down on Vivi, and the rubber ball dropped from her hand and rolled into the gutter. She turned, crying. A clod hit her in the face, knocking her glasses off. They fell into the soft dichondra, and she screamed, clawing at her eyes.

My father raced out of the house.

"You?" my father barked hoarsely. "You did this?"

Before I could answer—and what could I have answered? It was hard to tell whose clod had done the evil deed? That I had been seduced by Tommie? Neither of these moral loopholes would have grabbed it. Father yanked me up by one arm and threw me into the air. I was as high as the jacarandas. He caught and spanked me hard. He was shaking from anger and shock, and it went straight into me.

And what did I learn? my mother wanted to know later. I was too easily led. My amorous frustrations had reached a boiling point I didn't realize until it was too late. But now I think the lesson is harder. That innocent people are forever getting caught in the line of somebody's else fire—their pent-up love, their bitterness, their fanaticism—all over the world, and the best we can do is direct that fire out into the night. A punching bag. A pool waiting for strokes. A knight on a chess board. A dance floor. A hermit's cave, if nothing else works. A writing tablet. Is that not why Disneyland was born?

And so it came to pass that I began in the afternoons after school to write. Stories would come to me in the solitary hours picking up stones in the back and front yards—punishment, as if anything more was needed than the brute fact of what I had done—for nearly blinding my sister. Before dinner I would jot some of them down. One I particularly liked was called "The End of the World," and featured me and my dog, Sandy, living in a wooden barrel sailing down a flood that had destroyed the world. I had Deborah Nodnok drowning when the water crept up to the third floor of her old Anaheim house, and the last thing she cries out before the water enters her mouth is, "Pug, where are you when I need you?" As for Pug, he is cut to shreds by a buzz saw magically running in the swift current as he struggles to stay afloat. Gruesome indeed. My parents konk their heads against the refrigerator when the force of the water smashes through the kitchen window. Tommie Blaw is poleaxed by a streetlamp, Dickie Jo-cabs reduced to mush by a 1957 Chevy bearing down like a shark as he treads water. In spite of this havoc, Sandy and I are quite happy in our barrel, and I feel certain if we just hang on, the flood will recede and we will, as Noah himself, hit dry land and grab a dove or two.

At Easter, my teacher Sister Mary Mark gave me a holy card of Christ lovingly holding a globe of the earth in his hands. On the back it read, "Frank, you will one day be a writer. Please do some good with it."

When my father asked if I would like to go to Disneyland to ride the brand-new Matterhorn for the first time, I declined, retreating to my room to fill up another notebook with "The Epic of Stukabooka," about a happy-go-lucky midget who ingeniously uses a hot-air balloon to save a girl from being eaten alive by a coral snake.

But when my seventh-grade class got free tickets to mount the Matterhorn, distributed by Walt Disney himself to Orange County public schools and Catholic parishes (the synagogues in the area were not so graced, and if there was a mosque within a hundred miles, it must have been two hundred feet underground with no mailbox), I finally gave in. There was something about this phony mountain that was beginning to get to me. Nevertheless, I was drawn. To be a kid in Anaheim at the birth of the Matterhorn and refuse to ride its runners would have been tantamount to quitting a Little League baseball team after failing to execute a bunt. It simply could not be done.

And thus they did swarm, the Ford Station Wagons, the Nash Ramblers, the Woodies, the Dodge Darts, from East, West, South, and North to the mountain. They did come from afar, as far as San Diego to the south and San Francisco to the north, from Barstow in the East to Santa Monica in the West, called by a magnetic pole to the highest mountain inside the San Bernardinos, to see it, feel it, and rush along its cold aluminum sides. And the dwarfs and Mickey Mouses and Donald Ducks were irrelevant because all looked up for something greater they hoped was real, or if not real, at least with the pretense of reality, something so close to the real that it would trump the real, would out-real the real, would call each and every soul to a kind of hyperlife, one they hadn't had in their factories or traffic jams or vacant lots.

And we in our St. Boniface bus were among them, and in that bus existed one who was with them but not of them, or better, of them but not with them—in any case, an incipient outsider, someone beginning to develop a distinct sense that all was not right with the world, starting with himself, yet with a hunger for a better world and a better hide and like all Orange Countians hoping in his heart of hearts that the mountain all were traveling to might just provide transcendence, something that would redeem the futility of days, if only for a few seconds. For what was so stunning about Moses's Burning Bush on Sinai, but that it did not consume, that life could be lived even in the burning? So, too, the Disney Matterhorn gave hope that ice could live in the Southland, that a mountain could strut from the flatland, that Europe's own Alps could be owned by oranges. In this dance of the antimonies, I had hope, yes I admit it, I, too, was drawn with all my distrust to its promise of life beyond life.

And who of all people would I find myself with along those cold slopes in the sun alone, of all the students of seventh grade St. Boniface—but Deborah Nodnok? It was so written. *Maktoub.* She and I shared the last toboggan. There was space for another student or even a teacher, but none were left. Fate had placed us not in the driver's seat, but the caboose.

God, it was thrilling. The base of the mountain gigantic as the flanks of a prehistoric dinosaur, shining in the end-of-school sun. The brilliantly aqua toboggan, gliding along the rails, hidden carefully among the flanks of snowy alp. The spray exploding into our faces each time the toboggan hit the Alpine pools.

Deborah's hair flew behind her, now flicking scorn on my cheeks, now caressing my forehead, each tug of the toboggan drawing her closer to me than she had ever been. I yelled. And in the yelling expelled all the longing of the past year into the bowels of the mountain. Deborah screamed, too, and in the screaming the two of us mounted a leviathan duet, the children before us, the entire class a crescendo chorus flung down the slopes. But this was not hopelessness, this was Life lived with a Capital *L,* this I was certain was where I wanted to be in little life—the speed, the smell of cold water crashing, the sun on my cheeks, Deborah's hair. I did not want to arrive. I did not want the ride to stop. I felt safe in speed, a good American at a time my country could not only do no wrong, it hardly seemed to a lover in Anaheim that there was even an option. I forgot my sister's eyes tortured of dirt. Pug and Deb. My lies. My inability to embrace Jimmie Lou in a way she obviously wanted. Just don't stop, I whispered to the wind and the flag of Deborah Nodnok's hair.

We stopped at the peak of the last tall climb. The wild toboggans disappeared below. Behind, no toboggans either. Now that everything was bizarrely still, the illusion of a real rare mountain was broken, for now I could see what was only a blur before—the iron cables dripping of oil, the chain quivering above our head, the guts of the mountain not soil or gold or anything, really, but poorly painted Styrofoam. I could vaguely make out a man behind a window standing in the mountainside facing the rails and the cables, like someone far in the Battery Tunnel in New York, standing watch should anyone break down, mute and stiff as a corpse. Though we were clearly in peril, the figure behind the foggy window did not move, and I half wondered if he, too, were not a dummy.

Was this part of the ride? Why were we not falling? Deborah and I didn't move. We both, I think, thought we would jinx the ride itself. Surely, we were being taken care of. Some adult yelled below, "Just hold on!" Now I sensed the danger we were in—an instinct that has never left me and to which the writing life is intimately attached. Something had gone wrong, and the entire Matterhorn ride was malfunctioning. Above us, at the underarm of the mountain, a little red flag fluttered in the breeze, as if the thing were so new someone had forgotten to cut the manufacturer's label off.

But at that very moment of silent terror, something else gripped me—I was alone with Deborah Nodnok. Far from any adult, free, even from the control of the mountain ride itself. At this deathly peak, staring down at the ants of adults and the running water, out over the Magic Kingdom: I was in the catbird seat.

Deborah stirred. "Frank, is something wrong?"

It was the first time I had ever heard her say my name. It was never clear to me that she knew it.

"No," I spoke, my tongue thick and throat swollen. "No, it will go soon."

"Are you sure?"

"Very sure. This is part of the ride."

Her white hand gripped the aqua handrail. It opened and closed like a sea anemone.

I bent forward as she faced away from me, and I kissed, gently, the font of her hair, just enough to let her know I was there, but not enough to hurt her, for now I knew she was part of the ride, part of the ride of childhood I was about to leave, a world falling away quicker than freshets fall off the Matterhorn, just enough to let her not forget me. I went right for the top of her head, where the hair had its start, the place as an infant she was most vulnerable, the fontanel, a place I would kiss my children so often until they, too, grew hair, and the kisses lessened, the world of kisses became less Arab and more singularly American. I pressed her hair in with my lips, awkwardly, but as true a thing as I ever did.

She felt it. She looked to the side. Her blue eyes matched the sky. There was a small smile. Someone called out below to wait, hold on, which we were doing, better than anyone could know. And, as if she knew something I wanted her to know, and knew it the way I wanted her to, simply and truly, she turned to face the front, but put her hand back and touched my cheek. It was adult.

"It's not part of the ride, Frank. We're going to die."

"No, it's not part of the ride. But we won't die."

"Yes we will. It can't be helped."

"Maybe we will, but not now."

"Are you sure?"

"No."

Then she unbuckled her seat belt, turned, and kissed me on the lips. It was brief, but good. I sucked in the air. And then we fell. And I lost her in the crowd. How were we? What was it like? And my not once telling them the truth, listening to Deb say how happy she was to be alive and my thinking the same, dumb, beautifully dumb, with a sense that life was for real and that there was opportunity in the real and real disaster, nay, revelation far beyond all the illusions of Disneyland.

Just as I was about to press my advantage and break the Gordian knot of Pug and Deb, my father announced we were moving fifty miles crosstown to a place called Burroughs in the San Fernando Valley. We were gone just after school was out. I barely said good-bye to my buddies, to Jimmie Lou, to whom I entrusted a brand-new copy of *Emma* in Braille (hunted down by my mother as the other had worn out). As for Deborah Nodnok, I had no address.

When we drove out of Lincoln Park, I wrote furiously in a new notebook I had been given for my birthday. I tried to capture the angle of her elbows, the widow's peak of her sumptuous hair, and feel of her lips. And then, as we turned to enter the Santa Ana Freeway, I threw it out the window into a clump of sage. I thought I heard her yell, that marvelous scream as we fell, and I turned, my elbow hitting Vivian, who started to cry. Behind us, the Matterhorn grew smaller until it was nothing but a sunpoint.

The Chandelier

ukhlis drives up Asbury Street in Pasadena and brings his green Buick to a slow stop underneath the largest flowering eucalyptus in Southern California. The first door cracked is that of his wife, Wardi, who gets out as she has every week for forty years, as if she were with child. She has not been with child for many years, but her body at center is like the burl of a cedar and her legs are bowed as an old chair's. Mukhlis emerges from the Buick. He looks left and right for cars—a short, searing look. And the sun tries to plant its seed on the center of his bald head.

Mukhlis has made his money in real estate. He has apartment buildings downtown in Los Angeles, and many of his tenants are black or brown. He himself is brown, or rather almond, and his eyes, like those of many Lebanese and Syrians, are blue. A continent man, Mukhlis owes this hue to the Crusaders, the last blue twinkle of a distant lust.

What words there are to say, Mukhlis rarely says. His eyes and body speak—a body made to withstand. As he ascends the steps of his sister's home, his suit collar pulls taut around his bronzed neck, the nape standing in a welt of muscle. And that neck—thick as a porch post—welds shoulders to head. Nothing fat about the neck or the man, save a little bulge to the belly, testimony to forty years of Wardi's sweets, such as her *awami,* the Epiphany spoon balls she double fries year-round, epiphany to the point of stupor. Wardi (Rose, in English) does not react to compliments about her sweets; instead, she prefers to pay a compliment to the appetite of her complimenter. But not Mukhlis. He says not two crooked words about Wardi's *knafi,* or those date cakes they call *iras bi ibajwi,* or her famous *sillit bint al-malek,* the bird's nest rolled on a stick with the patience of Job before it's pushed off to form the prickly edge, then filled with pistachios as green as Mukhlis's Buick—probably greener—before the final touch: a drop of rosewater syrup.

Mukhlis kisses his sister, Matile, and booms a simple greeting to the air behind her. His large head, sapphire eyes, and corded neck all shake in silent laughter. And if it is a summer afternoon, with a large group of people chatting on Matile's porch, all will be aware of Mukhlis, though he will say the least, and when his hands come apart from their clasp on his belly, people will drag on their cigarettes and turn.

"No one wants to work, so the devil has his pick of the young people."

Wardi folds her hands under her bosom, nods, and sips coffee from the demitasse.

"Matile, do you have any cream?" Mukhlis asks his sister.

"Certainly, my honey," she sings. "Anything for you."

Matile's voice sings to smooth over rough spots in conversation; her feigned joy or fright has saved many a wounded soul. But when Mukhlis sang—the fact that he once sang is his most guarded secret—it was with the voice of the *hassoun,* the national bird of Lebanon, multicolored red, yellow, and black, prized for its rich warble, and fed marijuana seeds by children.

Among immigrants from the First World War, Mukhlis was prodded to fill the heart gaps after they bore the strange Atlantic, "the Sea of Darkness" in Arabic. Please, Mukhlis, sing the praise to the night! Sing of the moon and its white dress! Huddled on the stoops in Brooklyn, they asked for the song of two lovers separated by a river. The one of the nine months of pregnancy, in which Mukhlis pulled a pillow from under his shirt. Sing, cousin Mukhlis, for we are tired of the dress factories, we are tired of the mountain of silk. Sing of the land at the end of the Mediterranean!

Sing he did. His voice was effortless and sweet; it was made all the sweeter by the power everyone knew lay under it. Then one day this unschooled tenor, this voice dipped in rosewater, just stopped. It stopped cold after Mukhlis's mother died above a funeral parlor in Brooklyn. It died out as he covered for the last time the three white scars of her back from the lashes of the Turks. No one in California has ever heard him sing.

All of this is whispered behind Mukhlis's back. His usual response to any mention of the latest atrocity in Lebanon is: "How is your dog?" or "The apricots are too thick on the bough. Snap them off."

But today the large porch is empty, except for Matile herself and her oldest grandson, Mukhlis's great-nephew. This young man has been traveling for years, a restless soul, thinks Mukhlis, sitting on the legless couch on the porch, Wardi against Matile's pillow of faded flowers on the white wrought-iron chair. The great-nephew takes to the old porch swing. Noticing sun on a vine, Mukhlis says to himself, What is it about this day? The wind is hurting the grape leaves.

Matile brings a tray of small cups with the brass coffeepot and announces dinner is not too far off, and all must stay.

"It is never far off with you, Matile," Mukhlis says, blowing over his coffee.

"You *must* stay," she sings. "I am making stuffed zucchini."

"Never mind," he says. "Have you got a *ghrabi*?"

"*Ghrabi*?" Matile stands so quickly she leaves her black shoes. And goes into a litany of food that lasts five minutes.

"No, no, no," Mukhlis punctuates each breathless pause in her list. "*Ghrabi*—just give me one."

"One!" she cries. "I have hundred."

"One, please, is all I want."

She fetches a dish piled high with the hoops of butter, sugar, and dough, each with a mole or two of almond or pistachio.

"Eat," she says.

Wardi takes one. Mukhlis shakes his head and breaks off half a *ghrabi*.

"Isn't that delicious?" Matile asks, preempting the compliment. Mukhlis chews. "You look *real good* today," she smiles, her face brightening at his headshake.

Mukhlis turns to the young man. "What are you doing here?"

"Looking for work," says the great-nephew, a dark, slender fellow with broad shoulders. These eyes of his, Mukhlis thinks, have a dark sparkle. He's cried and laughed too much for his age; his laugh is a cry, and his cry is a laugh.

"It's time for you to get serious and stop this wandering and get a good job in business," Mukhlis says loudly. "You are playing with your life. When are you going to get married?"

Mukhlis gleams a crocodile smile and laughs silently at the great-nephew's shrug. Then he goes solemn, touches the pistachio on a *ghrabi* with a thick forefinger.

"Aren't you ever really hungry, Uncle Mukhlis?"

"Boy, have you ever seen a person eat an orange peel?"

"I've eaten them myself. They're good."

"No, no, boy. I mean rotten orange peels, with mud and dung on them. Have you had that?"

The great-nephew purses his lips.

"Well, I want to tell you a story. I want to tell you about hunger, and I want to tell you about disgrace."

Matile gets up again and lets out in her falsetto, "Don't go no further till I come back."

Mukhlis disregards her and squeezes a sun-bleached pillow on the legless couch, as if he were squeezing his brain. What is it about the breeze and the light today, the crystal light? Will he go on? He does not know. His great-nephew is too silent. Mukhlis does not like silence waiting for silence. He likes his silence to be hidden in a crowd. From the dome of his almond head, he takes some sweat and smells it.

"I was the oldest of us in Lebanon when we lived in the mountain," he begins, "but when World War I started, I was still a young boy. You see, the Germans were allied with the Turks who had hold over all the Arab lands. And so the Germans become our masters, too, for a time. When it was all we could do to steer clear of the Turks! In 1914, the Allies blockaded Beirut harbor, and for four years there was no food to be had in Mount Lebanon."

Wardi crunches a bird's nest. Matile puts a heap of grapes in front of her brother.

"Nothing like this purple grape, I can assure you! These were treacherous times. People were hungry, and hunger is the beginning of cruelty. The Turks themselves would tolerate no funny business. If people refused to cooperate with them, they would take it out on the children. I saw them seize a boy by the legs and literally rip him in half. I saw this happen with my own eyes; one half of the child flew into the fountain we had in Mheiti. The fountain was empty, but even after the war when it had water and the remains of the child were dried up, no one would drink there."

"*Yi!* You tell them, Mukhlis! You tell this to show what happen to us!" Matile's voice rises as she lays down a plate of Syrian cheese and bread. "It was terrible."

Her brother continues, "Food was so scarce people would pick up horse dung, wash it, and eat the grains of hay left. It was common to go days without eating or drinking, because the Nahr Ibrahim and the Bardowni rivers were contaminated by dead bodies. The Germans and the Turks would throw traitors into the river . . . Then there was the chandelier."

Matile clicks her tongue, "I could tell you story, boy, I could tell you story."

"Did you know 'Lebanon' means 'snow'?" Mukhlis raises his pointer finger. "It means 'white as yogurt' because in winter the mountains are covered with snow. That winter, we stay in. Without food, it was colder."

"What about restaurants?" the great-nephew ventures.

"Restaurant? You are an idiot, young man, forgive me for saying. Any restaurant was destroyed in the first year, any market plundered by the soldiers. We had to find food ourselves. Each day for four years was a battle for food."

"I could tell you story," Matile puts her eyes up to the stucco ceiling of the porch and shakes her hands. "*Khubz!* A crust of bread was so rare it was *mittle* communion. My mother, she had to go away for days to trade everything we had for food on the other side of the mountain—"

"Matile, I—"

"—she give us slice of bread before she leaves, and she shake her finger at us and say, Matile, Mukhlis, Milhem—you don't take this at one time. Each day you cut one piece bread. One piece! No more. And you cut this piece into four pieces—three for older ones, then you break the last one for the infant. You understand? Like one cracker a day for each of us. Little Milhem, he cries all day. He wants more. He too little to understand, and the baby Wadiyah . . . ah! Milhem hit us for the rest of the slice of bread. I hide it under my pillow one night. And that night . . . Oh, I could tell you story make your ears hurt!"

Mukhlis shifts in his seat and flings out his arms, "Now, when I went off in the snow—"

"The chandelier, you remember."

"Yes, Matile, of course I do."

"You remember, Wardi? You wouldn't believe it."

Wardi's eyes are large as a night creature behind her thick eyeglass lenses, and she nods.

Mukhlis clears his throat loudly. "My mother gave me the last lira we had and told me to go through the snow over the mountain to the village in the dry land, to fetch milk and bread. I was not as strong as my mother, but I was strong, and so I tried. But the first day out I was shot at by a highwayman, a robber. I hid behind a rock; still he found me and stripped off my jacket and took the lira. I was glad he did not kill me. But what was I to do? I could not go home. I continued walking until I came to a monastery. I would ask the monks for some milk. They were not there."

"They die."

"Matile, please. They were not there. Maybe they went to Greece. They were Greek monks. The place was empty. The door to the chapel opening with the wind that moved it back and forth. Inside the candles were snuffed. And the candlesticks were cold, and the pews were covered with frost. It was winter inside and out. Up above was a—"

"Chandelier!"

"Yes, Matile, a huge crystal chandelier. In all my life I have never seen one larger. Its branches were as far across as this couch, made of solid gold. Inlaid in the arms were rubies the size of your eyes, nephew! I remember standing in the chapel that day thinking how we had come to worship there with my father when I was a young child; the chandelier was something I would worship. I would look up, and its great shining light would say to me—God. This is your God, Mukhlis, here on Mount Lebanon. He brims with light, and He will sit in your eyes, in your dreams. I had never thought of touching it. For one thing, it was too high. It was at least ten feet above my head. Well, so help the Almighty, I was hungry. And my mother was hungry. And so were my brothers . . . and my sister. And we had not heard from our father, who was in America for two years. Before God and man, I committed a sacrilege. See, the mosaics on the wall were shot out. I crawled up the wall where the tile was gone. I crawled up that mosaic until I made it to the crossbeams of the ceiling. And I had to be very careful not to knock loose more mosaic. A mosaic of Our Lady it was, and who knows? Maybe my foot was in her mouth."

"How sad!" sighs Matile.

"But I hoisted myself onto the crossbeam and slid—like this, yes—slid across the beam. It was cold enough to hold my hands fast as I tried to balance. But finally I made it out over the nave of the chapel, to the chandelier."

"*Yi!*"

"The chandelier was held to the ceiling by tall iron nails. Slowly, carefully, I put my hands through the crystal teardrops, to latch onto the gold arms. And then you know what I did, young man? I was a monkey. I swung free on that chandelier! I pulled up and heaved down on it, trying to loosen it. I yanked and yanked with the crystal hitting my eyes and the rubies sweating in my hands. And I swung back and forth in the cold air. The chandelier would not loosen. It seemed like God Himself was holding it through the ceiling and saying to me: 'No you don't, Mukhlis! You do not take this chandelier from the church. This is mine, Mukhlis. And you, a puny human being, will rot in hell for this.'

"I am not talking about playing in the acacias. I am not talking about swinging from those miserable apricot trees, which need to be cut back by the way, Matile."

"Anything you say, my honey."

"I am talking about a tree of crystal and gold. I am talking about food."

"Wardi, would you like more coffee, dear?"

"Matile, I am talking about food."

"So am I!"

Wardi's enlarged eyes close, and her big bosom vibrates with mirth, like a dreaming horse.

"Oh, it's useless. Why talk about it?" Mukhlis folds his hands, as if to tie up the story once and for all and leave everyone hanging on the chandelier.

Matile speaks with alarm: "Please, tell them, tell them. I won't get up no more. This is story you never heard the like of before. It can't be no worse!"

Mukhlis gets up, paces the clay porch, and goes over and breaks off a branch crowded with apricots.

"Here, Matile, here is your dessert."

Shaking the stick of fruit over the rail, he spits out, "Finally, I heard it come loose. The plaster dust rained on my face, and I heaved on this chandelier one more time. And then I fell."

Mukhlis drops the apricots, raises his forearms, and grips the air.

"It breaks, ah!"

"No, Matile, it does not break. Please, you are killing my story at every juncture."

She laughs and gets up for some rice pudding that is cooling in the refrigerator.

"I fall with it. I fall with it, and I fall directly on my rump. This is why I walk slowly to this day, young man. Because of the chandelier. That chandelier had to become milk. It was going to save my life, our lives. What did my bones mean? Nothing. But I was a tough fellow—not like you soft people today—and not one teardrop of that crystal was scratched. I got up, and my hip was cracked a little. But I got up. I carried the chandelier to the entrance of the church. No one was around. No one saw me do it."

"God finally let go?" the great-nephew asks, with a smirk.

"God never lets go. I yanked it out of His hands. But I could not carry the chandelier far—it weighed a ton. In the vestibule of the chapel was an Oriental rug. I placed the chandelier on top of that, wrapped it in the rug with the cord, tied it around the branches of gold, and dragged it onto the snow. No, Matile, no rice pudding. For the next three days, I dragged the chandelier over the snow to get to the hot land of the Bekaa. For three days I walked and pulled it behind me."

Mukhlis stops and wipes his brow. He is sweating heavily now, though the California air is dry.

"I was exhausted by the end of the first day. I lay down in the snow by a cedar. I did not want to damage the chandelier, so I left it on the rug and tried to sleep on the snow with as much of my body as I could against the cedar. I was so tired and fell fast asleep."

"Did you dream?" asks the great-nephew, taking a spoonful of the sweet rice pudding.

"I don't remember. No, I don't dream. Dreams are for soft times," Mukhlis grunts. "You've dropped some pudding." His listener takes up the white spot on the porch with a finger. For a while Mukhlis says nothing, listens to them chewing, sipping. He stares out past the apricots, past the flowering eucalyptus, to the cloudless sky.

"I awoke to the sound of licking in the dark. I felt warm breath near my face. I sat up. There were six eyes, six greenish eyes in the darkness. My blood went cold. Wolves. I got up fast, grabbed the chandelier, and swung it around and around, turning inside it myself. It made a tinkling noise that was loud in the dead forest, and the wolves howled and scattered back into the night. I was breathing so hard my heart felt like it would come out of me. I was too much awake now and decided to go on dragging the chandelier in the dark. All through the night the teardrops clinked against each other and the rug rubbed over the snow. My eyes have never been so wide as that night. I looked on all sides and hurried until dawn, then rested. I remember lying down by a boulder, hooking the chandelier with my arm. When it dawned, the sun sent it sparkling. It made rays of red all over the snow, and the rubies looked like drops of blood. I rested a while, my eyes opening and closing, but I did not let them close completely. No, not again!

"The second day I met a family trudging in the snow—a mother, daughter, and two babies. The mother asked if I had any milk. I said I was going to get some for the chandelier. She shook her head and kissed me on the head. Her daughter's eyes were rimmed with blue, and she was shaking. She had nothing on but a nightgown and thin sweater, and her toes showed through her leather shoes. They went on—they were going to Zahle, they said. I said I thought Zahle had no food, because my mother had been there and had bought the last scoop of flour in town. The mother asked where my family lived, and I pointed up the mountain. They said they would try to go there, to Mheiti. I said, Please do. The mother stared at me a while with her own blue-rimmed eyes. One baby had blue lips. The other was whimpering and breathing quickly in the daughter's arms. I went on. I went on and on, with the snow wedged in my shoes and pants. That night I slept with my head inside the chandelier, my arms hugged it, my legs hooking it so that if wolves came they would not want me, for they would think I was part of the chandelier. It worked. I was not bothered by wolves that night.

"The third day I descended from the mountain. I saw the dry lands in the distance—the rust-colored sand and rock of the Bekaa—and I was so happy I broke out laughing. But I descended too quickly, and a thread of the rug snagged on a bush. The chandelier slid off and down an embankment of snow that the sun had turned smooth. I plunged down the cliff after the chandelier, cracking the shelf of ice. But when it reached the edge it fell. It fell about twenty feet. I cried out and rolled like a crazy dog down the snowbank and fell on my face in front of the chandelier. Luckily, it had landed on snow that had not iced over, that had some shade from the ledge. I moved it slowly. One of the gold arms was bent, and some teardrops were shattered. I turned it and stepped back. With the broken part to the back, it did not look too bad. The rug was still above, so I fetched it and carefully laid the chandelier on it, like a wounded human being, and went on. Slow down, Mukhlis, slow now. I did not let myself be excited anymore by the nearness of the Bekaa. I have never let myself be excited again because of that chandelier breaking over the ledge.

"That afternoon, I reached the small village my mother had told me about. The villagers there were healthy. They still had some fields producing corn and wheat and lentils, and the road to Damascus was open. When they saw me—a little runt dragging this chandelier on the dry, dusty road—they gathered around me, asking questions. I was too tired to answer. I just said, 'Take me to a cow farmer. Please, as soon as you can.' They led me to such a man. I said to him, 'Look, I have come from the mountain where it is very cold and there is no food. My family is starving. I will give you this chandelier for milk and anything else I can carry.' The farmer inspected the chandelier, God damn his soul. Our people! They will try to strike a deal no matter what. You may be flat on the ground, your legs chopped off, and they will throw dust in your eyes at backgammon. This farmer held up the chandelier with the aid of another man and said, 'It is broken. It can't be worth much.' I said to him, 'Please, sir. It is made of gold and rubies and crystal.' 'Where did you get it from?' he asked. I said, 'I got it from the mountain.' He nodded. He did not want to ask me the next question, the how. 'I'm not sure,' he said. It was then that his wife, God save her soul, slapped him on the eyes. He pushed her away. 'All right,' he said. 'Two jugs of milk, and we will put a pack of bread on your back. Can you carry all that?' I said, 'Yes, yes, I can carry as much as you can give me.' And he gave me two lambskins of milk and hoisted the bread on my back. The wife put in two bags of dates and dried apricots when he wasn't looking. And she kissed me on the head.

"I stayed in that town to rest for the night. They fed me a good meal. It felt good to sleep, to sleep thoroughly. But by morning I was ready to go. I walked back up the mountain, rising from the warm air to the cold, walking back into the snow world and the dark forest. I walked steadily, though my back and pelvis were hurting. In a few days when I made it back to Mheiti, I found myself running through the worn path in the snow up to my little house—a house made of limestone blocks, a good, sturdy house in normal times. My mother spotted me through the window and came running. She shouted in a hoarse voice, 'Mukhlis! Oh, Mukhlis, you've come!'"

Matile is standing rigid. She does not speak, or offer food. She watches her brother's sapphire eyes melting in their own fire.

"My mother threw me above her—*ya rubi*, she was strong—and then carried me into the house before she saw the milk. When she did, she tore it off my neck. She gave some to Matile, to my brother Milhem. But there was the infant to go—my brother Wadiyah. She frantically squeezed the lambskin's tip into his mouth as he lay in his crib. It was a wooden crib. A small wooden crib. I watched her force it on him. I saw that his eyes were stunned open as if he had seen a large rock toppling on top of him. She kept squeezing the lambskin of milk until half of it was dripping out of his mouth to the floor. '*Immie!*' I called to her. 'Don't, don't! You're wasting it.' She wouldn't stop. I had to pull it out of her hands. She squeezed the infant's cold cheeks and then took her nails to the wall. She claws it, yes. The wall. After a while she put a sheet over the crib."

Mukhlis looks down, then to the ceiling of the porch. "I never knew him."

"*Akh!*" Mukhlis stands slowly. "Let's go, Wardi."

"No, no," Matile wakes from her trance. "You must stay for supper."

"We can't. I must go pick up a rent."

But Matile will not be swayed. She lifts her urgent voice, as if the food were gold and they were turning their backs on precious things. Mukhlis relents while shaking his head. All move into the dining room.

They sit under the chandelier, and pass the grape leaves, the stuffed zucchini, the swollen purple eggplant. They eat in silence, the unlit chandelier struck by the descending California sun, breaking into light above the food, pieces of light on Mukhlis's almond head. When he finishes he stands, and ticks one of the crystal droplets with the thick nail of his finger, and does not speak.

"You hear what we went through?" Matile says after they are gone. "That was not all of it." She hugs her grandson, but not long. Even before she is through crying she has opened her mammoth horizontal freezer and said, "We need more bread, more bread."

Get Off the Bus

maybe it was the newspaper lying on the porch that got Frank Matter going. It was September 17, 2001. Frank hadn't been reading much about the attacks, caught up as he was in his mother's car wreck the very day after—September 12. The banner head arrested him. He stopped on the family home's circular drive and unfolded it: LOS ANGELES WAS ON THE HIJACKERS' HIT LIST. Subhead: *San Gabriel Arab Shot in His Store.* Frank refolded the paper, tucked it under his arm, and went off on foot into the Valley's hot streets.

As Mother's car was totaled and lying in state in a junkyard in Carson, the bus was Matter's only way to get to the hospital. He walked out of the Burroughs hills that morning across Ventura Boulevard, the sun bouncing off the windshields and car tops as people snaked through that deadly crossing at Reseda where his mother had taken a left turn as the light turned red. Frank Matter threaded his way through cars stuck in the intersection, one man calling out, "Fuck you, asshole!" as the light again turned red. Frank couldn't tell if the driver meant him, so conspicuously free on foot, or the car ahead of him who was trying to back up to let the cross traffic through.

Quiet came quickly past Ventura, a quiet morning in the Valley, a klatch of Mexican women walking south to swab the homes on the hillside where his mother lived. A boy on bicycle headed to school; a Vietnam veteran fanned his hat out to the traffic at Burbank Boulevard. At Oxnard, Frank approached the brand-new Orange Line Busway stop. The orange canopy, the orange message on a wall—Ride in Ease—the orange painted benches all sporting the color of the lost groves, now it seemed squeezed to latex.

35

An old woman with knobby elbows, her hair newly frosted, clutching a gold lamé purse, walked slowly up to the platform, her sunglasses propped like a periscope on the powdered nose.

"Good morning," Frank nodded.

She grunted, nodded back, and then looked straight out at the smooth roadway as she sat. A duck appeared out of nowhere, leading her ducklings across the busway, presumably to the L.A. River one block up. The old woman's shielded eyes followed the duck family until they disappeared. She glanced over as he unfolded the newspaper, then did eyes straight again.

Frank fixed on the cement pad of the busway and thought of his mother driving that car, the door from the passenger's side thrust across the console into her hip. How was she going to make it? At seventy-three? Unconscious for four days? Seven broken bones, torn spleen and kidney. The urn at the foot of her hospital bed was still filling with blood, though its color was more rose now than red. The doctor said she might be turning a corner. Now it was all on her heart.

A small breeze came. Tall palms clicked like Arab women at a wedding. And then in the distance a light grew in the light of day, until the long Orange Line bus stopped in front of them. The old lady got on first. Frank went to help her, but she tucked her hand away and uttered something about "myself." Before he could follow her, a small boy jumped in front of him with his book bag.

On the bus were only two others: a young white man who looked like a college student, with green hair, and a girl beside him, with blue hair. They were smiling and holding hands. Otherwise the bus was empty. Los Angeles had just begun to build a few aboveground subway lines, a late-in-the-game attempt to siphon off some of the maniacal car traffic of the freeways. Of course, freeways had built L.A., and so had Detroit. No other city in the country was so in love with its cars, nor had poured so much circling cement in their honor. Everyone loved his own iron box. Everyone cursed that there were so many other iron boxes in a row, but few could break the habit, even with the Metro and busway beckoning. For a city adverse to crowds, built on the right to situate oneself in ever-widening space apart from others with one's own nuclear family, the attacks on New York and Washington wouldn't encourage convening anywhere, not the least, on the new freedom-stealing busway. Never mind that they were ripping along quite beautifully at sixty miles an hour with no lights to stop them and no jams.

Frank Matter enjoyed it. For years, he'd ridden the Metro in Washington to work, and gotten used to it. But after fifteen years of getting squashed by fellow riders at rush hour, and the studied dreariness on everyone's faces, he'd given it up for a car commute when his government job moved to the suburbs. The irony: just as L.A. got its first Metro lines, D.C. began to propagate thick car traffic. There was no release from it. Too many people in too small a space. But this busway, sparsely populated, was something of a dream, and he thought for a moment, leaving off that L.A. might be next on the hijackers' list, maybe there was hope for his hometown. Maybe this steel monster will thread us together, like a surgeon's needle.

Us. Not many willing to be threaded.

The busway stopped its orange blur at Tampa. There a black man with a snowy crown got on. He limped to a seat across the aisle from Matter. Thin, with hollow cheeks and pensive, amber eyes, the black man was dressed neatly, with a dark tie over a short-sleeved white shirt.

"Terrible what's happened," he said after spotting the front page. "I read that this morning."

"Yes," Frank said, looking at him. The man scoped out Frank's eyes carefully. It made Matter suddenly want to hide the paper or throw it out the window. Then he thought: *I can't do anything unusual with it. I must continue to read it as any burgher would read it, calmly, wanting to be informed.*

"Imagine!" the black man smiled craftily. "What do they target in our town? Disneyland?" Then he leaned over, looking back at the old woman and the smooching young couple, and whispered, "Not much of a loss there, eh?"

The bus driver looked in his large rear-view mirror in the center of the windshield. Frank glanced back briefly at the old woman whose back was as upright as a pole. Lines were deepening on her brow.

"Tallest thing there is the Matterhorn," Frank dropped out of the corner of his mouth and wished he could grab the words back.

"A fake mountain!" the old man crunched his own laugh so that it swizzled into his nose. "There's not much else tall. City hall? Can't be fifteen stories. Coupla tall new buildings downtown like that nasty U.S. Bank Tower, but it don't stand out. None have any symbolic value. Same thing at Century City. I work at a library here in Canoga Park. Three stories. I figure I'm safe. You safe?"

"I guess. I'm going to a hospital in Northridge."

"Oh, I know it. Oh, yeah. You'll be all right."

The busway zoomed along, sliding the palms like butter, blurring the dogs and their masters, the artwork of gangbangers brought to societal purpose, people who would never topple a tall building.

"People got a lot o' hell inside 'em," said the man, lifting the snow off his eyebrows. "We ain't so innocent, either," he concluded with the authority and brazenness of age.

Suddenly the old lady was passing them, passing a phalanx of empty chairs, holding pell-mell to the railings.

"She all right?" the librarian leaned.

The woman gripped the money changer at the front of the bus and spoke sternly to the bus driver. Soon the bus was stopping. There was no stop.

The driver got up off the new vinyl seat. There was no sound to his rising. Those were brand-new springs. The floor of the bus was new, too, and provided no squeak. There was nothing to indicate damage, wear, the deterioration of the infrastructure. Frank feared the driver was approaching his voluble companion of the morning.

"Sir, I have to ask you to get off this bus."

He was a heavy-set white man with dark glasses and a mole on his cheek. He was looking at Matter; the old woman standing behind him also directed an accusatory stare, one with no eyes, protected from the sun.

"I'm sorry?"

"This woman says you have been discussing terrorism."

"To some extent, but . . ."

"This is a very serious situation. You can't talk like that here."

"Like what?"

"Like attacking Disneyland!" the woman shrieked. "Who are you? Get out of here!"

"Now wait a second," the black man defended Matter. "We were only talking about the headlines." He pointed to the newspaper. Frank opened it on the banner head.

The man scanned it.

"I'm not talking about him," the old woman pointed at the black man.

"I understand, lady," said the bus driver, waving her to calm down.

Frank stood. "You're worried about me? I've lived here my whole life!"

"Now settle now, mister."

"You settle down. This is a public bus. I have a right to ride it. I have paid taxes in this country for thirty years."

Matter's self-defense seemed to sink him further into a hole.

"Just step outside, please. You have caused a great deal of anxiety to this woman."

"How?"

The lady with the gold purse looked down, and muttered, "This is how they are. Don't you understand? This is how they are. They have lived among us for years. They will make us believe anything."

"I don't have an accent. I was born in Los Angeles! I've been to more Dodger games than I can count!"

"Anything," she muttered, turning her head behind the large rounded shoulders of the driver.

The two young people were now gathered around. The boy with the green hair spoke: "Maybe you ought to go off even if you're innocent 'cuz we have to get to class."

"Innocent? Is this a trial?"

"Let me help you off."

"Off? What if I stay? What if I refuse to leave?"

"Mister, this woman has a heart condition. I am two seconds away from calling the police. And then you are in real trouble, because I have the authority to ask you to leave."

"How's that?"

"You've got one second."

Here he took out a cell phone.

"Let me have it!" the lady cried out and snatched the phone out of his hands. "I'll call it myself!" She punched 9-1-1 and started talking to a dispatcher.

"All right," Frank said. "I'm leaving. Fuck you! Fuck you all!"

"This is a disgrace!" the black man yelled. "He gets off, I get off!"

"Well, then get off!" yelled the bus driver.

Soon two passengers were standing out in the empty busway, long between stops, standing in the fumes of the retreating bus.

"Why'd he do that?" Frank asked. "What did we say that was so horrid?"

"It wasn't what you said," his companion said. "It was the look of you."

They looked at each other. For the first time in his life, Frank thought, I see a black man. Not a man who is black. But a man whose blackness is part of him, in spite of everything he might want or feel. Frank saw the ridges of his face bones, beautifully reflective in the sunlight, the lips dry, full, but wanting, cracked, the pepper in the skin, the eyes, lit of amber, wolverine, small, knowing, full of old pain, the pulls of skin laughter and sadness had made. And Frank knew him now for the first time. And he knew Frank. This stranger knew him. He was not just a man; he was a man who knew what it was to be a thing. To be taken for a thing.

"Well, I guess I did the opposite of Rosa Parks," he laughed softly.

"Maybe you did, maybe you didn't," Frank smiled.

"What's your name?"

"Frank."

"Mine's Oscar. Where you headed?"

Oscar walked his new companion a few blocks north up Winnetka, then turned to go to his library, where he checked out books.

Frank kept on, grateful for the buffering. But the longer he walked alone, the more it crept up on him.

What was the look of me?

He approached a parked van and went to look in the long vertical mirror on the driver's side. He was dark, yes, but plenty in California were dark, and how many times people in the East would see him after a family trip West and exclaim, "What a nice tan!" But it wasn't just the dark. Nor was it just the nose, bony and large in the mirror. It was the eyes! That's what the old lady with the gold purse had seen. Frank Matter stared into his own eyes. They were very dark, so dark there was no pupil, or rather the pupil had taken over the iris and this because he was humiliated, told to leave by virtue of his eyes, the eyes that had become so black to this woman and perhaps at least for a moment to the bus driver and who knows who else besides Oscar in this world.

And he did not know what to do with his eyes. He wanted to pluck them like Gloucester and present them to anyone on Winnetka: *Look, these are just ordinary eyes. They don't want to kill. They happen to be dark, very dark, like the night, and who knows what I am supposed to do with pupils that swell up too fast, that envelop the brown. But here you take them, you there on your way to school. Take them and learn from them what it means to be overheated in this land of the lukewarm.*

And after Matter had taken his eyes out he began to punch the air, blindly, the bus driver, bursting his mole, the obsequious college kids, making their head hair red, the old lady, blistering her powdered nose and punching his Washington wife who hated the West and didn't like his chest hair and punching his children who had the temerity to ask for something else for dinner, and punching women who turned on a heel and men who said take a walk and the general who dismissed the Arabs as kibbe heads and the waitress who throws the cream at you, the candidate who lies and lies, the columnist calling for war, the old girlfriend holding the fetus, the bend in the L.A. River dry as his trembling heart.

"My name means rain!" he yelled out. The streets were empty and dry. "Rain!" he yelled again. "Give me your parades, your huddled masses, and I will rain on them. How many things you have said I could dampen, I will dampen. I will question every proposition of war, those telling me who I am in less than a second. I will rain until something true grows. I have rain for East and rain for West. And for myself I keep a Dead Sea. Or Lake Tahoe. Or the L.A. Wash."

He stopped calling out and flailing his arms. No one witnessed him punch the air. He could see all too well no one was there. Then he realized why he was there: to help his mother in intensive care. It hung on the heart. Shamed, Father Matter walked furiously toward the growing sun.

Fabiola

harder!"

Lately, I haven't been able to get her out of my mind, and when I look up at the gritty window after unsticking the soggy diaper of our new baby, I half-think that he knows that my vacuous, searching stare out the alley is not for baby things, but for Fabiola Diaz Ponce. I call our little son "the Judge." He has a habit of tensing the flesh under his eyes, pursing his lips, then the spittle. None of my own facial contortions will change his judgmental look. Yet just when I've given up trying and stare out the window, his cheeks indent and he has me by the tail of a smile.

My wife—an eminently practical girl with eyes deep as lapis—says I must be careful changing him that he does not get a cold by the window. Since autumn rains are falling, he sneezes. We both vow to move his changing table to another side of the room. But for some reason, it doesn't get done. So I attach his diaper, rush an undershirt over his head before he cries while my wife warms his bottle downstairs and bags my lunch.

The window is fogging up and the Judge is sneezing and Fabiola is pulling my bathing suit off with her teeth.

Psychologists may call this sublimation or regression—but somehow I do not feel either adequately explains the appearance of Fabiola Diaz Ponce in the hard gelatin of my memory. We are older than first parents used to be—bearing our child after our first back problems—so at end of day there is not as much coal in our tender. I am an anchored dolt compared to the vagabond years in which I met Fabiola, happier too, if happiness may be defined as a lack of a need to seek it. But by day's end our bodies are worn out; my wife is still sore where the child came. Though she certainly hasn't purchased slinky black negligees, I did spot her reading one of those women's magazines with a cover story—"How to Turn Your Man into a Mystery Lover." My wife is not to blame, nor am I. Nor is the Judge.

Fabiola, lust at first sight.

This was no simple undercurrent. It was a riptide carrying me out to the starfish. I was just out of college, free of required books and exams, with not much notion of what I would do in the world. My kid uncle, Harry, sensing that I was gullible enough to do anything to while away the time, gave me employ as a maid at his beach pad in Marina Del Rey. He was living with William Haddad at the time, a fast-moving stockbroker who had once been a leader in Junior Achievement.

The vacuum cleaner was roaring on the chartreuse rug the day Fabiola happened into the front room, with no knock. She didn't stride as if she owned everything. She just appeared. I shut off the vacuum.

"Where's Bully?"

Though her dark skin and fire agate eyes indicated the southern climes, her peculiar accent sounded almost Russian. I couldn't place it. I wondered if she meant Billy.

"Yes, Bully."

She said her name without looking at me, peering into Bill's bedroom. The *b* she softened to a *v*. Her bare feet went on tiptoe as she leaned, and her black tank top dipped abundantly. A scarlet bikini rose out of the black like a blush.

"He's at work. So's Harry. Who are you?"

Bill had been seeing a succession of women, and I wasn't sure where this one stood. He was a handsome fellow, tall, with midnight-black hair combed immaculately with water. He had one physical drawback, however—a beak shaped like a toucan's. His constant effervescence was, no doubt, a hopeless attempt to shorten it.

"Are you Bully's brother?" She pirouetted.

"No, I am Harry's nephew."

"What chore name?"

"Frank Matter."

"Matter what?"

"It means 'rain' in Arabic."

"Hmm. An *Arabe tambien,* no?"

"Yes. But American."

"Oh, *Americanos,* they all talk about freedom. I think it's too easy." She pointed to the dull jade Pacific.

"Can I go out there?"

I looked up from twining the vacuum cord on hooks.

"Sure."

She pulled the sliding glass door open and stepped out into the warm breeze.

"Heez beautiful."

I began polishing the end tables, snatching glances of her. She bent over the white wrought-iron railing; her legs were short, but tanned and flawless, the Achilles tendons jutting as if her bare feet were unafraid of heights or stones, shoes, or men. Harry had a Louis Icart lithograph in his bedroom, which I had just dusted. It pictured an ingenue in slip bending out a window just this way, her long, pale legs touching like dove wings. Fabiola was no dove, however. She was a ruby-throated warbler.

"So you an *Arabe* like Bully?" she asked, reentering.

"Yes," I said, catching the hint of Spanish. "But I was born here. We're all Californians."

She drew her lower lip down by a finger. "I yam a Californian, too." And she began to stroll toward the door, looking up at the ceiling as if she had found some secret. "Bye-bye."

I stood in the sea air coming in with an idiot's smile, then went to wash the dishes.

Later that afternoon, Bill came home. Stockbrokers have short days. By three o'clock his tie was thrown on the floor (which I would pick up), his swimsuit donned (it later would be thrown on the couch), and he was off to the beach to play volleyball. I did not tell him about Fabiola's arresting entry that morning until that night after I had cooked Bill and Harry and their dates a soufflé and served them a fine cabernet. For a few moments, I was allowed to join them, and we toasted the wine. The dates—statuesque German sisters with smoky eyes and full figures Bill had met playing volleyball—laughed at Bill's corny traveling-salesmen jokes. Diminutive and demure, Uncle Harry impressed them with his newly learned French. I cleared the dishes, lit the candles, and watched the four of them sit back on the leather couch, arms wrapped around each other like octopuses.

"It's getting cold tonight."

Bill got up to slide the balcony door.

"But—heez beautiful," I whispered to him. He looked at me with a noncommittal smile, and asked if I could fetch some Courvoisier. On his way back from the bathroom, I poked him in the ribs and motioned him back to the hallway. "There was a girl here this morning. Name of Fabiola. Said she knew you."

His black eyes went wide. "Keep her away! I've been suffering from her for two weeks." He stuffed his hands in his pockets and pulled up. I followed him with a tray of brandies.

The women retired with the men to the bedrooms, and I got out my sleeping bag, laying it out on the chartreuse rug, cracking the sliding door to feel the fine mist come in off the beach. I read Kazantzakis's *Saviours of God* by pen light and tried to hear only the sea's moans.

A week later, Fabiola appeared again. I held up my dust pan, speechless, mumbling that Bill was not in. She didn't seem to hear, but walked through the open balcony door, exclaiming what a beautiful day it was, and would I like to go bicycle riding? I undid my apron and told her to give me a second. In the garage I found Bill's bike. Fabiola swung a lithe leg over her seat, and we were off.

We headed down the shore road to the bicycle path along the sand. Her short golden hair flecked with darkness flew up in the wind. I called out, "Don't your bare feet hurt on the pedals?" They were stripped of rubber.

"No," she smiled, pumping faster.

We passed the paddleball courts at Venice Boulevard and stopped to get a hot dog. Fabiola said, "I like lots of mustard, heh." The plunger of the mustard jug spit like a wheezing sailor. "Then gimme some of those pick-lays," she said and laid on the relish. "And some *tomate, por favor*."

At Muscle Beach, a man with outsized biceps and deltoids was clanking twenty-five-pound weights on his dumbbells.

"Ridiculous," Fabiola said, licking the ketchup off her arm. "They look like—how do you say?—bears. Big bears."

"Don't you like big bears?"

"I like skinny bears," she smiled. Her eyes were sunspots. Another man lifted five hundred pounds, his face turning purple.

"I should go tickle him," she mused.

We bicycled far down shore, until the path was swallowed by sand. I raced her to the waves, dove, but the tide went out and I slapped on the foamy sheet, scraping my chest on the sand.

"Oh, Francisco, I am sorry!" she touched my shoulder. "You are really hairy."

"And you are really beautiful."

"Lie down here. I will fix your chest."

I lay on the warm sand, and she ran to the sea, scooping up water, running back to smooth it over my raw body. I jerked from the sensation and turned over. She ran to get more water. It dripped through her hands to the point that she was giving me a rubdown and faking the water. I couldn't stop laughing. "Eet hurts so good I bet," she said, then slapped me on the rump with a "heh." Her body was clefts and dunes.

*

The other day, taking a long morning shower to stave off the day's responsibilities while my wife, exhausted, hid in bed from the baby's first gurgles, I bent to wash my feet for the first time in years. On the instep of my left foot sat a white scar the shape of an incisor. It had been cut by a jagged rock, but it was the Mark of Fabiola.

The day after our bicycle ride, Fabiola came to fetch me for another ride along the beach. At the sight of a fishing boat she raised my arm as if it were a spyglass and sang, "Look, go to the tuna!" Then she dropped the arm as quickly as she had picked it up and ran to the sea: "I want to be a fish that is catched and they take me to La Paz."

"Bolivia?"

"No, La Paz, Baja California. My home country."

She swam south away from me. When I caught up she spied a jetty, declaring, "We go they-er." The way she said it did not sound Mexican, but rather Deep Southern. She took my hand to mount the first rock, balancing on green slime and avoiding the mussels, then let go as she hopscotched from one slippery rock to another. "Careful, Favvy," I called out.

We sat on separate rocks at the end of the jetty, watching a tuna boat melt into the horizon.

"Favvy, are you sure you are not part Swedish—the blonde hair and all?" I thought I caught the long, sonorous *o*'s of a Scandinavian.

"You are craisie! Are *you* Swedish?"

I sprinkled her with water cupped in the rocks, and she gave out a "heh."

"What brought you to Los Angeles?"

"I want to study . . . to be a nurse. I am taking the English at the Santa Monica College, but the chemistry, heez too hard."

"Where's your family?" I asked, figuring she'd say La Paz. She ignored the question, pulling a piece of seaweed stranded on the rocks around my neck, and then another around hers, like a necklace.

"Beautiful, no?" She purred, "I would like to be mermaid."

"You are!"

Off came the tank top, and the pores of her chest grew to goose bumps, each with a fine, almost invisible light hair that made her skin downy. Alone over that skin was a red stripe. She eased herself down the slippery rock into a cleft. Water surrounded her. Buoyancy personified. The sea curled into her ravines, and I responded, blood swimming from the interior to the extremities, as if it were on alert that it might be transported completely into someone else who—the blood itself seemed to sense—might spill it if not careful. That's why it was both a surge and a halt. Fabiola noticed, breathed out, "Heh," before sinking, her hair swirling like an anemone.

I rushed down the rocks, slipped and fell, slashing my foot. Fabiola put her arms around my waist, and I slid into the sea, the pain suddenly transformed into her and obliterated. I tried to kiss her aqueous shoulder, but only caught the sea. "Let's go out far," she announced, and began swimming toward a buoy. When she left, the pain came back, and I cried out, "No, Favvy, I'm going back."

My foot was bleeding in tributaries through the toes. Fabiola swam to me, fetched her tank top from the jetty, and made a tourniquet for my foot, her arm wrapped around my waist as we hobbled back. Our free hands walked the bikes as if they were our children.

Bill Haddad scowled when I told him later I was going up the coast with a young Mexican woman named Fabiola. He warned me about catching disease and said she was common. But had he been strung with seaweed by her delicate hands? I kept my secret.

Soon we were headed north on the Ventura Highway, which, two hundred years before, had been the El Camino Real, "the King's Highway," the six hundred–mile path trodden by Fr. Junipero Serra mostly on foot, though he was made part lame by a painful scorpion bite his first week in the new land. Pointing to a bronze church bell in Woodland Hills marking Serra's path, Fabiola called out, "Ring it!" I honked.

"*Ayie,* not that way!"

Past Oxnard, migrant workers stooping to pick summer squash and strawberries, we turned a gentle curve to find the Pacific shining like a hammered metal sheet. A road bell signaled Mission Buenaventura was close. Salt air filled our lungs as we got out, Favvy in her cut-off jean short-shorts and red sweatshirt, and me in jeans and T-shirt of the Los Angeles Dodgers.

"Francisco, I cannot wear like this to see *Madre de Dios,*" she said, glancing at the mission's arched door and adobe bell tower. Up went the trunk, and Fabiola fished out a skirt and scarf. "You watch for me while I change in the car." I did.

Entering the church, she touched three fingers in a font. Crossing herself quickly, she genuflected and entered the last pew. I knelt next to her. Soon she began to sob quietly, and I reached in my pocket to fetch her a handkerchief. "Are you all right?" I whispered.

"*Si.*"

She hid her eyes in her hands. Then she turned to get a holy card of Our Lady of Guadalupe, and murmured in Spanish the prayer on its back. I stole a look at her marvelous calves; the light from the stained-glass window of the Good Shepherd filtered blue and red onto the smooth amber skin. While her focus was heartfelt, mine was getting increasingly profane. I buried my own face in my hands, but received no Guadalupe but Fabiola. With Teilhard de Chardin, the Jesuits had made God into a process. Processes do not answer prayers.

Fabiola got up. After her long séance, the air was heavy with the breath of old adobe and the odor of candle oil. Her faith seemed more than habit, but cracked open by suffering. When we came out, the sun hurt.

"Favvy, we have a history in California older than the Pilgrims."

"Who are them?"

"They were the Englishmen that first came to America back East."

"Was Jorge Washington with them?"

"No."

"I must study more history to become an American," she murmured.

We walked underneath palms lining the mission, nodded to an old padre in Franciscan brown, and I told her about the visionary Serra and Crespi, his sidekick, who constantly complained about the effect of coastal fog on his bones. Crespi was Sancho Panza to Serra's Don Quixote. Fabiola pronounced me Serra. "I am Crespi," she said.

When I told her about California's namesake, the seductive heroine of a novel popular at the time of Cortés who ruled over Amazons in an earthly paradise, she said, "You are *absolutemente* Serra."

"And you are Queen Calafia!"

She nuzzled my arm, coming close on the midnight-blue velour seat; those were the days when American cars still had a complete seat, not buckets separated by a console, and lovers risked accidents rubbing up against each other. Her knees touched, curled on the seat. Was skin on kneecap ever so bright?

At the Rincon speed trap, my foot got heavy, the water dazzling my eyes, Fabiola caressing the nape of my neck. Her breath smelled of sweet corn. The policeman caught me doing eighty-five. I let Fabiola speak to him, figuring her accent would throw him off and convince him we were foreigners. He didn't even take off his shades. A hundred-dollar fine or jail. Thank you, officer. Isn't she something? Isn't that water gorgeous?

The highway narrows along the sea in front of a little settlement known as La Conchita—three flat, short streets of oil and gas workers up against a cliff. It would be half-buried in a landslide twenty years later, the oil platforms, too, shut down after the Torrey Canyon spill and Unocal itself pretty much gone broke, a small part moved from California to Texas. But then the platforms were still churning away, Unocal was Union Oil and the sponsor of the Dodgers, "the sign of the finest, the sign of the 76."

Suddenly, Carpentaria sprouts in eucalyptus, pepper, and bougain-villea. A citrus orchard moved the hill back, a new lemon grove with waist-high trees then, now thick with lemons. We passed the Big Yellow House—famed for its chicken—and a strand of rocky beach signaling Santa Barbara around the bend.

Today Coast Route 1 flies through Santa Barbara unimpeded by lights. But then this was the one spot in the five hundred miles between San Fran-cisco and Los Angeles where you had to stop, and the lights were very long, so that you had to inhale the lemon air, the gardenia and the jasmine. You had to be captured.

"Oh, Francisco, you can smell this town."

Father Serra himself gave thanks for the odor of wild roses he found here, reminding him of the roses of Castile. The friars had prayed to Saint Barbara when their ship had almost wrecked in a storm off San Diego, and the sea had calmed. So this east-west strip of land drinking the sun all day against the mountains was named for the saint who had saved them.

Passing the house with a bronze statue of a dog on its lawn—he drowned saving his owner—the road welcomed us to the Queen of the Missions.

Fabiola ran immediately to the rose garden. She put her nose to blos-soms of each type—Gloire du Dijon, American Beauty, Tea—exclaiming, "Heez beautiful," continuing her conversion of everything she loved to a male.

"Can I pick one?"

"You're not supposed to, Favvy."

"Oh, please, just one." And as she asked she did, looking up at me with sin of which only the innocent are capable. She stripped off her sweatshirt as it was getting hot near noon, took the red rose from her hair, and placed it inside her madras blouse.

"Come, smell." Her voice was powdery.

A young lad threw a Frisbee too far from the green, and it landed in the rose garden. She ran to retrieve it for the stranger and let it fly. It flew all the way to the Roman facade of the Queen of the Missions, the only one of the twenty-one never to secularize, with sandstone the color of flesh.

We happened on a stone trough once purged of water by a bear's head gargoyle. Favvy lay down on the bottom of the empty trough used to wash clothes, melt fat for tallow, and grind wheat. She called out, "Grind me like the wheat!" I laughed, snapping a picture. I took another of her hanging onto the branches of a giant Moreton Bay fig tree, as if she were tugging at the neck veins of a man.

"Oooo, look at this!"

She ran her hands up the flanks of a lemon eucalyptus, the smooth bark rippled at joint like a flexed arm or leg. She took a picture of me kissing the knee of the tree, and gave out a "heh," which I was beginning to realize was the closest thing to a laugh Fabiola possessed. She smiled; her teeth had the dull sheen of abalone. But she didn't laugh.

Once again, Fabiola went into a church, taking her place in the last pew, burying her face before lighting a red-cupped candle. She reached for a tiny pink-bordered handkerchief as we left.

Now the road veered away from the coast past Gaviota, then reached it again at Pismo Beach, where fog blots out the sun. From there we continued north on Coast Route 1.

"Oooo, look at that! Big as—how you say?—what the head is when it is dead."

"You mean 'skull'?"

"*Si.*"

It was Morro Rock, the Gibraltar-like boulder, an ancient man with cavernous eyes. We got out; the surf hissed. A trawler passing in front of a barge got a sorrowful blast.

"I would like to live at the top of that rock, you know."

"Why?"

"*Pero* I be away from the freeway and the people, and I can see only the water. But *es frio,* no? You are hungry?"

I rolled my hand over my stomach.

"Good," she said. "Where is the closest mission?"

"Back in San Luis Obispo, inland."

"Take me they-er. Pray first, then eat."

As we passed The Buccaneer with its sign of a juicy hamburger walking the plank, I said, "No. Eat first, then pray."

Favvy scowled. But after moving around the blue leather round booth, she ordered fish and chips and I a double-decker burger. She went to toilet, returning with her hair tied in a barrette and lips daubed persimmon.

The conversation was an underdeveloped one, as most were with Fabiola. She was not confident of her English and rarely verged further than two sentences at a time. I showed her pictures out of my wallet; she asked me to describe what each of my cards were, from Social Security to banking. In those days I had no credit cards—paid cash for everything—and, except to my parents for my education for which they would take nothing, owed no one a dime. Fabiola played with her fork as we waited for our meals, shearing the spaces between tines, barely touching metal. She also proved she could bend her fingers at the knuckle in a certain grotesque way.

"Is this what they do in La Paz?"

"You are craisie. They fish in La Paz for abalone and many good things."

"How many brothers and sisters do you have?"

"A lot." She flipped a fry into her mouth. Then she wiped her lips and asked, "What do you love most *en la tierra*?"

It halted me in midchew. I thought: Mother, father, sister, brother. The sea. The mountains. Poetry. But each seemed to entail too much talk, and I ended up sticking her in the side of her ribs. She jumped and gave out her ironic pant.

"Do you want to be a doctor? You are *mui inteligente*."

"No, I kind of like to spin fables."

"What?"

"Fables, stories. But I will probably be a newspaperman. You can't do as much spinning there."

"I would like you to spin *fabula*."

"Do you spin?"

"If you want me to spin! I like that."

"Every time you fix my foot, I will spin you."

"But I have to fix other foots if I become a nurse."

"Then I will spin you every time you fix another foot."

"*Bueno!*"

We went about Mission San Luis Obispo in silence, noting where Father Serra signed its first register in 1772 in the shadow of mountains whose twin peaks look like a bishop's miter. This was *La Canada de Los Osos,* the valley where bears were once plentiful and tore up the bushes.

This time in church Fabiola did not cry, though she started a candle. Her amber eyes lit with the candle wicks, but she seemed distracted, not covering her face for prayer but looking out through a stained-glass window, as if seeing a signal of someone lost at sea. This time I prayed; I prayed that I would make love to her. I begged God to turn His head and let me do everything there was to do with this young woman from the Far South of my home.

"Do you know how the Indians made those tiles?" I asked her, pointing to the arcade's roof.

She shook her head.

"They shaped the wet clay around their shins before baking them in the sun."

"Oooo," she said, rubbing her shins.

That afternoon, past fields of peaches and avocado, we turned off the road to sand dunes surrounding Oso Flaco and Oso Gordo lakes. Fabiola shed her skirt and tank top and ran up a dune in her emergency-red bikini. I gave chase.

The sand was blistering. The afternoon sun had slapped the stones with heat. Strands of yucca and sea oats brushed against my shins as I followed her trail out of the rocks into the perfect blonde sand. I crested a hill; she was on another one, looked back at me, then disappeared downslope. In the distance, a thin strip of blue showed the Pacific. East was a deeper blue, one of the lakes on the other side of the high dune.

I ran to keep from burning my soles. What was Fabiola doing? She had lured me far from the road; undulant sand now blotted any view of water. I was sweating and breathing hard. She was quick on her feet, even in sand.

Cresting another dune I found nothing; Fabiola had disappeared. I ran around shouting for her. Then I heard a low growl and turned. Red emerged from the sand, then a head.

"So, you're burying yourself!"

"No, no!" she shrieked, starting to flee.

I lunged, tripping her by the calves.

"Oso Flaco!" she squirmed, smiling. The sand flew as if hit by a rattler. She dug in her ankles. "You know what that means? Skinny Bear."

"Then you are Oso Gordo!" I cried, and bit her neck. I grabbed the tie of her top. Her squirming slowed as I loosened and pulled it off. Sky. Ballooning blue. A spume of cloud trail dispersing like a jet stream. Her breasts were caked with sand, nipples like the stems of figs. She lunged for my mouth, her tongue cayenne.

Her head thumped left and right as I pulled off her bottom, throwing it like a bull who has hooked the matador's cape. I went down on her and tasted a rank mix of sand and sweat and vulva. Her eyes closed as if praying. Then as I crawled up over her, she bit my neck. Out shot the cloud trail. The sand was steaming. Too soon!

"O Flaco, Flaco, you are so hairy!"

It took a loud report from an intruder to realize my skin, our skins, were burned.

"What was that?" she coughed.

A dune buggy roared toward us. Fabiola leaped to fetch her bathing suit. As did I. Then he turned. Two more dune buggies appeared in the distance, rising and falling on the dunes like giant soldier ants.

"I hate them," Fabiola looked up at the sky. "There is more cloud now."

Up the highway, she spotted another mission, the only one you can see from the main road. It was San Miguel, but we kept moving.

"You no want the greatest angel?"

"We're running out of sun."

"I want to sleep by the sea."

I checked the map. It was a dull, long ride to Monterey on 101, and I knew that Coast Route 1 at night is treacherous with fog on the high cliffs and no hotel shy of Ventana.

"Okay, back to Pismo."

Fabiola smiled. "Heez got a flat beach."

By evening we had pulled into "the Clam Capital of the World." Pismo was firm and wide, cars and Jeeps driving up and down. It was misty and cold, but still I dunked myself in the sea, along with the sun. Fabiola stood onshore, hugging herself, one leg slithered around the other like a crane.

Clams for dinner. The steamed windows of the café made me think: We are the clams. We are eating ourselves. Fabiola barely looked up, lapping the juice.

Before signing Mr. and Mrs. at a motel—a terribly quaint thing today but a required subterfuge then—I walked with Fabiola along the firm, wet beach. She shivered, gripping me. Banked fires swirled smoke into the night. The low chatter of campers grilling their hot dogs and marshmallows. The wind ate a stray guitar's lonesome tune. The surf hushed.

"I love whales," Fabiola murmured.

"Have you seen one?"

"*Mucho*. In my country near La Paz, they come at there to mate. Scammon's Lagoon."

I nodded, stopping to pick up a broken piece of a conch shell, pointing to the smooth, pink lip.

"But it is dead," she said, looking up at the gray sky.

The room was cold. Fabiola pressed the back of her hand to her hip as she shivered, then gathered extra blankets for the bed. She closed the drapes and went to the bathroom to take a hot shower. I got in bed, heart ajar. Silence. The sea soughing at the window. When she returned she was naked. For a while, we lay undercover, unmoving. Then she whispered, "Flaco!" And came over me, kissing my eyes and neck and mouth, as if anointing them. She moved down with a "heh." I lurched, and she held me. She covered it and began jerking up and down fast, like some cricket-headed oil rig. She sucked and sucked and sucked. She did not draw back her teeth. It felt like being ground down! Her teeth and tongue worked at cross-purposes, but they stopped an early explosion.

I turned from her angry, knowing passion. And moved down her body, catching the nipples.

"Harder!"

I gritted my teeth like a boy forced to pose for a picture, wondering if I might bite them off.

"Harder!" Her voice was raw.

I raised her breast like a tent. She began to shake as if electrified. She shook like a motor. She seemed to want me to thrust to her mouth.

But I was a young man with less experience than I would have admitted then. Sex was a kind of unspoken required college course that everyone took and thought they got A's in and wanted to repeat, so I was no virgin. But I had had few repeats, and, I suspect—free-love clarions aside—more passion was spent on antiwar yelling, weed smoking, and harmony seeking than repeater courses for sex. And love? What sex we did have certainly delayed or confused that plenty. In short, neither were we promiscuous as we appeared to be—with the same shynesses and shallownesses of most American teenagers when confronted with the real thing—nor did we have the guts for love.

Fabiola introduced sex as a force, not a requirement. I had attached myself briefly to mild coeds, and with the Pill, not to mention the semester system, we dropped off each other as easily as you'd change courses. But the girl from La Paz was educating by fire. Her unleashings were something different, even frightening. Teeth bared, tongue relentless, body centrifugal in power, something drove her, and it wasn't peace, love, and harmony. It was dark. For a moment, I thought of Billy's warning, but not of disease.

After two repeats, we lay spent in the darkness. The waves lulled us to sleep.

Now beauteous Carmel beckoned, where my parents had spent their honeymoon after the war, conceiving me supposedly in the little town of artists and writers. Carmel contained the final resting place of Serra at Mission San Carlos Borremeo.

We were bird chirping with each other, Favvy calling me "Oso Flaco" and me calling her "Oso Gordo," stopping at the wharf of Steinbeck's nearby Monterey, the old capital of Spanish California. Here was the famous oak Vizcaino had marked in 1602, which took Portola 150 years to stumble upon after getting lost in the fog. On its branches Serra hung two bells in 1770, as he did on a tree at each mission's start. He began his first mass at this third mission, singing the Te Deum to the swish of pines and Monterey cypress. A month before, lost at sea with Portola, he had written, "We are out of the world." Lonely, drunk, the Spanish soldiers wrecked this foothold in the north by molesting and raping the Indian women. Serra would be plagued by the wretched irony up and down the coast: to save souls he had to travel with the protection—and the satanic abuses—of a colonizing power. Trying to shake off the demons, Serra moved his headquarters mission from Monterey to Carmelo, his final resting place in 1784. There, crying out a *Tantum Ergo* with lungs beaten by asthma and the stone he hit his chest with, he gave up the spirit.

We drove the six miles from Monterey to Carmel Serra had walked, a few of the eleven thousand miles he had traveled in the New World, half on foot. Fabiola kissed the hands of the sarcophagus containing Serra's body, and then she knelt.

"Favvy, this is not the church."

"But I love him. He gave us our places."

Later, on a stone wall back in Monterey, I spilled some wine from our bottle on my shirt. Fabiola tried to suck it out. I fell over, laughing. "Flaco," she poked my ribs. "Gorda!" I grabbed her buttocks. By afternoon she was tipsy, eating the pepper balls off the trees and spitting them out. "Where is the bell? Where is the bell?" she threw her arms in the air.

"There!" We ran to one of the roadside bells, and I swung it. No sound.

"Heez deaf and dumb," Fabiola said, finding no clapper.

I went to the car for a tire iron, and banged the bell with it.

"You are craisie," Fabiola looked around us. "You didn't have to ring the bell that way."

"Why?"

"'Cause you did it the night before," she smiled.

Dizzy, we fell into our Travel Lodge for the night, and I opened up a flask of Fundador brandy.

"The Arabs and the Spaniards met at Granada!"

"Granada!" Fabiola sang, pulling down the coverlet.

She flicked on the television. "This is how I learn English!"

"*Yo te quiero et te necesito et te amo con todo mi corazón.*"

For that one memorized line of Spanish learned in some locker room of the past, Fabiola tackled me.

"Why you no go to the war?" she asked, sipping the nut-colored liquor.

"Because I breathe too heavily." I inhaled to demonstrate. "I am an asthmatic, just like Serra."

"But what if they pick you. You go?"

"No. I would not serve in this war."

"But they put you in prison."

"No. I would go to Tahiti."

"All the other *Arabes,* and the Yewish—they like to fight."

"It ruined my generation, this war."

"But you are not ruined."

"Yes I am. I am aimless."

"Except for spinning Fabiola."

"*Si.*"

"Can you make a living spinning Fabiola?"

"No. I will probably become a gigolo."

"What's that?"

"It is a man who makes money off of rich old women who have not gone to bed with their husbands in twenty years."

"How much will you charge?"

"One Rolls-Royce."

She put her finger to my lips: "No cars. I hate cars. Gold."

"Then I will charge gold."

"Good, then you can give it to me and we can make babies."

"You will make babies with gold?"

She tipped her glass till it was drained, then looked out the window.

"How come we didn't go to San Gabriel?"

"What do you mean?"

"Mission San Gabriel. It's the one in L.A. They rape a lotta women there, a lotta Indians. That was the worst. Why we no go there?"

"It was too close."

"Yes, it was too close!" Her agate eyes flared.

"You know some history, don't you?" I drained my glass.

"More than you know I know."

She grew sullen, holding her hip, going to turn the heater on as the night winds lashed the motel.

"Why do you always hold your hip? Are you hurt?"

"I was."

"How?"

"*O Dios!*" she whimpered, crumpling a blanket to her chest, rocking.

"Favvy," I said softly, leaning over to rub her back.

"It was the day. We were coming back from seeing the whales make love. My father and sister and I. We were driving fast back to La Paz. My father, he sing. He loves to sing, and my sister play *guitarra* for him in the front seat, and I . . . I was singing, too, in the back seat. The car is not a good car, and it start to shake. Maybe he is going too fast, and I say, Stop. *Padre,* stop! There is another car coming, and our car is shaking. It shakes like craisie. And we are smashing. And our car is going over and over and over."

Her cries were broken by silences. They made me tremble.

"My father was killed, and my sister. *Muertos. Todos muertos, Dios.* I crack my ass."

"Where was your mother?"

"*Madre* die long time ago when I was small. We have no money for medicine. We are poor. O Flaco, *estoy sola, sola!*"

I embraced her in her torment, trying to mend her with my hands. She began to shake and at the height of her excitement gave out a yell that branded itself on my memory:

"Fry my yeggs!"

"What?"

"My yeggs, fry them!"

Appropriate enough. I was, in fact, a housemaid.

In the middle of the night she moaned, "I am not good feeling." She got up, clutching her stomach, and ran to the bathroom, throwing up the wine and brandy and sausage. I listened to her wretch. It was pitiful. I helped her get into the bathtub afterward to clean off. The hot water ran down her back as she sat, doubled up, whimpering. Then came the most startling of all Fabiola-isms:

"I feel like a table!"

There was nothing to say to something like that, so I enfolded her in towels, dressed her in a nightgown, got her in bed, and went to find some hot tea. When I returned she was sleeping. I drank the tea, looking out the window at the boats bob against each other in the harbor like restless children.

On the way back, Fabiola was silent, curled to one side of the car, in and out of sleep. She read me a passage that struck her from the Serra historian King about the legend of Serra seeing the Holy Family in the California desert one day, and then returning with others to prove it, finding only three cottonwoods in the wasteland. She turned to stare at the blurring El Camino Real.

The only mission we stopped for going south was the most dilapidated, timeworn of all twenty-one missions.

Soledad sat by itself in a dry plain of the Salinas Valley, a crumbled wall of adobe sloped to one side with an eerie blowhole that appeared like an eye. The church was gone. The arcade with tiled roof was gone. Most of the walls had crumbled to dust or melted in the rain. There was no road to Soledad. To reach it, you had to hike through a field of nettles.

Fabiola did not know where to pray.

"Soledad" was the first word Father Serra thought he heard uttered by the Indians of the parched region to the Spaniards. From out back of the crumbled adobe wall, a man emerged and shooed us off. "There's nothing here," he drawled. "Why did you come?"

Favvy shook her head as we walked in wind rattling the nettles, "*Soledad* will be much between us."

*

Last night, my wife set out a fine meal in our dining room. She had chilled white wine in goblets, an excellently sautéed scrod, and salad with her own tart dressing. For the first time, our wedding finery was brought out—the china, the embroidered tablecloth and napkins. Just as we toasted, the baby began to cry. We looked at each other, put our goblets down, and stared mutely at the wall, our heads cocked to take in the ancient, mindless, bottomless wail that you wait to end but does not end. We both knew any effort to retain the romance of the evening was fruitless. I got up to get the Judge, a silent tear edging down my wife's cheek for an effort well tried. Soon he was with us, cheeks all puffy.

His was not unlike Fabiola's cry in the bathtub that night so many years ago, nor the way she cried—though muffled with a handkerchief—at the airport the day I left for Alaska.

I had continued to see Fabiola in the warm weeks before leaving for pipeline work in the Far North, an oxymoronic bent for which I have no explanation. When we went to my parents' home for dinner, Fabiola donned a flaming-red low-cut dress that instantly raised my father's eyebrows. I had never seen her in a dress; she appeared as lovely as the Naked Contessa smuggled into the satin of Old Granada. All that was missing was the black fan. My father and she hit it off. They danced in the den to a cha-cha of Prez Prado: "Aaaaaaaah!" He did the side step, the turnabout, all the while not once looking at her, a genius of the dance floor. Favvy told him of Scammon's Lagoon and the whales; he was fascinated and vowed to visit there on his motorcycle, a vow he kept. Mother and my sister chattered in the kitchen about how gorgeous were Latin women.

Adjusting to subzero temperatures was not easy, and Fabiola's passionate letters helped. She wrote: "Dear Flaco, Where are you? Oso Gordo is *soledad* without you. The beach is cold and windy, *mi amor,* and you are not here. I need your hairy fur to protect me. I want to cure you from the cold. I am still being almost a nurse. You will like me dressed in white, but maybe not as much as bikini. O Flaco, fry my eggs tonight!" The back of the envelope was imprinted with her red lips.

I began to get a terrible, burning sensation whenever I urinated. The doctor judged it nonspecific urethritis, or NSU, a common imitator of gonorrhea. Bill Haddad, alas, had been right. The price of Fabiola's oral ardor!

I wrote that I missed her immensely, but that for her to come to Fairbanks would be crazy. If her bad hip gave her terrific pains in California fog, what would it be like in fifty-below-zero weather? She wrote back that she understood, but was sorry and hoped that someday soon I would leave Alaska.

"Are there other *Arabes* in Alaska?" she asked when I returned for Christmas to the Southland.

"No."

"Then you are craisie. It is not natural for you to be there."

"Maybe you are right. Maybe I am beating myself like Father Serra, except with the snow."

I did not tell her about the NSU. Nor could I admit to myself that I was not yet a man. That I fell into that excuse of distance because I couldn't give her or anyone what was richly deserved by such revelations as she had given me. I had graduated from college, but that was all. I was afraid of her endless school.

We did not make love, but took long walks onshore, listening to the sea.

*

The day my father and sister died, I told my wife about Fabiola. After a stretch of remoteness—as people enter when they are assessing whether they should take something as a threat—she pointed to our little boy and said, "Heez beautiful." I think I fell completely in love with her that day.

In the morning we hear the first gurgle. We know we have about fifteen minutes before the day draws us out on the spur of his mindless need. She tickles and curls into me, whispering, "Harder!" that I may continue to spin Fabiola, and it is as if a beauteous one long ago could claim a part of every lovemaking after her father and sister were killed. And she had told me the story.

A Perfect Stranger

people never ask why you became a doctor. Politicians are asked what made them run, writers what urged them to put pen to paper, athletes when they knew they could not live without breaking the record. I guess people assume doctors are born that way—in love with mucous, syringes, the hammer-on-the-knee. Not to mention blood. No one seems to want to know why you would choose a life where you have to put your hand up someone's fanny every day.

Well, it came to me the night of my late-bloomer near-wedding to Carolyn Smith—I'm thirty-two—that it all had to do with a little pickup basketball game when I was fourteen down by the sea. Just before starting high school, I was at Ocean City, Maryland, where my family had rented a little board-frame summer house four blocks up from the Ferris wheel. I had no more care in the world than throwing a ball into a leather hand or a hoop. Girls? They had begun to catch my eye with their hint of ravines, but not much. I had no words to say what they did to me anyway, and fourteen is a good age to take your wordlessness to the courts.

It was a great day. Sea wind was blowing sand from the dunes. It fell like grace on the slippery asphalt. I was in a mean two-on-two with my pal Sandy on my side. Our opponents were these two local black kids who stunk as badly as we. The sand didn't help visibility or movement to the hoop; it caked our sweating bodies. We were down eleven to ten (scoring by buckets) in a game to eleven, but you had to win by two, so I was pressing to get inside. There was a feeling I used to get at a peak moment in a basketball game that I was playing completely on my toes, that in fact, with the right amount of spring, I could vault not just to the rim of the basket but over the top of the backboard, an illusion of pure antigravitational force that shot up from my ankles, through my calves and chest right to the sideburns of my head. My anger made me buoyant. Sandy used to say at the end of a game my eyes grew mean, drained of their blue till they were icy.

"You look like everyone else on the court is an insult," Sandy laughed one day when we were having Gatorade after a pickup game. "Then you're tossing this marshmallow to the lions, and they can't block it and we win. How do you do that, Stevey?"

"I don't know," I told him. And I didn't. And I still don't, though mine is mostly a passing game now. As a teenager, anger on the court made my fingers soft as a cat's. It's when I was lackadaisical that I'd throw the bricks up there. In those days, I thought myself the best white guy on the D.C. courts, at least under fifteen. I was so cocky: I OWN THIS HOOP! It was in my walk, squawk, and eyes.

Usually, facing a tall guy with a goatee skinny as I was, I'd have gotten a pass from Sandy, taken his screen, and put in my ten-foot jumper. To go inside with players taller and faster would have been suicide. Mine was a perimeter game anyway. (Now I'm all inside, all rebound and out pass—no shot, except a cripple. Don't have enough stomach muscle.) In fact, my life to that time was on the perimeter. I met everything and everybody out in the foyer and invited someone inside very carefully, if at all.

Something called me inside. Sometimes, you head fake, the court is a blur of bodies, inside it's packed with sweating hulks, and you'd no sooner go there than you would drive a car into a tree. But sometimes, you head fake and the blur of bodies disappears. You use your head like a wand. Go left, people there. Come back right, they're gone. Just for a second, the middle is open like, well, daylight.

I saw it. The rim like a tabernacle. I've always felt something holy in basketball, and I'm not punning. Certainly ever since that day by the sea. That day, a wave mounted behind the rim, and for a second I said to myself: *Dive in!* So I drove inside. And that's where it happened. That's where my life changed forever. That's where, without knowing it, I started to die.

As I twisted upward to glance it off the backboard, the tall fellow with the goatee kneed me in the stomach. Coming down I slipped on the sandy court and fell. For a time, I didn't move. It was three seconds forever in that lane. It felt like his knee had gone through me. I upchucked. The guy with the goatee yanked me up, trying to help. I had no smile for him, but somehow stayed up. Sandy was so mad he charged on two straight plays, and we lost.

Didn't think much of it going to bed by the sea that night. My stomach was sore, but I figured I'd be better in the morning. The drifting waves gave off a scouring sound, then a hissing. Soon my whole insides felt invaded. I couldn't sleep. My folks pumped me with aspirin, to no avail. I threw up blood. By morning, my mother came into the room and said, "You're white as a sheet." She called the local doctor. By the time he got there I was vibrating like one of those old malt shakers my father likes. I almost blacked out. The doc was shaking.

There are things that go on inside us—I mean physically, too—that just never make it into the medical books. They taught us in med school to be calm as a lighthouse. Try that out with a five-year-old hyperactive kid who is bloodying his head against a wall to avoid a shot. Or a heroin addict who is begging you for one, choking you for one, before he opens up his fucking mouth. In some ways, I became a doctor because I had to. Luckily, my dad had enough of the shaking local yokel with his wild stethoscope and called 911.

"He's in shock," the husky medic said, wrapping me fast and tight, then giving me a quick hypo. I was up and gone in seconds, leaving the nervous doctor behind. My pop was right alongside me, looking a little tense, before beaming his luminous smile. I always thought he gave heat with that look of his, and I needed it, as I was still shaking. Funny, of all the people I know, my almost new wife Carolyn looks like my father— both blonde with eyes flower-bed brown.

"Steve, I know you like to dance, but isn't this too much?" he said, pulling the blanket up around my neck.

Only my pop could crack a joke at a time like that. It helped. I began to subside. The shot was taking hold. They never taught us humor in med school, but it would have been as valuable as slicing up the cadavers.

The rural hospital in Salisbury had a crude MRI, a thin tube in which I lay still as stone, listening to what sounded like a machine gun shooting me. Maybe it should have. I had a tumor the size of a baseball on my liver that the knee kick had ruptured. They poured blood into me. I'd lost a couple of quarts internally and was nearly dead. Nothing bleeds like a liver. Just take a look at the cow liver in the market and press it, and you'll get the picture.

There was not one tip-off to that tumor in the months before that pickup game in Ocean City. Frankly, I was rarely sick as a child, the picture of health and hardihood on court or field. When they stabilized my heart, they medevacked me to D.C. Children's Hospital. More MRIs, more CAT scans. All kinds of radium going in and out of me. I read my folks' faces. Even Pop's face was drained of its inner light. Liver cancer is extremely rare in children, more common in older men who drink a lot. Hepatitis can cause it, but I never had that.

People said, "This is so rare." Who wanted to be rare? I wasn't interested in entering the *Guinness Book of Records.* I just wanted to live to shoot a free throw.

Pop took my hand that night after the revelation of my fellow traveler, the tumor. "That basketball game was the most important game of your life," he said softly. "Thank God you drove inside." I nodded.

"Ever find out who kneed me?"

"No sir," Pop said. "A perfect stranger."

It took us a week to find a doctor who had ever seen a malignant tumor in a child's liver. He flew down from New York City. If I had stayed with my game, said the doctor, played it safe, put up an outsider, I'd'a been dead in a month. That's how fast that thing was growing. I liked Dr. Craig. I liked his frankness and the way he twined philosophy with biology. He was also very good with obscure baseball facts; for example, he knew not only that Ty Cobb was a bastard but that his uniform sported no number. When I was out of my mind with pain, it was Dr. Craig who forced me to figure out how Three-Fingered Brown lost his two digits.

Eventually, two more docs consulted with Dr. Craig, trying to decide what to do. Finally, they cut half my liver out with the tumor. Filleted me like a cod. They cauterized a tricky little item of a smaller tumor attached to my big abdominal artery. And then they began to kill me with the chemotherapy for six months. Something I called Big Platinum. Kind of like industrial cleanser. I hated it. I could barely sleep at night. I trembled. I cursed God, whom I was beginning to feel Present for the first time in my life if, at first, as some kind of mute judge holding me in the scales. I've treated children with the Big C, though not in the liver, and it's always my best patient and my hardest assignment. I confess a tremble and even a smoke after my revelation to the parents. Won't confess what I did when one died. Just that it was a long, long drive, and the woman at the end of it was beautiful and held me hard.

The hair loss. The eyelashes falling off. The puking. The feeling that you are being scraped inside with very coarse sandpaper, cored like an apple, as if you're not only not going to get better but going to die like a piece of paper, something that would blow away. I hated every drop of that poison. That's, of course, what chemotherapy is. They poison you to make you better—in that sense, it's not too much different from the seventeenth-century leeches they'd attach to someone's body to rid him of a high fever. Or bleeding someone. Chemo attacks the blood and everything else in your body.

I looked up at my mother one night. She's all gray now, but then was a shining brunette with the tenderest touch; she looked up with those wide blue eyes they say she gave me. They were rimmed in black—that I remember. All the smiles in the world didn't take that black away. And I said to her, "Do you believe in God?"

She hesitated. Then said, "Yes."

"Well, why don't you go to church? Pop went back to church." My father, a man of infinite rationality, had suddenly shed all his Thomistic need for proofs of a deity and began going to mass daily, kneeling in the back row even when you are supposed to stand. He showed me the knobs on his knees.

"I don't know," she stumbled, coughing. She teared up, using the cough as her cover. "I guess I'm afraid to ask for something I won't get."

"Ask."

"All right," she smiled and cried quietly for the first time since I was stricken, leaning her pageboy hair over me as she kissed me. Her hair felt like mist on my hot forehead. In our dark hair, we are joined—the darkies in a light family—the huskies of the brood supposedly able to bear subzero weather or humanity. They say I have my mother's heart and my father's head, but at that time my body was nothing but a hollow.

During the carpet bombing of my blood, I got especially close to my old buddy Sandy. He's one of these people who has a great natural unorthodontic smile with an incisor turned outward as if to say, "For you, I sheathe the weapon." We've been friends ever since first grade at public school when he broke my nose during a spelling bee. Sandy was the second-to-the-last kid standing, facing the brain of our class, Margaret Kemper. I didn't even catch the word he muffed before he collapsed in his desk chair and reared his head back just as I was about to mouth some words of consolation. Got me right on the bridge. We both ran for the door, howling. Center field on our school's field was almost not big enough for both of us. We collapsed near each other, he gripping his head, and me my nose.

"What word did you lose on?" I asked him, smearing my hand with blood.

"'Hello.'"

"How did you lose on 'hello'?"

"One *l*!"

From that point on in life, we were rock solid, though people underestimated easygoing Sandy, figuring he'd always come in second. But from way back I liked someone who underplays it, who looks sideways while he's planning the most incredible assault.

"I haven't got your killer instinct, Steve," he said once.

"The hell you don't. You forgetting my nose?"

He laughed. Took him a while to make the team, but by our senior year, him at second base and me at shortstop and pitching, he was leading our league in stolen bases. "You're a goddamn thief," I said. He smiled craftily, "We try harder."

Once while he was staying overnight in my hospital room sleeping on the floor, he looked up at me about three o'clock, as the Platinum bottle was changed by the night nurse, and said, "Stevey, why do you always have to be first in everything? First picked for the all-star team in Little League. First to strike out eighteen batters in Eastern Regional history. Now this!"

"First with cancer?"

"Yeah."

"I guess some of us are meant to be lucky. What you wanna be—second?"

He looked at me with swollen eyes. He was someone who, while not easily serious, when he decided to be, could be.

"Sorry," I said. "Some of us were meant to lead, and others to . . ."

"Hello." This was his way of shaking me out of my voice cracking and finishing the statement darkly.

I told him I'd found out—no one dared tell me—that I had a one-in-three chance of surviving. It was on the National Cancer Institute Web site.

"Remember," he said, sitting on the corner of my cranking bed, pulling one of the four IVs to the side as if it were a veil, "Coach Shorely told us—remember him holding up the ball and pointing out the seams like infinity?—this is the only sport where you can fail two times out of three and be a huge success."

I started sobbing like a damn fool.

"Look it," he grabbed me by the bony shoulders, and I suddenly realized I was skinnier than him, far skinnier. "You're a solid .330 man. You're gonna make it. Who else am I going to flip to at second? I could close my eyes and know where you'd be."

"Close your eyes."

I took his hand and guided it to my belly. That was the scar, an inch wide and two feet long. It looked like a motorbike tread.

"What girl's gonna love me?" I hit the lowest point of my self-pity.

"Are you crazy? The minute you got the cancer you are assured of the best-looking girl in the land. Women love tragedy."

I slugged him, even with my IV, in the bicep.

"Hey, man, you're supposed to be asleep!"

With that we both bedded down, him to the floor, and me to my IVs.

From that high point came the low. The next day, I thought I'd come apart. It was from the medicine they gave me to counteract nausea. I shook like a fucking motor. It went on for hours. I stood up, unplugged my IVs, shouted, "Stop me! Stop me, God!" My mom cried out and called for the nurse. My pop came rushing in from somewhere, and they got me into a straitjacket. They apologized. It was the wrong medicine. When you get the C like I got the C, they try everything in the books and some things not in the books.

Sandy came down and calmed me.

"One *l* or two?"

Over the weeks Sandy read to me *The Pickwick Papers,* complete with accents, and recounted for me each of his favorite double plays in glistening detail. He told me, "Look, you save yourself. And you let God take the credit." I had a hunch it was the other way around, but I didn't let on. I just nodded. A shortstop has to trust his second baseman, that he'll be on the bag just so, before pivoting. And he has to trust you'll loft it to him in such a way he isn't cut in half by the runner.

Sandy was right about the C drawing the gals. And it came to pass that, when I had to fly all the way to California for an operation that would cut out a new growth where they had cauterized along the big artery, I met my first love and what I pretty much figured was my final love. She was a candy striper. Her name was Star Williams. She was a beautiful, glow-worm-eyed mulatto whose mother was a Mexican actress and whose father was an insurance magnate. She was doing the rounds of the cancer ward of the great clinic in San Francisco as part of her community service. What I didn't realize till years later, she hated it. Her lizardy green eyes were not dedicated to community service. She responded to me because I wouldn't let her not respond to me. I grabbed ahold of her heart like a handrail.

The new growth turned out, shockingly, benign (presume the worst about anything in life and you're rarely let down) and soon, after a year of chemo and operations, I was pronounced cancer free. My pop and mom took the news quietly, hugging about 5.0 on the Richter scale. Part of their muffled excitement was superstition—we had five more years to go before any such prognosis would be bankable.

I thought, stupidly, Star was the reason for my miraculous—that is exactly the word—recovery. After all, she had been there by the Bay when the last tumor was gutted. We wrote for a long time, throughout high school. She wrote letters that were full of "news," and I'd greedily scan it for one love word or phrase that usually occurred, if it did, in the last sentence.

But that emotional parsimony I took as special favor—the pearl of great price that I, and only I, was given, after weathering four pages of commentary about the 49ers and the Giants. We certainly had sports in common. She was a champion backstroker. She came and visited me for a summer. Her skin was brown velvet, buttery to the touch.

But there was something about her that Sandy did not like.

"She doesn't look at you directly," he said. "You say something meaningful, and she looks away."

"Maybe she's just shy," I said gamely, "especially with you in the room. She's not good at competition."

"C'mon. I'm not competition. We're not gay. I mean, when you love a girl, really go down into her with a look—you get me? You expect it to be returned."

"How do you know? Florence?" He'd been hanging around a girl we grew up with who had these Grand Canyon dimples and liked to be tickled. I found her a little flimsy.

"Yep. Hard-core experience." Sandy shook his head. Then he fixed his eyes on me. "Why doesn't she put her arm around you? I like a girl who wraps it around, you know?"

"Just because you haven't seen it doesn't mean it hasn't happened," I snapped. Sandy's inspections began to rile me.

About halfway through my senior year, all internal signs clean for four years, the big C chased from my insides like a battered pitcher, a boy my age on my block died. Stan Gaynor had been hooked by a brain tumor not long after I was kneed in the liver. I'd never been friends with him—he wasn't athletic—and I sure didn't get used to sirens up the street that year and actually stuffed pillows into my ears the night water filled his lungs to choking. Days later in the rain I walked by the funeral cortege. It was one of those bone-cold rains in Washington, D.C., that run off the tops of the old stone churches and the monuments and even the Jefferson cupola so that it seems Jefferson himself and all grand ideas of the pursuit of happiness and life and liberty are nothing but water running down marble.

Hands in a warm-up jacket and poncho over my head, I stopped and listened to the rain plink the hood. There weren't many cars in that gray procession. Gaynor had taken years to die, and I think many who had cared for him, even, had fallen away; he'd fought valiantly, but unlike me, he wasn't winning, and most everyone knew he wasn't. It's hard for even a close family to hold on to such hopelessness for so long. I'd heard he'd been a good bunter in Little League. I heard talk since my own striking down that maybe there were malignant electronic waves coming off a transformer on the power lines on our street since Steven Thompson and Stan Gaynor lived only three houses apart. There was talk of an investigation by the local city councilwoman, but nothing came of it.

I watched his mother get into the black car at Holy Host Church. She was Jewish and his father Catholic, and that in itself, so word around the neighborhood went, split them apart early, too much righteousness from opposite directions. That had all occurred before the cancer. Gaynor's tumor festooned from a ball at the back of his neck and spread in tentacles over the top of his brain. They got the tumor, but they couldn't ever get all those tentacles. So they bombarded him with all they bombarded me with, but more, and with less effect. He shrank to sticks, sleeping on his couch in the living room most of the day, tossing at night. Oh, how I knew that toss! But I didn't want to compare, no, not face-to-face! I didn't want an iota of his downward spiral to latch onto me.

"The boy Gaynor's mother is making him into a Holocaust victim," said a woman on the bus one day to another woman. I hid my face and pulled my cap down over my eyes. "Why don't they just let him go?"

She looked at me, Mrs. Gaynor did, just before entering the limousine. And I looked away again, just as I did that day on the bus. I took myself in the pelting rain to the church. It was empty. The sanctuary candle seemed an urn of blood.

I dropped on the red-cushioned kneeler. A woman up on the altar was snuffing candles, all but the one of blood, which must stay lit forever if we are to know this is indeed a Catholic church, one founded on the transcendence of mindless suffering.

"Dear Lord," I prayed. "I'm no good." The church glowed in amber, like the belly of an old ship. The woman at the altar disappeared into the sacristy, and I was alone.

"Why was I spared? Do you have a box of tumors up there and play them like checkers over the land? And I got the one that didn't kill? What do you want of me? Haven't I earned at least some illumination? You kill Stan Gaynor and take from me all heart toward him. Bring it back! Let me understand why I am here, hurting my knees on a rainy day in November, and Stan is being shoved in the earth.

"Damn it," I looked around, embarrassed, "don't let me be just a witness to suffering." And then I added the crux of the matter: "Please let Star fall in love with me."

Two weeks later, in response to my inviting her to our senior-year homecoming, at which I was going to propose marriage way past my parents' pleading, Star wrote that we were through. She had fallen in love with a breaststroker: "We just lived too far apart, Steve. You are my dear friend, Stevey, but it's just not romantic with us. I'm glad I helped you through your illness. But I can't help you for life." She planted her red lips to her signature, her most passionate gesture to date.

I went to college at Cal-Berkeley, Star's school, thinking, perhaps, I might inhale her. But my first semester she got pregnant by the breaststroker and moved to his hometown in eastern Montana. Sandy wrote me some joke about "he should have been a backstroker." I never saw her again.

For ten years, I hurt women. One was a nurse in med school who became pregnant and had an abortion. I found her the right doctor. Another fellow med student begged me to marry her, insisting I make love to her on Mount Tamalpais. I cut it off three days before the wedding. I told none of these good women about my liver cancer. When they saw the scar, and felt it, stroked it, I just told them it was a bad appendectomy.

Why I lied for so long about something so boiling inside I do not know. Maybe it was that telling Star everything and receiving nothing in return violated intimacy to such an extent that I pushed it all far down. The physical cancer was replaced by a spiritual one. The minute I sensed love ready to chain me, I took the bolt cutters out.

Not that the Great Giver and Taker of Tumors refused to answer at least part of my pleadings that night of Stan Gaynor's burial. I attached myself to a clinic for migrant workers in the wine country and ministered to their children. It has been great work. The mothers call me "El Doctor Grande." But I lost my faith in my own cure, or rather, the meaning of the cure, at least as I had hoped it to be. The love of a good woman eluded me—or I eluded it. Every possible outcome, every wayward gesture I dissected as coldly as you would a spleen. I deluded myself into thinking that my calling was general welfare and not specific to any one heart.

Then on a day off caring for the Mexicans, I stood in the mist under a cypress tree overlooking Point Lobos. A hat flew by me. It was a purple hat. It belonged to a woman in mock distress who gripped a railing and watched the hat alight in front of a barking seal.

"Well, it'll look better on him than me," were the first words Carolyn Smith uttered to my ears. Her brown eyes made her blondeness real, earthen, grounded. And they looked me straight on without speaking for about ten seconds that was a year. Or lifetime.

She turned out to be a teacher of seventh graders—the calling of a saint. She had a patience for my silences (which I would fall into when, for instance, she'd put a finger to my scar and ask, "What is this?"), and even more patience with my enthusiasms. I liked the way she smiled to herself, closing her eyes, humming over crackling eggs on the stove. Her father was, of all things, a cement contractor. We'd drive up and down the steep roads of San Francisco, and she'd point out foundations he'd laid.

"Since 1906, it's all a gamble, of course," she laughed. "One good earthquake and his foundations are all split. But it's good cement."

"I'm sure it is." I liked that 1906, the teacher in her. But she didn't lecture; you don't lecture seventh graders.

"Take that," she said. And she slugged me. Strange to say, I liked that, too, even when I realized she could hurt you. She was someone new to me, someone who subverted, even attacked, my fantasies, and because of this it was hard to dismiss her after the inevitable letdown (a belch? an opinion? a look?). We were already on the earth. The first woman I'd ever taken to who didn't make me want to fly away with her or from her, but stay.

She cried one night when we found her mother on the floor, a bottle in her hand.

"She drinks," Carolyn aspirated in a wheeze I recognized as asthma. "For every foundation that starts to pour, she drains a bottle. I can never figure out if she's celebrating or pissed at his unwavering dullness."

"I find him charming," I said.

She closed her eyes and smiled. "Maybe I'll drink some day."

"No, you won't. I'm not dull."

"Oh, you are. You are dull as a wall."

I liked her little insults, her fey comments on some aspect of my physiognomy, as they always preceded lovemaking.

We entered the little chapel at the Mission St. Raphael Arcángel six months after the lost hat. Everyone back home was excited for me, and Sandy flew out to be my best man. I had finally not thought to death a love, not attacked it with the chemo of my high-mindedness. My parents were shocked when I told them I had not told Carolyn anything about my cancer. I promised I would, but I couldn't get it out before the ceremony and knew it was going to cost me.

She walked up the aisle that day in the old Spanish chapel, her hair twined like gold rope along her neck settling on a tan collarbone. That sinuous torch made her seem exposed—flammable even—beside the white net of her face. That whiteness cast a shadow; I could barely make out her eyes. I thought my own surge for her might light that shining thatch on her shoulder and destroy her—the thought of a late bridegroom.

Suddenly, I saw something strange. Maybe it was the ray of blue light from a stained-glass window (later confirmed by the priest to be Mary's robe) as it hit Carolyn's netted face. A watery, dreamlike figure appeared. Stan Gaynor's englobed head come close to Carolyn's, as if he would kiss her. I touched my face.

"Stan!" I muffled a cry. "What are you doing here?" It was like Banquo's ghost. But what had I killed? Only the memory of someone who meant nothing to me, whose fate I had long ago skirted. To what purpose, on this good day this specter?

His encephalitic visage perched like some white crow on Carolyn's shoulder, and his funereal robes blended into her wedding dress, making them seem Siamese twins. I lurched from Sandy's side off the altar, down the aisle toward the approaching bride. Startled, Carolyn looked up through the white net and tripped on a warp in the chapel's rug.

She fell, gashing her forehead on the oak pew. She bled over the carpet, which soaked it up as if it were part of a masterful painting to which she was contributing her precious color. There was no time for the priest to marry us. I stitched her as we flew to the hospital in an ambulance. She took ten good stitches. I gave her a strong sedative to konk her out, shooed away relatives and friends, and got a pillow to sleep on the floor near her, like some dog. I reminded myself of Sandy.

"Am I still alive?" she asked, finally coming to.

"No. You are on Mars. I am a Martian."

"Oh, it's good to be Martian. Will you lay your head here?" She pointed to her chest.

I crawled into bed with her.

Her fingers searched me for the truth—the long scar. And I gave it to her, as we enfolded. I told it in long detail, and when I told her of the knee she touched her head. Deep into the night when I finished and we both lay in a long quiet I told her, "We can't make love. You'll burst your stitches."

She took my face in her hands and looked at me hard enough that my eyes blurred, "You must always stay inside me, lovemaking or not. And there's only one way—don't hide what's far down ever again."

"I didn't think you'd—"

"Are you crazy? How's a marriage going to live if you hide the source of it all? Whether it hurts or not, tell me what's burning."

Swinging her legs over the side of the bed, she called out, "Oooo, my head!" And then she insisted, "Let's be married tomorrow for breakfast. Call the priest."

"All right," I said, hardly myself now, or a self now known by his wound.

Carolyn nixed our planned honeymoon to Lake Tahoe. She had another idea. We are flying to Washington, renting a car, and driving to Ocean City, Maryland. You see, there was this black guy with a goatee who lived a different life. I am sure of that. I could tell by the hardness of his hands and the menace of a knee that saved me long ago. Carolyn wants to find him and take him to dinner.

Brother of Figs

Tie loose, knot tight over his heart, Ben stood in the fig tree.

"Best ones, the fat ones, right up there." He pointed to the top of the branches. "And I'm going up there."

"Don't know about this, Ben," said brother Frank. "I don't want to lose any more than I've lost."

"*We've* lost."

"Hey, those dress shoes are gonna slip."

Ben mounted a rung of the fig tree. But the limbs weren't thick, and the gray bark was gnarled and slippery. His brother was halfway up the tree when Frank saw the sagging.

"C'mon, Bennie, we've got some beauties right down here, right under my nose." He leaped up and pulled a purple fig from the branches.

"Man, dee-licious. I've never tasted better."

"Try this." Ben snatched a large, swollen one. Frank put his hands out, then shielded his eyes from the August sun. The prized fig fell to the sidewalk.

"For christsake, that was the best one on the whole tree," Ben shouted. "Calm down."

Frank picked it up, dusted it off. Nectar oozed out the broken nipple.

"See? No problem." He plopped it into his mouth.

"Yeah. What are we worried about? Germs? Germs didn't do him in."

"That's right. No. Wait, Bennie. Figs aren't meant to climb. They're too short." Ben rose to the thinner branch.

"This one ain't short, it's humongous. I've never seen a fig tree this big, especially here in the Valley."

"Gram's tree was small, right?"

"Right. Hey, grab onto the branch, will you?"

"Gram's tree looked like a troll. But the figs were good. Say, remember Dad's no-hands driving while he'd sing the Hawaiian War Chant—or was it the Love Song?"

"Oh yeah. *Tal a wa ala wa ala wa ala. Hee hee-a binga binga loo-a-loo-a-la.* But it wasn't no hands. Dad wasn't that crazy. He'd drive with one finger."

"Yeah," Ben looked down from his picking and eating. "I remember that now. Maybe I was too short to see the finger when I was young. But I remember it. We were going to the beach, you know."

"You said."

"Can you guess," Ben asked, opening the inner purple hair of a fig outward with his thumbs, "what a fig looks like on the inside?" His dimples creased deeper, and for an instant as he looked at his brother he smiled. It was his first in three days.

"Sure. You said it. Ever tasted that?"

Ben stuffed his smile with the fig, and nodded.

"The beach." Frank looked off at the rusted sky.

"Zuma. Zuma Beach. Dad was going to take me—you get that? Me. He was going to take little twenty-year-old Ben, the baby of the family—by himself—to the beach. With no brother and sister, aunts and uncles. No cousins. No secretaries. No shipping clerks. No neighbors. Just *me*."

Ben's eyes grew dark and wet. He licked off his knuckles a sweet salt.

"Aw, c'mon, Bennie. It's smoggy out. Get down now."

"When isn't it smoggy? This is August. The whole month's a smog alert. Everything happens in August in this family, right? Dad dies in August, and you'll be what? Thirty-five in August? You're an old man, man. Catch. Great. Finally you caught one. Good one, eh? Just like a woman's . . . aah. Who wants to talk about sex? August. You were married in August, and Aunt Janine was born in August, and our illustrious Vivian offs herself in August about two minutes after Dad."

"Stop it, Ben."

"Tell me something." Ben asked as he gorged himself. "Did you ever go with Dad alone to the beach?"

"Just Dad?"

"Yeah. Without the horde."

"Let me think. I'm not sure."

"In Anaheim maybe? Before I was born. You had to."

"Well, maybe. Dad used to snorkel dive a lot with Hutchy—you never knew him, did you?"

"How could I know him, goddamn it? That was ten years before I was born!"

"He was Dad's best friend."

"I know it. I wish I'd known him. He didn't come to the funeral, did he?"

"No, he didn't."

"I wonder why. That's a strange thing. Aah, Dad never had any best friends."

"He had Hutchy."

"Yeah. And where is he?"

"Maybe he didn't know about it."

"Hell, half the world knows about it. It's all over the front pages."

"Hutchy's in San Diego. They don't get the *L.A. Times* down there."

"What's he doing down there?"

"Watch it. You're slipping, man. Those figs fermented? He retired from the marines to work on cruise missiles. A consultant, I think."

"How could Dad be that man's best friend?"

"He was. They were both in the war. Hutchy was on Bataan, and Dad was at the Bulge. Bad spots. They shared the bad spots—I guess that's what makes the best friends."

"Speaking of bad spots, is it okay to eat a fig that's half eaten by birds?" He showed the crystallized maw. "The problem with this tree is that it isn't guarded by Thatee Matile's tin-can lids." Frank matched Ben's terse grin.

Ben gazed out over his brother's head and pointed. "But we're all guarded, aren't we? We're protected as hell."

Frank turned around and saw by the white walkway of a fine green lawn the sign "Warning—Armed Response." It stunned him. Ben broke the trance, holding two figs as if he were holding up a dress by the shoulders: "Now here you are, ladies and gentlemen. This is a real—"

"Zinger."

"Yeah," Ben laughed. "Zinger!" He rotated the figs from pecked maw to smooth purple skin. "This dress is neat. Remember how Dad said 'neat'? I never heard anybody say the word that way. If he said 'neat' he meant 'tremendous.'"

"Yep. It was his one understatement—'neat.' It's like he collapsed all his heated-up life in one word—'neat.'"

"If you don't like the back, how about the front? That's the California look—a plunging neckline! Seersucker straps! How 'bout it? One hundred of five to fifteen? Leave it to me. I'll fill in the colors, the breakdown. Yeah, the breakdown. The breakdown!" Ben cried out, coughing. He hung from the fig tree by one hand.

"Ben, get the hell down here."

"I'm just putting on, Franky. I never saw Dad sell dresses. I was only eight when the goddamn business went under, you know? I learned all that rot from Vivi. She was always mimicking him, you know that. She wanted to be Dad; that was her problem."

"Yeah."

"You know my last memory of the three of us together with Dad and Mom before Vivian went crazy?"

"When?"

"That Christmas with the records."

"And we all danced, and you, you were the disc jockey, Ben."

"You bet I was."

Ben got excited, gripping limbs of the fig as if they were rails of a diving board. He shimmied his hips and called out, "Rollin'! Rollin'! Rollin' on the river!"

"I had it nailed that Christmas," Ben said. "I knew from experience Dad's top-three rock songs to dance to, and I lined the albums up right alongside the books in the family room, knew exactly where the right cuts were. I was rarin' to go. But I didn't dance."

"No."

"I wasn't a dancer."

"I know."

Ben described how his father's dress designer, Sam Peltzer, hastened to answer the clapping on the first cut by Creedence Clearwater.

"Sam broke the ice. He was a real dancer, and boy, those hips were jumpin' to 'Got a good job in the city! Working' for the man every night and day!' Shit, he knew. He was working for Dad."

"A hard taskmaster, our father," Frank said.

"Yeah. But the dance was reward." Vivian, who had begun to lose her confidence or was slowed by the pills she was taking to calm her down, came out on Sam's urging, Ben remembered, Sam's arms pulling her. And Ben quickly slipped in "China Grove."

"Vivian really liked the Doobs," Ben said, rubbing a fig. "It was that dang fuzz bass lead. It was like electric shock. She had to stay in it."

"You're pretty good at music trivia."

"Nothing's trivial with music. You'd be surprised, Frank, what I know about bars and clefs. It comes from being a wallflower."

Ben then described how their father made it a threesome on "Every day is a new day dawning," and Peltzer faded, joining Omar's and Vivian's hands, and soon it was father and daughter alone going at it. Omar knew swing from the forties, and Vivian would try to ape it but she didn't know the steps. She just used her natural rhythm, which jiggled her top and bottom and made the audience clap louder as they wanted to cure her, to keep her from falling over that ledge completely, as if the music and her father were lubricants to a life of increasing metal-on-metal, a handrail before the cliff.

"And then you would join, Frank, and oh! How I wanted to, too!" Ben sang, playing the fig branch as if it had frets. Vivi faded, he remembered, leaving Frank free-form with his father and Ben himself leaping over the couch, back and forth, like a circus monkey.

"That was my dance," Ben admitted.

"It was a fine dance."

"It was ridiculous. But it was the only way I knew how to join you two. For that one song that was coming, that one song, I was grown. I was like you two."

Ben put on the big one. And everyone, including his grandmothers, Nazera and Matile, got up and danced. Nazera added a little Arab kneading of the air, and Matile moved her hands back and forth, a fey acknowledgment of the absurdity of it all.

"I like the way the Who started—tentative, that light Moog synthesizer, the keyboard like they were moving lightly in outer space. No hint the blastoff was coming, except it was almost like a musical countdown. The sweet 'Whooo are you?' almost hummed at first to Keith Moon's light sticks on the cymbal. Till Daltrey rasps, 'I woke up in a Soho doorway . . . God's there's got to be another way!"

And pretty soon, Ben related, as the music intensified and Townsend's guitar crashed and crashed, one by one they dropped off, exhausted, to the couch or the floor or the bar stools, where Mae's husband, Henry, cried out, "All right, Omar! Crank it up! The Poison Dance!" And, stripped of his shirt now, pulling the air like some Kirk Gibson after the one-legged home run, Omar Matter danced alone, perfect in rhythm, twirling his invisible partner, the Who's other for a few wonder seconds revealed, and to his sweating chest held in his arms—the You, You, You—known and one with him, known the center of his beloved ocean.

"Oh, God, what are we doing? How do we know who anyone is?"

"Bennie, get off that branch. It's too thin."

"That was Dad's downfall. He thought his love so powerful it could know another. Even Vivi in all her mania. And he thought if he knew her he could rescue her."

Ben swayed unsteadily back to the trunk.

"All right, Ben. Hold on, will ya?"

"You haven't told me."

"What?"

"When you went swimming with Dad alone."

"It might'a been at Laguna. If it happened at all. Maybe I went with him and Hutchy. Dad let me carry the masks. I remember them walking out over the rocks with their masks propped on their heads, and maybe a wet suit jacket. Their fins were slung over their shoulders. 'Let's go, troops.' One of Dad's favorite expressions—anyone worth anything was part of the troops. Maybe he was talking to the pelicans, or the swallows. Capistrano. They took me in springtime to see the swallows come back to Capistrano. We fed them with Aunt Mae and Uncle Henry. It was a good childhood."

"My childhood stunk."

"I know it."

"Listening to Vivi screaming to one of her devils all night long."

"It's over now. She's not screaming anymore."

"And we won't hear 'neat' again. Or 'Let's go, troops,' or 'Who Are You?'"

Ben was hanging by one hand, again threatening to free-fall.

"Wait," Frank yelled, surprising himself. "I do remember. Yes, I was once alone with Dad at the beach for sure. And I will tell you about it if you get a grip. That's better. All right. It was in Santa Barbara. Where you and I both escaped to at different times. And Dad escaped there just before he pulled the plug on the dress business. He came up from L.A. on his Harley-Davidson. And we went down to the shore—a good long walk from my old place at Micheltorena and Bath. 'Member that? I was living like a pauper in one room trying to write. I think it was a Sunday. You know that place down under the tall palms in the grass where they folk dance?"

"I think so."

"In a circle."

"Yeah."

"Dad and I sat back in the grass propped up on our hands to watch. This was at the tail end of the hipster days just after the last helicopter lifted off the embassy in Saigon. Hitchhiking was dying out. Guns were coming in with the heartbroke vets and druggies. And the kids whose pops were gone and couldn't study or find work could get one just for the asking—like water with your meal. 'One gun, please.' Vivi got hers right down the road here. I'd like to blow the place up.

"Well, there we were watching the blur. These hipster gals with hair down below their butts and pottery-making guys with ponytails all moving in a circle, kicking up their bare feet. The gals' breasts were bouncing. Dad liked that. It was like the Poison Dance writ large. But what he really liked besides the curling blue water that he'd go down into with Hutchy, whom he didn't see anymore because of embarrassment at having no money, was this tall, straitlaced looking guy in army fatigues and paratrooper boots. Can you imagine? And this dude was leading! I kid you not. He'd grown a scraggly beard, but his hair was crew cut and his dance step was impeccable. Perfect. Graceful, even in the boots. He held the hand of the flower child to his left firmly, but gently, too. Sometimes he'd close his eyes, and his rough beard would jut up to the blue on top of the Santa Inez range. All the time not missing a step! Behind him you could see the Channel Islands like private worlds bobbing under his arm. Yes sir. And Dad says, 'Look at that fellow. During the week he probably hauls freight, or stacks boxes, or pushes paper. He's a nothing 99 percent of the week. But for this one hour here on Sunday afternoon he's a king! Who's to say he hasn't got the big shots beat?' Dad regarded this guy for a long time, clapping him on. You think he'd seen the Savior. He went back to L.A. and closed the factory. That was it. Kaput."

Ben was now turned away from his brother, breathing heavily. Frank could see the tall frame with its slender shoulder blades vibrate in the white shirt. When he turned around, tie dangling like a noose, he seemed to emerge from the figs themselves. Frank sucked in his breath. Ben had smeared his face with the insides of figs. He let out a ghoulish scream and flew to the ground, hitting a carpet of rotted figs dark as midnight.

"Now you've done it."

Ben reeled, blood spurting out his nose and mouth.

"I want to die."

Ben ran into the street. A parakeet-yellow Cadillac in the slow, mindless cruise of a Valley dweller swerved over the curb to avoid the man with the camouflaged face. The driver rammed his horn, shouting out the window, and punched it past the strange twosome.

Frank ran after his brother, grabbing him by the neck in the middle of the street. Ben slumped.

"C'mon. Sit over here." Frank pulled him to a brick frill over which peered black-eyed Susans.

"No smell to those flowers. No smell to any flowers in this whole god-forsaken place!"

"You jerk, you *wanted* to draw blood. But why your own?"

"Whose else am I gonna draw? Yours? Ah, Franky. Always with the handkerchief, just like Dad."

Frank Matter cleaned up his brother, figuring this handkerchief was going to be stained forever.

"You're lucky. Looks like only a cut lip and a nosebleed."

"What about my hands? It was worth it."

The two walked back down Wells Drive past the public grammar school that had been shut down for lack of children to the little cul-de-sac of their childhood, Early Place, a street of fine long houses with curving green front yards inside circular driveways, nonbearing pear trees, sego palms, palms shaggier, older, a place of quietness since they had grown up. No one throwing the football or baseball in the streets anymore. No children. Tall iron remote-controlled fences. But good neighbors, more or less, whose wives walked furiously in the morning as one by one their husbands faltered, then fell. Lily Matter was suddenly among them. Early Place had become the Street of Widows.

"You don't want to die," Frank said to Ben, cresting the hill, looking down at the line of cars on both sides of the silent street up to the circle.

"How do you know?"

"Because when you called me back East to get out here, you told me you needed me for the rest of your life. Well, 'need' means 'be here'!"

Ben showed some blood on his teeth as he grinned. "You know why I took you to this fig tree? This is where I came right after I went to the store and saw the blood on the floor. I smashed the sign that said 'Sale—2 1/2 cents a copy.' And I wandered all over the back streets till I found myself before this fig tree and started eating from it like a nut. Did you see all those rotten ones? Nobody was picking this tree! It just a waste. Of the sweet and the good and Dad. Pure waste! All these ripe little bodies lying on the pavement. And no more orange groves or lemon or fig groves in the whole San Fernando Valley. People just waiting in their stores or their homes to get killed."

He was hyperventilating. "I had to take you here."

"Glad you did."

"To eat."

"Uh huh." Frank caught the fig and put it in his mouth.

Out past the funereal cars, the rock-strewn or fake clay-tiled roofs, past the listless pepper trees, the junipers and unstrummed telephone wires, beyond the breath coming off the pools and the boulevards of selling and buying and sirens, they both saw the haze of the San Gabriel Mountains like the far limit of a tomb.

"It's all changed for us now," Ben said. "Everything matters. Every drop of this world. Because nothing matters." He drilled his finger into Frank's ribs. "Can't waste a minute from now on."

"I'm with you."

"Because it's all gone."

"Or going."

"What the hell's the difference?"

Many in the murmuring crowd at the family home hushed at their crazed, blasphemous smiling. It was assumed they'd been running in the smog.

The Epistle of Barnabas

ying under a hemlock for the night did not keep rain from soaking through the hitchhiker's clothes. Along the hard gray vein of Interstate 5, thumb pointing sideways like a wisecrack, the morning air chilling his skin, Benjamin Matter remembered standing up in his first bathtub. A draft through the door made him hug himself. And Mother? Far away in the house.

Rain misted Ben's maroon wool cap, swung like old blood as cars and trucks passed. This was Oregon, whose solemn, innocent children grew up in rain and damp and a green that made anything not green seem ugly to them. Ben had seen plenty of green in his year here. Velvet cracks in concrete. Green mold in slippers. Oregon rain entered everything. It invaded bones and told them as they ached, "Be silent." The rain made a rust case against guns, slipped up the robber, all too soon cooled the sweat of the marriage beds.

An eternal cold sweat—that was what this rain was about. The people were aloof, but pliable. Their soaked-to-the-bone spirits made for compromise, but not for young wrecked marriages. They were with you in every way until you broke.

Few cars were headed south this morning. Every now and then, a hoot burst the gray morning, and Ben'd wave at a passing cab. He read the names of the huge trucks: P*I*E, SAFEWAY, UNITED VAN LINES, BOISE CASCADE. The trucks streaked lines on the wet pavement, but it was impossible to determine if they followed each other's tracks. A rain world was not precise; it did not define a self. It slid things together, then apart.

For an hour, Ben held his thumb out, even with no one coming. Perhaps a bird would pick him up, like the swan hoisted Leda! He wasn't Leda, and there weren't swans in Oregon in January. There were swans where he was going, where losses were distinct, brazen, and expected, where he might start over again. He thought: *I can even bear what my crazy sister did after what's happened up here.* He rested his thumb every now and then. Slowly, he learned.

After an hour, he began using the European method, forearm swinging up and down like a train signal. Hitchhikers in Europe looked like they were beckoning toward a real bargain. Over here! In the woods! A girl undressing! It was effective.

The European method with the blood-colored cap soon drew a dented, trout-green pickup to pull off the road. The truck missed Ben by forty yards. Bad brakes, the hiker thought. Perhaps it was an ice cream truck, or the psychedelic jalopy of a professional drifter. The truck started weaving in reverse toward him.

He grabbed his pack and ran down the road shoulder. As he pulled near, Ben saw the signs on the back well:

JESUS IS YR SAVIOR (in red)

END TIME IS HERE! (in blue)

BARNABAS=WIZDOM (in yellow)

A little door to get inside the sayings had a combination lock. The hitchhiker took it all in quickly.

"Where you headed?" he called into the passenger window as the driver rolled it down.

"Lord . . . wherever the Lord wants me."

"How far south is that?"

"About to Sonora, Mexico."

The driver sized him up with eyes that looked like the winter sky trapped in a circle. Ben glanced back for a second at the colorful slogans. He came back to the cab; the driver's eyes riveted straight ahead as if he were driving. He gunned it in neutral, then the engine coughed. The man's neck was scrawny. Ben felt the cold soaking into his joints and the rain on his own neck.

He squelched air in his throat, pulled open the rusted door, and jumped in.

"You want me to shut this window?"

"Don't matter to me."

"Can you let me off in San Francisco?"

"If it's in the Lord's path."

"It's on the way to Sonora, isn't it?"

Without irony the driver said, "I believe." The thin, cock-headed man twisted a look out the window, waited for a truck to rumble by, and took off. Slowly.

The driver picked up the flashlight on the seat between them, reached over, and stashed it in the glove compartment. Crumpled papers kept it from closing, and on the lid sat a small New Testament, its red marker hanging out the gold-leaf pages like a snake's tongue. It was not forked.

"Would you say the Lord's way is the main road of any place?" asked the hitchhiker.

"Well, of course it's the main road. There ain't no other road but the Lord's."

"Well, that's good." Ben watched the blue badge pass by. "Interstate 5. That's good." He wiped the cold water from behind his ears.

For a while they drove on in silence and the squeaking of the old truck's shock absorbers. Only the wiper in front of the driver worked. Shortly, the hitchhiker grew weary and hypnotized by the blurred green that was Oregon. He kept the side window cracked for a one-inch-by-one-foot view of the world. All else was the truck and a growing green vapor. How many lumber yards was the cold thread covering? How many people trying not to wake?

The driver spoke first. A ripped seam in the air.

"Been driving for twenty hours now, and didn't stop till you. I'm as clearheaded as can be." His high voice pulled itself down. "I saw you standing there a long way back. I've got the mission of the Lord because the Bible says, 'Ask and it shall be given unto you,' and yesterday 'round dinner I asked and said: 'Lord, I've got to get to Sonora like You told me in the dream, so give me the righteous power,' and He did. Praise the Lord."

The driver gripped the wheel harder as he talked, never veering his head. To the hitchhiker it sounded like the Dow Jones Industrial Average.

Praise the Lord was dropped low and final, yet hung in the cab indifferent as the rain.

"What Lord are you talking about?" Ben spoke to the glass.

"Jesus Christ, praise Him."

"I just wanted to make sure. There was, of course, the Lord of Monmouth . . ."

"Who?"

"Not to mention the Lord of Northumberland."

The driver looked aside for the first time, then frontward, stone-faced, as if thinking.

Edging near the door, Ben felt rusted metal flake in his hand.

But no answer came. Words swizzled up the driver's rosy neck, muscles taut as a cord of Venetian blinds. Then he seemed to be swallowing. The hitchhiker watched the one good wiper slap in front of the driver. He opened a book, but the first page blurred. The driver's teeth were knocking and grinding.

"Render unto Caesar the things that are Caesar's, and unto God the things that are God's!"

"I never was much on money, yeah," Ben laughed nervously.

"You're talking about the people who rule here on earth. And I'm talking about the Ruler who rules everything: the trees, the earth, the roads, us—everything."

"Does he rule the rain?"

"He rules the rain."

"Can you tell him to turn it down a bit?"

"I can't tell Him. He's the Master."

"Well, what do you pray for?"

"For salvation and righteousness."

"How far are we from San Francisco?"

"Oh, I'd say about six hundred miles."

A long silence passed. Except for the one wiper slip-slop-slip-slopping and the shocks creaking like a hobbyhorse.

The driver turned on his radio and turned it off quickly. Only static.

Past Roseburg, the truck swung off the road. The passenger looked up from his book. There was a black figure in the watery window.

"Roll it down,' the driver ordered. He leaned over.

Another young man stood in the rain in a black raincoat, holding a black duffel bag with both hands. The passenger thought: Mr. Hyde.

In breath that smelled of sour milk, the driver asked, "Do you know the Lord?"

"Yes."

"Praise the Lord," said the driver.

"Praise the Lord," said the black-coated man.

"God," thought Ben.

In the newcomer climbed, squeezing the original hitchhiker into the middle.

"I can put your bag in the back if you want," the driver offered.

"No, I'm not going far. I'll keep it on my lap."

The driver positively ignited back onto the highway. He bounced on the seat, getting position. The three touched shoulders in the close quarters: dry canvas, old suede soaked with rain, wet black nylon.

"I was just saved last night," the newcomer said.

The driver pivoted his head spasmodically, like a pigeon thrown seed. The driver's large bucked teeth emerged as the newcomer spoke.

"I was in Roseburg. I was driving down from Eugene the other night and something pulled that drive shaft. Wow, jus' cruising into Roseburg at midnight, without knowing why or wherefore I was there. And I came to this little mission house, and the fellow there said, Sure, you can stay here. The next morning they had a meeting, and I couldn't help it. I was saved. The Lord must have guided me to that spot. All kinds of people were testifying, and this big man with a deep voice just got to me, I guess. I stood up. I told them everything. Hell—Lord, take that word from out my mouth—why, Christ, I was a heroin addict until yesterday."

"Praise the Lord," the driver said.

The newcomer glanced at the man in the middle as if to say: the *regular* world, hah!

"Where's your car?" Ben asked.

"It doesn't matter," the newcomer smiled.

The driver opened up. Yes, he was an evangelist who went from mission to mission around the country and, in fact, the world, spreading the

Truth. He lived in the back well of his truck, inside the words. He never worried about money because—the Lord will provide. He had seen alcoholics turn dry inside of an hour. He had seen women give birth *naturally,* Praise the Lord, and not a whimper. He was not surprised that the man on his far right had happened along the road in the rain and flagged him down. They were brothers, in Christ.

They talked about an hour of Oregon going by, exchanging revelations and Bible passages, the driver's face incessant with information but set as rock. The newcomer's talk was as clipped as his new haircut; he didn't want to lose the power that had only recently come over him. The driver's face flared under his short-cropped, creek-bed blond hair.

Between them, soaked hitchhiker Ben stared ahead. A stud of the driver's seat-belt buckle was digging into his side. He thought of the Zen masters who could walk over hot coals in bare feet, silent.

The newcomer said he'd be getting off just around the bend.

"Uh-huh," nodded the driver.

"There. Wolf Creek."

The brakes screeched.

"Someday I'm gonna get them brakes fixed. The Lord will find a way."

Slamming the pedal down, the driver threw everybody back.

"Praise the Lord," the driver said, his gray eyes taking the light.

"Praise the Lord," uttered the man in black to the floor as he got out. And then he said to the driver with a cryptic smile, "Don't let this guy get too close."

Containing his relief, Ben slowly slid back into the shotgun seat. The truck clanked down toward Grants Pass. Rain beat heavy as they neared California, the sky darkening. Then it let up, and for a while an inhuman silence became a pleasure for Ben.

"Aei ayo atowanna bee yo ayah egaho aei!"

Ben turned to the driver. His neck muscles were bulging, his lips pulled back like a monkey's, exposing the large teeth.

"What?"

"Aei ayo buwanna fweeya te gonoda woopee!"

Suddenly, the driver's face deflated.

"I was speaking in tongues."

"Pardon me?"

"Tongues."

"And what were they saying?"

"I don't know."

The driver's eyes flared steely; his nose arched over the wheel. This was neither delight nor consternation. "I don't know," he repeated, grabbing the wheel close and staring into the highway ahead, as if his answer were just around the bend. A third time he spit out, "I don't know," as if he really didn't want to know.

"That is the greatness of tongues—not me, not me, but the Lord—the Lord is speaking through me!" He rocked back and forth and accidentally lit the turn flicker. For the next ten miles, the hitchhiker felt the corner of his eye blink red. After a while he said, "Hey, why don't you hit that thing?"

"What thing?"

"The turn signal."

"Oh."

It was nice to collaborate on something with the driver. It wasn't much, but they had communicated. The hitchhiker relaxed and took the book out of his pack.

The pleasant wisdom and calm of Thoreau. The rain increased to a plopping on the rusted roof of the truck. Ben gripped the book like an umbrella, occasionally looking up at the blurred window, splattered by wheels of water. No windshield wiper for him. But he had cracked his vent. The other had not. The other had to continually wipe his window on the inside, and did not seem to make the connection between his warm breath and the vapor. He did not open his side vent. So here they were with separate blurs, one caused by the rain, one by himself.

I should tell him, Ben thought. I should . . . but perhaps he wouldn't want it too cold. He is sweating. There are beads of sweat on his taut neck.

Another blessed silence grew. The plopping of the rain and Thoreau's green vision. He could see Walden, the perfect glassy lake top in winter, the huckleberries with the very dust of ripeness on them, the *how der do* owls, the *sky water* needing no fence. The hitchhiker relished Walden growing in the cab of the truck as they rumbled through wet Oregon.

"Circumsize the hardness of your heart, and harden not your neck."

The reader looked up. Wheels of water.

"There are people uncircumsized in heart."

The driver grinned monkey lips again and dropped just as quickly into solemnity.

"That is the Epistle of Barnabas."

"What epistle? I don't recall that one."

"And you won't. Barnabas is not in the King James Bible. Or any other Bible but the one that matters."

The hitchhiker thought about this, and closed his *Walden*.

"Look in the glove compartment there," the driver pointed. "Right in there. You'll find a copy of it. I had three hundred copies printed up. That is the last one. I've got to get more. The Lord will provide."

Ben put the little Bible on the seat between them, then fished through maps of Mexico, California, Washington, Oregon. A pamphlet with epithets similar to those on the boards covering the truck well said: "Mr. Bob Lonen will speak tonight about a powerful NEW MESSAGE FROM GOD, a lost text of the Bible!" Then the hitchhiker found an outsized sheet of newsprint. He unfolded it. It was the entire Epistle of Barnabas printed microscopically on one large sheet of butcher paper.

"Who was Barnabas?"

"He was Saint Paul's friend. They traveled together all over the world."

"You don't say."

"Uh-huh."

"Circumsize thy heart. Tell me, have you ever loved a woman?"

Lonen, who spoke in short, direct sentences about his life and faith, suddenly could not finish a thought. He stammered; his face turned more red; his eyes bulged with their held-back light.

"Let me take over the driving. You really ought to relax your neck."

"No, no. CIRCUMSIZE THY HEART. That's—. I found it. I am the only preacher in the West, maybe the whole continent, who has taken up the great banner of Barnabas. He is unique! He was humble. He wasn't—intelligent. No Saint Paul. But, but—he was inspired. And there's a conspiracy among churched Christians to blot him out, and he will not be blotted out!"

"Are you sure?" the passenger asked, still thinking about driving.

Rocking against the wheel, the one wiper whipping more furiously, the driver reached over: "Barnabas—you read it there. Right there. That's it. See!"

The preacher did not wait.

"It says Barnabas was talking to the old Jews who kept up their outmoded practices. They were still circumsizing themselves. He wanted to show them the emptiness of their old practices. He said, 'Circumsize your heart! Don't worry about . . . that other thing.'"

"What is your name?"

"Bob."

"I'm Paul."

The driver met Ben's extended hand with one gloved in sweat. Fingers held tightly, it felt to Ben as the head of a barracuda might feel if placed in a hand. The hitchhiker's resolve took a profound dip. His little ruse hadn't worked. The fictitious "Paul" struck no recognition in the driver. The humorless rain flicked on Ben's cheek from the wind wing. It was a long way yet to San Francisco.

In the late afternoon the truck veered across four lanes of rain down an off-ramp.

"Gotta get some gas. Can you help?"

"Yeah. Man does not live by talk alone."

The driver steeled himself.

"You read this while I get the gas. Make sure you read it. It's important."

Ben gave the driver ten dollars. He grumbled to himself, took the news sheet of Barnabas with him to toilet.

There was someone already on the pot. Ben waited by the sink until he heard a flush. His eyes absently wandered up the gray stucco wall to a few messages of strangers requesting solace of one sort or another:

I HAVE A BIG, LONG, HARD

case of the clap!

SCREW ME I'M LONELY

—quit bean liturary Mary es mui bonita puta

SPICS SUCK THE BONG BONG

"Say, is that today's paper there, son?" the man coming out of the toilet spoke as he hit the Boraxo lever.

"Well, uh—"

"You wouldn't give me the sports section, would you? Just want to find out how the Trailblazers did."

"Well, this is the Epistle of—"

"Heck, that's all right. I gotta get going anyway. You haven't read the sports section yourself, have you?"

"This isn't the Sports Section."

"That's okay, don't mind me. I gotta get back to the truck. Take 'er easy now."

"All right."

Ben stared at dull-green mold on the wall. Did the incessant rain beg for speech, he wondered, as he sat down and opened up the epistle full-length.

"All happiness to you . . ." it started. Ben skipped down to the "new look" at unclean animals. It was all right to eat cuttlefish and lamprey, really. Just don't talk to people like these fish "who are altogether wicked and adjudged to death. For so those fish are alone accursed and wallow in the mire."

Why were hares banned from the dinner table in Mosaic Law? Because they were born adulterers. Every year the hare "multiplies the places of its conception." So this, Paul thought, was the origin of the phrase, "She screws like a rabbit." The weasel's problem? "It conceives with its mouth." Hence, Barnabas exhorted, do not let your mouth commit wickedness with impure women. Apparently an early no-no against oral sex. Then he read in the renegade text that Jesus said, "My face I set as a hard rock." Barnabas must have caught the Savior on a bad day. A curious combination, thought Ben—the epistle wants a hard face and a raw heart.

Outside the rain had lessened. The hitchhiker stood still. Moisture settled on his cheeks like talc. It calmed him. He should get off here, he thought, and chance a quieter, less proselytizing ride.

Bob the driver was fiddling with the broken wiper on Ben's side.

"Aaaah. Can't get the thing to go. Can't afford a new one. You'll have to bear it."

The driver looked at Ben with ice that seemed suddenly to melt.

"I used the money, Paul. I put it into gas and oil."

Ben gazed down the road into the coming darkness. Two semis went whooshing by. He took the clear talc on his tongue as if it were communion. He knew now the way Lonen had said "Paul" that the driver believed him. He felt he owed him something, if not faith in Barnabas, companionship.

"Sure. Let's go."

And so they ascended in the darkness of Grants Pass. The driver kept on his argument. Notice how up-to-date Barnabas is? How he talks about birth control—"Thou shalt not destroy they conceptions before they are brought forth"?

"Funny about that word *conception*," Ben dropped, trying to get Lonen to laugh. "It means an *idea*."

The driver was undeterred: "Barnabas told it like it is: "Thou shalt not be double-minded, or double-tongued; for a double tongue is the snare of death."

That stung Ben. Lonen—or was it Barnabas?—had caught him being something he didn't like in others, a smart aleck. The mountains began swallowing the road, the lamps, the road signs. Out the side window, the rain grew. The sky and the mountains and the earth descended, even as they ascended. Ben took out a bag of pink pistachios and shook them toward Bob. Please, leave off of me, Ben thought to himself. Take this peace offering of a cynic.

"Huh? No, I don't eat but once a day, Praise the Lord."

"But they're especially good for you because they're pink." Total silence for ten minutes. *Can't you kill it, Ben, can't you just kill it?*

"Do you know," Lonen nearly shouted, "Chicago will be the end of the world? An atomic bomb will be dropped on Chicago."

"Barnabas visited Chicago?" Ben's breath was now short, hot.

"No. I saw it in a dream."

"Who was in Chicago? Was Bartholomew in Chicago?"

"No—he went to Samaria."

"Well, who took care of Chicago?"

"An atomic bomb will take care of Chicago!'

"O Suzanna" suddenly broke out in harmonica from the shotgun side of the cab. Ben was fighting fire with air, not nearly the right retardant.

"Barnabas says the world will end in six thousand years!"

"—*O don't you cry for me, for I come from Alabama*—"

"Chicago leveled—"

"—with a banjo on my knee—"

"*Aei wo gotta bangaloosa.*"

"Six thousand years from when?" Ben barked.

"Wha—?"

"When you counting it from?"

"Why six thousand years from the beginning of the world."

"And when the hell was that?"

"When Adam and Eve were born."

"If you don't know when the world was created, how are you going to know when it is going to be destroyed? Six thousand years from what? Jesus, give me some peace!"

Ben's anger silenced the driver, and he put *Walden* behind his head against the door, and tried to sleep. It didn't work. The rain increased. He heard each drop now, each strike against the metal roof and the glass, each needle of water. And then in half-dream, he saw the watery face of his sister Vivian surface in the family pool, and Ben laughing and splashing her, hoping against hope she would crack out of her meds and smile. But she didn't. She touched her eyes where his play had shot, and she thrust forward in the shallow end and slugged him right on the jaw. It felt like a hammer. And he dragged her underwater for half the pool, not caring if she'd drown, and when she came up, gasping for air, she was his wife, saying to him, when she finally had her breath, "You're cruel. You've got a cruel streak, Ben."

The rain fell with a mad determination. His ears puckered as they went higher and higher in the darkness. It must be the Siskiyous now, he thought. The cab grew colder. Out the driver's side of the front window, Ben saw a lurid white form come out of the dark, and he wanted to ask it forgiveness but it went by too quickly. They were nearing the summit.

His eyelids grew pink with light. Ben felt a leveling off. Then a dip pulled his stomach, and the truck's timid pace quickened, the brakes screeching on and off. Everything got darker, but louder. They were driving down into California.

Before they had descended much, Ben heard a strange whimper alongside him. Then another one. He opened his eyes.

"Look," said the driver.

The headlights were failing.

"God," Ben said unconsciously.

Cones of light flickered on and off, now illuminating the pelting rain, now giving in to darkness.

"I thought they'd last one more night."

"What? Are you crazy?"

Quickly, Ben rolled down his window. The rain pelted his eyes.

"This cap is nothing. Have you got a regular hat with a brim?"

The driver's nose and eyes were nearly touching the glass, his knuckles whitened gripping the wheel.

"Under the seat, Paul." Ben dropped down and searched frantically.

He pulled out a greasy army baseball cap and secured it. He craned completely out into the rain.

"A flashlight! A flashlight!"

Lonen reached over and pulled one from the glove compartment.

"Christ! They're going!"

The lights were weakening.

Ben shouted, "Over! Over!"

Slowly, he steered the driver across four lanes into the slow lane.

"We'd better stop," he called to Lonen.

"No, let's keep going," the driver yelled back. "You keep telling me where I am. We'll make it. The Lord will provide."

"Well, he better provide soon."

Ben shouted directions, practically sitting in the window.

When the lights held, he would get a fleeting picture of the lonely road—no cars ahead, the distance to the ditch on the right, the needles of water breaking against the pavement.

But when the lights petered out, it was blackness, utter blackness. Only a pin or two of light on the other side of the highway.

The truck veered far right and hit gravel.

"Over! Over!" Ben shouted, flying his hand at Lonen.

The lights went on again. They were a foot from the ditch, clipping along at seventy miles an hour.

"Can't you slow down?"

The brakes screeched in agony. They filled the night with the sound of metal on metal. The downhill grade steepened.

"I'm trying!" Lonen cried out hoarsely.

"Downshift, damnit!"

"I can't. It's automatic!'

"First, for godsake. Haven't you got first?"

Lonen tried the gearshift.

"It won't move!"

Slamming the brakes made Ben's door swing open. The young man grabbed the rim of the car top and leaped down on the running board. He was holding on for dear life, still shouting directions.

"Watch out! A sign coming . . . A pole! Keep 'er steady. Brake! Brake! More left! Back right! There! Keep it there. Don't punch the brakes, keep 'em steady."

Halfway down, the headlights failed completely.

Lonen hit the brakes, but they were wet and nearly worn through, and the truck's speed kept them from stopping.

"Lord, let me remember where I was! Let me remember where I was!" the driver cried frantically.

Ben said to himself: *Jump.* The darkness rained in on them as they careened down. But a light from behind caught his eye. A car speeding at them!

He woke, and regripped the truck.

"Give me the flashlight!"

Lonen handed it over again, still driving as slow as he could in the borderless dark.

Ben aimed the flashlight at their rear. The car was really traveling at them. Now he could jump and save himself. Now was the time.

But he couldn't do it. He couldn't leave Lonen, this strange, sorry fellow who believed in something he once believed in and now felt thrusting into him like radium. Riveted, he aimed the flashlight to the rear.

Kicking up water, the car blared its horn and slid past into the fast lane. Soon it disappeared.

God, Ben thought, it's very late in the high mountains. Good there is no one else out now.

Now he trained the light on his right and found the white line. They had veered two lanes left. Ben called Lonen over, slowly.

For the next two miles they followed close to the white line, by the hand flashlight. A steady application of the brakes put an emergency whine in the night, as if they were guiding their own ambulance.

Ben was drenched. His coat felt like the weight of the whole soddened earth on his shoulders. He swung back into the cab, managing to grab the door and close it. His hands were bleeding, his back ribs cracked from the door swinging on him.

The hand light still poured on the white line. He didn't veer his head from the cone of light that was saving them until Lonen sang, "Yreka!"

Now they were close to the bottom. Beyond one more black bend, city lights shone in the darkness like another planet, one seething gold and quilts, a planet of hot showers and dry beds, of dry arms that could enfold you, of legs that would hold you prone and let you dream, of dry skin and good sleep. A planet of skin and dawn.

"We're making it! We're almost there!" Ben slapped the seat with his free hand, hopping the little Bible.

He looked over at Lonen, whose stiff neck and face loosened, giving the hint of a smile, but whose eyes were still surrounded by winter.

Ben was overcome.

"Say, how did you keep us from going over the divider? You know, when I was facing the rear with the light?"

Lonen's first smile appeared.

"I kept my eye on a pair of car lights coming up. I figured where the fence was from them and where I had to be from the fence."

"You don't say. Downright scientific."

"Yep."

Suddenly, the noise of the brakes stopped. Lonen's foot went all the way to the floor. All the redness of the driver's face drained. He put his hand on Ben's wet shoulder.

"They're gone."

The lights of the city flashed boldly, before they were swallowed by the mountains. The truck was going down fast. The flashlight was useless.

All now dark. All silent.

Except for the ripping water under the tires and the flimsy shock absorbers squealing like a crushed squirrel.

Just before the end of the grade the careening truck swerved to miss two red taillights. A tire hooked in the ditch, the truck flipped and crashed into the slough.

The two men were thrown out of the truck on Ben's side and slammed into an embankment. They lay on the soft, cold earth, their arms crudely intertwined, rain hitting their skins like it would hit two boulders or two calves wandering out of shelter. A black slough rushed at their feet.

In a while strong lights of a Mack truck passed over the scene enough to show the grass very green, a trout-colored pickup resting on its side, some multicolored signs fallen off it.

Thinking better, the new truck driver hopped out a mile ahead to see who might need a ride. As he walked back up the hill, he could see the darkness fading, the light coming on over the mountains, gray at first, blue, then a swift gold. The rain had now stopped. The earth seemed to be lifting. To the stranger, everything was moving upward, even the two sodden bodies he found hugging on the wet green. At a critical angle, in the morning mist, they seemed to rise as he went down, hoping to save them.

The Life of a Nail

At the turn of the nineteenth century, in front of the Pyrenees and the wool-producing village of Tarbes, a six-inch black nail was brought into existence by the hands of an old blacksmith named Roux. With hands thick as oak burls—beautiful outcroppings of sickness—Roux hammered and cooked the raw iron. He sang songs of the Revolution, raising the heated shanks as they turned orange to a face charred by years of sparking metal. His thick eyebrows jumped like crows.

One spring day Roux's eye was taken by something else—a girl from Tarbes walking in the meadow. She was not wearing wool, because sun irradiated her white scarf. Had she been to Paris for silk? Roux couldn't identify the girl's face. Her skirt, too, unlike Bernaise woolens, was not impervious to sunlight, which showed the shadow of her legs as she bent to pick jack-in-the-pulpits, buttercups, and small carnations. Roux, eyes gleaming in a way they gleamed over his best-formed nails, hit down with his hammer on his soot-filled thumb.

The shout carried to Lourdes where the old chapel bell shivered, thence to Pau, where Henry IV's tortoise-shell bassinet was set rocking. One pained glance showed the girl was not on the upland.

Roux examined a nail head poorly hit. It was to have been his last forging smash, but a cleft marred the side of the nail, a crook that made it appear to be—if one squinted—a thin female with one hip against the entrance of a cottage. Roux muttered a Bernaise curse, *"Dieu Biban!"* Forever it was wedded in his mind with a fingernail that would turn purple and fall off, and with the diaphanous girl of the upland. He washed the crooked nail. As all nails, it cried out at its baptism—a furl of steam from the bucket of water!

104

A sack of the new nails clinking and nudging each other in a paradise of unknowing was taken the next day to the nearby village of Lourdes. Roux bartered with a carpenter there who was head of the local guild that planned to renovate the old church.

"They are, Monsieur Foualt, the finest nails in all of Navarre," Roux announced, holding up with bandaged thumb a good one.

"You have tapered them, Roux," said the guild master. "I am not sure this will work."

"Monsieur, this is the new style from Paris, and none can equal their force."

Foualt jumped some in his hand. The others tried to poke through the burlap sack.

Roux grew impatient and massaged the muscles of his chest. "*Cinq francs* for the lot or nothing!" he announced.

"*Cinq francs* it is!"

The next day, Foualt strapped the nails to his donkey and was making toward the old church when a small tear opened in the burlap and out tumbled the crooked one, along with one well shaped. They dropped into tall grass by the Gave du Pau rushing indifferently by. Foualt did not hear them fall. Most were saved for his project. Chances are, he would have thrown out the product of Roux's momentary intoxication anyway. The misshapen nail and her mate were left to molder for fifty-eight years.

They lived an idyllic life there on the grassy earth. Worms crawled over them. Birds lit down to feed. One day a very stupid robin tried to pick up Crooked. He dragged the nail along for a yard or so and fell over on his wings before letting go. Thus, Crooked was separated from Straight, though they shared many experiences together, anticipating the union, perhaps, of Simone de Beauvoir and Jean-Paul Sartre in their separate apartments.

In the spring the Gave overflowed, and the two were awash in silt until the summer baked them clean. In the fall leaves from the cottonwoods covered them. Winter and they were in hibernation, protected under two feet of snow. Neither complained or could complain. Their mission in life was to be alongside the icy green Gave and provide a birthplace for moss and lichen and a small jacket of rust.

One morning in 1858 the fog lifted like a drape. The crooked nail began to tremble. A radiance set into each water drop in the air an atom of light. Voices humming played with the breeze. All things—cottonwood, oak, worm, grass, river—seemed for the first time to be known, even by the nails. The voices were the voices of a woman and a young girl. The woman in white robes talked in even tones from a niche in the rock along the Gave, glowing like someone who had drunk light. The girl was dressed in a blue woolen of the *paysan,* and a basket looped her arm. The lady soothed everything. The wind itself was kneeling, the cottonwoods in early bud. Trout huddled in eddies like gleaming ears.

The woman spoke of love, which never fails to seize up human beings or sever them like bits of iron. She spoke about a time unlike the time of peacefulness that permeated the green country of the Pyrenees. She said it was no longer enough to tend sheep, stack stones for shelters, or light small fires at sundown. She wasn't pleading with the girl—who only said, "Yes, Madame"—the lady had the voice of light, a direct beam that awoke everything. There was a war coming, she said. She said after one war a more terrible war would come, and after that, one that would destroy the earth unless she, the little girl, spread word of the niche by the Gave and asked people to look for their maker and pay homage to him in all things. If the nails had the ability, they would have taken off to Tarbes, pricked Roux in the ribs, and told him to get on his horse and head to Lourdes. But they couldn't move unless they were moved. Passive, they waited with their capacity for binding and holding unused.

Then an orange flake of rust fell off the nails. The radiance faded. Voices went into the *tilleuls,* silenced.

Some days on, a small boy hunting for worms named Emmanuel picked up Crooked and Straight. The two had an ecstatic reunion in the boy's pocket, touching iron shined by the lady's appearance. Straight made it clear his companion's disability not only didn't matter—it pleased him.

The boy handed the nails over to his father, who was designated as builder of the new chapel near the Gave in honor of the lady. They were thrown into a box of others, Crooked propped as if a leader to appeal to them that the tall grass near the Gave had been pulled up from its roots, before settling back into the earth. But the nails made no gesture.

And so it came to pass that the two old ones, whose mission—as all nails—was to hold things together, found themselves with an original black luster. As good as new, they were put into service in the top beams of the new chapel. What a pleasure it was to be driven into the yawning planks of oak! Crooked squealed. Straight shimmied. They shared the same plank in the rafters—over the altar. In the wet evenings, when a veil of mist dropped over the Pyrenees, the chapel went cold and the wood sagged and made them shiver. In the hot summers, the beams tightened and nearly strangled them. Straight preferred winter to fall; Crooked liked the hot spells, so reminiscent of her birth and Roux's flashing eyes. Her painful curves made her move in warm weather.

Under their watch old Guido, a pilgrim from Rome, came with a bad back and was cured. Ecstatic, he scooted along the floor on his back, kicking his heels like a crab in reverse. He collided with Cardinal Linguini, who was blessing the confessionals. Linguini fell over and was hobbled from that day forward. In effect, one man's miracle crippled another. Linguini never came back to Lourdes, but he went high in the church. Gossipy prelates who came to bow their heads near the grotto ended up chattering about Rome and Linguini. If the nails could have played back these conversations, more than one saint would have been found a sinner, more than one priest defrocked.

As for Guido, he became the chapel's custodian and was nicknamed "the Crab" for his unique action after the miracle. There were many things in the chapel that no one but the nails witnessed. One night Guido was changing the candles on the altar. After being cured he became somewhat bold, and holding high one of the beeswax candles, he slipped and fell backward into the canes and crutches, which covered him like dirt. Guido shouted, "Mother of Christ! Save me!" Guido was greedy; he wanted to be saved twice.

During a hard winter snow when no pilgrims were in the chapel, the town poacher, Ignacio Roselle, crept down the aisle. He crossed himself in front of the altar and muttered a few prayers. Sheep lice crawled off his blue pantaloons; he tortured his Basque nose as if trying to rub it off his face, and looked up with limpid gray eyes to the statue of the Lady. He seemed to be trying to imitate her, in supplication to the cross above her.

He began crying, rubbing his eyes, wanting to know why the Lord had abandoned him, why did he have so few sheep? Could anyone explain why he had to sleep on rock while his brother, Almedo, slept on meadow grass, with his wife as a pillow, no less? Roselle walked onto the altar, as if testing the powers of the Almighty, hesitating, then advancing, bowing his head to the floor, then craning it with the eyes of a rascal to the transom above all where Christ was gilded in gold, and, yes, *nailed.*

He slobbered some more about how his own wife no longer believed in God and lay in the arms of some Catharist who wooed her on Sundays with a handful of ripe blueberries. Hoisting himself up the side altar of St. Bernadette, he huffed and puffed his way onto the transept of the chapel. Sunk in the center beam were the two old iron nails.

Fuming, batting away his demons, eyes wide as those of a spawning fish, Ignacio Roselle slid over to the exact center of the transept and plucked the gold cross with the weathered grip of a man made to be a thief. His eyes looked like they would drop out.

"Oh you are mine, mine, dear Lord!" he hugged the cross, then crawled forward.

Now Crooked heated up; Straight burned with anger. Roselle's hands gripped them hard, and he cried out like a dog, dropping fifteen feet to the stone floor. The cross fell free and landed in the glass cup of the sanctuary candle, shank first and upright.

Roselle picked himself up and looked at his hands. Each had a circular burn! He looked up at the beam and shook his head. Glancing side to side wildly, he ran from the chapel.

The next day Father Philippe, the pastor of Our Lady of Lourdes, came in for morning mass and noticed the cross in this curious position. He declared it "the Day of the Sacred Descent," and sent off papers to Rome about the new miracle. Father Philippe told the congregation that as a result of this untoward occurrence, Christ was telling the people they had strayed from the life of righteousness. The Lord might soon rescue the world from the clutches of the Commune of Paris, and the loss of Alsace-Lorraine to the Prussians. In short, the Second Coming was at hand. From that day attendance at Lourdes increased twofold.

Once some pilgrims from the Far East took their place in the back pews for a few hours—people with the gout, blindness, paralysis, boils, carbuncles, and "*le can-say*," as the French put it. A Japanese priest sat with his congregation alongside a Dominican nun from Paris. She held her head in her hands. After a while as she prepared to go she began searching under the pew, in the prayer racks, all over the nave of the chapel. "I've lost my rosary," she said to the Japanese priest, who helped her look. The rosary couldn't be found, and the nun was distraught. To come all the way from Paris to lose one's cherrywood rosary! The Asians left with no miracles, and the priest shrugged his shoulders. The nun stayed and prayed furiously. At sundown, the Japanese priest returned alone and knelt alongside the nun, who was quite beautiful, with green eyes and pink cheeks. After the chapel emptied but for the two, the priest noticed the nun's hands were trembling on the pew. The priest put his hand on hers and said something in broken French. She looked up in supplication. "*Voici le rosaire*," he said quietly, and reached underneath the front of her white robe. Her eyes widened. "*Voici le rosaire*," he repeated, his eyes closing. Hers closed, too. He felt the roundnesses there and the two pilgrims murmured words not in the French or Japanese dictionaries. "*Voici*," the priest said again with a cluck in his voice, and touched his lips to her neck; her lips vibrated like flower petals in the wind. She slumped into him, and they proceeded in this way, until he got up and found a plank to lodge and secure the chapel doors from entrance. Returning to the pew, he pulled the nun's cowl off; her red hair appeared like a sudden fire. The nails warmed in the wood as the two sank to the floor. Later the priest left. The nun followed shortly after, her rosary knocking softly along her robed hips.

It was a good life up there in the rafters, forever above the miracles and the nonmiracles, the sick and the quick, the blessed of God and those cursed ushering in and out of the sacred place. Termites did not last long. They gnawed on Crooked or Straight and died instantly.

But the state of grace did not last. The calling that bound them and for which they bound others was thwarted. In 1890, a hurricane blew off the Bay of Gascony and pummeled the town of Lourdes. Giant oaks collapsed on the chapel, and wind broke the stained-glass windows. All through the night the storm raged and their plank gave out, crashing to the ground. Everything in the chapel fell, except the altar.

Pilgrims and peddlers, the ecstatic and the shysters all descended on Lourdes to carry off what they could of the holy chapel for treasured souvenirs, for talismans against evil, or for simony. The priests and nuns could do nothing about it—a wooden carving of the Fifth Station of the Cross was carted off by a German, a marble font by an American. No one left without a sliver of the beams or a pebble from the walls. The two nails were among the holy contraband. As Straight was pried out, he gave out the first great cry since his birth. He had always been a quiet nail, alive or not. But to see her stranded in the wood while he was taken away made him die inside, made him only metal.

As for Crooked, she felt the full force of the strange, mute life she was given so many years alongside the Gave. For the first time she felt spurned by the power that brought her to tremble; she wanted to tear something, to burn holes in the hands of the entire human race! Crooked was a misshapen nail, but now as her companion was clutched to the bosom of a woman from Tarbes, it was obvious their existence was not the norm for nails. Was consciousness a curse?

Later, Crooked herself was pried from a fallen beam by a Parisian count. She spent the long carriage ride north alongside a pistol in his leather valise. Where was the Lady? Where was the blinding light?

In Paris, Crooked was placed on a mantel in the living room of the founding member of the French *aviateurs* corps, Count Alexandre Balotte. Madame Balotte nodded. She was a shrill, puffy-limbed woman with a tangle of silver hair that she put on for formal occasions. But when she came to bow her head in front of the nail, the bald spot in the center of her pate screamed.

This bowing was done willingly by Madame Balotte, not so willingly by her three children, Phillippe, Beatrix, and Michel, and not at all by the count. They placed two candles on either side of Crooked, and every Sunday evening the madame would say her rosary and gather the waifs on cushions, looking up as if the nail were blessed. The nail would have been pleased to have been hammered into something and given rest.

The count was a busy man. He was one of a new breed of men taken to the air in strange mechanisms. He also was an inventor of aeroballistics and often had the aristocracy of France over to his chateau to discuss the need to be ready to counteract the "German demon." To the nail, the only German demon was the gent who carted off the station from the chapel at Lourdes. There he certainly was not alone in his malfeasance.

The men and women who came and went at Chez Balotte were refined and spoke a kind of French different from that of the Bernaise and Basque of the Pyrenees. It was a rapid-fire French, a French full of intolerance that turned in the air and withdrew itself into the voice box of the speaker before the sentence was through. The head of the Parisian munitions factory, a Monsieur Roux (he placed his card on the mantel), was addressed as Monsieur "Roo." The x in the beautiful name of the blacksmith Roux was cut off in Parisian pronouncement like an appendix.

Life was a series of embarrassments at Chez Balotte. Arguments between Madame and the count were constant, though Madame had a testy sense of humor that made them bearable. The count, who could be gone for many days, was invariably answerable for his absence.

"And where have you been now, Alexandre?"

"Madame, I have been in the air."

"Where in the air?"

"In the air above Paris."

"For twenty days you've been in the air above Paris?"

"Yes, Madame."

"I understand it is impossible for an aeroplane to stay up in the air for longer than one hour without adding more petrol."

"Madame, I have been involved in experiments of a sensitive nature."

"I'm sure you have. On the ground or in the air?"

"Madame, are you questioning me?"

"Since the children are asleep, you are the only person here. Yes. I am questioning you. Who else would I be questioning at this late hour?"

The count sighed, tugged at his satin cutaway jacket, and went to the mirror above the mantel to curl his mustache.

"It is of no consequence to you concerning my experiments in thrust and counterthrust," he said to the mirror.

Beginning to boil, Madame pulled off her gray wig and threw it at him.

"Indeed! And does a corset come off more easily in the air or on the ground, Monsieur?"

And so it went until Crooked was rescued from this impossible condition by the youngest Balotte, little Michel. Always the one to pull away first from prayer before the relic of Lourdes and take cuffs from Madame, little Michel found Crooked to be of use in his project of building a doghouse. When the other children were off to lycée, Madame out shopping, and the count flying around, Michel nabbed the nail from the mantel and with dispatch that gave her delirium tremens hammered her into his wood shack for Cocu.

Cocu was a nervous Afghan hound who hid in the corners of the house whenever strangers came to visit. He slunk by nature and would try to run under sofas. If anyone came close he would slither along the wall, screeching more like a bird than a dog. In back of the chateau, Michel put together a credible domicile for this frightened creature, a work of art for a ten year old. He nailed a sign on top, "*Cocu, Le Roi.*"

In fact, the Afghan lived in a perpetual state of misery, a dog with tail drooped permanently between his legs. The Balottes never tired of telling guests how Cocu had mated once with the poodle next door, Fifi, and was hit on the nose by Madame for digging a hole under the picket fence. He spent most of his hours with his tongue hanging stupidly out the side of his long mouth, watching Fifi being mounted by every hound in the neighborhood from Great Dane to Silky Terrier. Madame put bricks along the fence to frustrate the Afghan. Hence the name "Cocu."

The night after Michel had completed the doghouse, shouts and shrieks filled Chateau Balotte, and Michel came running out of the house, chased by his mother with a paddle.

"Where is the relic? What have you done with the relic?!"

"Nothing, *Maman*! Nothing! It disappeared! It went to heaven!"

"You are a liar, Michel. I am going to paddle you until your bottom turns red!"

Little Michel—who was a good actor—got down on his bony knees, brushed his auburn hair aside, and pleaded with her. She held the weapon high and shouted, "You were here alone. You must have seen where it went! You've hidden it, Michel!"

"No. Maman, not me—it was Sophie!"

Sophie was the English maid. Madame glared at him as he squeezed his eyes closed. She spat, then she stalked into the house. Sophie was never seen after that day. Michel came over to the shack and petted Cocu, who slobbered all over him, while he patted the doghouse and waltzed back inside.

Sheltering Cocu was a fair job, and tailored to Crooked's needs. Early on she recognized not only that the other nails that Michel had used were as dumb as the ones in Emmanuel's father's shack at Lourdes, but they also looked different. She tried very hard not to withdraw, to hold the wood firm. The newcomers—streamlined, with definite heads—made her sink. Next to them Crooked appeared cumbersome and crude; her head, her body (even with its hiplike crook) were all of a part. She was, in a century, out of step with the world.

Too, there was Cocu's stench. He was given to violent dreams and whines for the nearby Fifi, and in the middle of the night would urinate uncontrollably. To live in the fumes of a dog? It was still better to be of demeaning but real service than to be an object of dubious worship. It was a burden borne in the service of the Lady of Light, who was . . . where?

Then came the talk of war. Using this word, whose treble was new to the nail, people scowled and puffed up like cocks of the roost. They shook their fists like Madame had done with Michel.

"'The Prussians are at the gate, and so is *le guerre,*" the count told a friend one day. "They are vermin. They will wreck civilization."

"Indeed, we should assassinate the kaiser!" said his friend, sipping on a glass of rosé.

"We ought to put the helmets of Prussia on their chairs so when they sit they will be buggered!" the count laughed, and they clinked glasses.

"I think," said the count, turning serious, "we must use the aeroplane."

"But it has never been used before. Wouldn't that kill too many innocents?"

"Bah! What are innocents to the kaiser? So many head of cattle. We must strike first, or we will be destroyed."

They walked into the house clenching their fists. Cocu urinated on himself.

Late one night, there was a rustling from the bushes. Laughter, then a hush, and whispers. Cocu peed in his sleep, turned over, and bit his own ear. A woman came rushing out of the bushes and was pinned against the doghouse by—the count! He muffled her panting, as the moon shone on her pearl-white neck and long red hair. And green eyes. Yes! It was the nun from Paris who had searched for her rosary at Lourdes. She had on no Dominican robes, but rather a red velvet floor-length gown that dragged in the mud. The count bit her neck and put a hand on her mouth, and when he heard the dog stir, he let go and chased her back into the bushes, out of moonshot. She made feeble attempts at a yell, and then the moans started, before she cried out, "*Voici le rosaire!*"

Where was Madame Balotte? Visiting members of her tea set naturally, after which she slept with a pillow over her face. There was an increase in shouts in the ensuing weeks, and a window or two was smashed. The besotted count was made to sleep outside. Leaning against the doghouse, he dropped his head right on the nail. After more than one hundred years on this earth, and crooked since birth, the nail wasn't flush with the wood, and she cut the count's scalp. He yelped, and Cocu licked him on the face.

"You like blood, don't you, Cocu?" he said. "Taste! Taste, *mon chien.*"

The count peered closer. In that second, each other man and nail knew. Maybe he thought he could make amends with Madame or Michel or the world, for he went to get a crowbar and spent most of the night trying to pry Crooked out. But he was drunk and kept slipping into the mud of the red-haired nun. Finally, he collapsed, exhausted, and fell asleep with Cocu in the shelter.

Crooked was lolling in the sun, head topped with dried blood, the day the bombs fell. The pigpen got it first. The chicken coop flew upward. Chez Balotte exploded; *le deuxième étage* dropped like a spiderweb unhinged by a prowling animal. A large gray cloud was hailing down destruction, something called a dirigible. Prussian. Though she could not move on her own, the nail trembled like no time since the day by the Gave when the radiance brought her alloys to life. Screams came from the chateau, and the children ran out of the sagging back door. Suddenly, Crooked was on the ground covered in blood, the doghouse splintered. Fifi should have been far from the wounded Cocu's mind, but when a bomb took out part of the fence, through it he slithered, only to find Fifi cut in half.

The Great War. *Le Premier Guerre Mondial.* It was what the Lady had spoken of.

In the days to come, the count was killed in his bed, not having a chance to enter the cockpit of his beloved flying machine. Madame Balotte suffered a severe gash to her head; the oldest boy, Phillippe, died, but Michel and Beatrix escaped injury. Soon the survivors left, including Cocu. The nail remained, as she had before, on the wet earth, gaping out of the plank the little boy had given her. She was hit and hit again by rain, in weeds entangled. To Crooked, the world had become instantly foreign.

Years passed, and the chateau lay in ruins. Lichen grew on the nail. One rude spring morning a crew of men threw the remains of the dog-house into a lorry. They went about hoisting beams and stone, glass and iron rods into trucks and took the whole lot to the center of Paris, where the fate of the nail looked to be sealed forever. The men were sorting stone from wood, glass and iron, and Crooked went into the scrap heap of iron. Rods and ratchets and poles and nails, all refuse from the war devastation. She searched for Straight. But no iron gave her a sign.

In the scrap-metal plant, Crooked waited to be thrown to a molten end. Was this how the odd being of a nail would finally be lost? In a flaming liquid metal like the day of birth? Crooked warmed as in the burly hands of Roux.

As luck would have it, a worker picked Crooked up and, throwing her to another worker, shouted, "Look at this one!" He overthrew the man, however, and the nail sailed over the wall of the plant and into the alley out back. The worker didn't fetch her. Sounds of gratitude and futility clattered on the cobbles. Crooked was old and no longer a relic.

Prams and parasols, mendicants and motorcars, Clemenceau and *La Tour Eiffel* standing over the horizon like a man with long arms at his sides—this was Paris of the twenties. The nail lay in a tuft of nettle growing through a crack in the cobblestones. The steamy life of a huge city passed by. This was her intellectual period—everyone from Cocteau to Sartre walked by and dropped bits and pieces of a philosophy that man was only himself and alone in the universe, that empires were crumbling and lights were no longer lit by gas but a force called electricity. One rotund raconteur declared to his companion on a sunny day, "Why, man has become no better than a nail!"

Privy to the loftiest and most despairing thoughts of the greatest minds of the age in that alley, Crooked was also able to see that whatever these thoughts, men and women evidently lived for moans pressed against walls late at night. Lovers walked on the nail. Winos sat on her; urinating dogs touched her. Motorcars spat smoke. Everything went swiftly. Even a nail can be brought to despair. She witnessed robberies. For a few francs, a man was knifed and left howling. The gendarmes came and drew chalk around the blood. No one picked up Crooked. No one even bent to pluck the little flower that curled from the nail's tip.

People began to live in dread of what they knew was coming, and when it came there was nowhere to hide. The cobbles of the alley were blasted to the sky. A black dragnet droned over the city—Count Balotte's dream was unleashed. Bombs fell and toppled tall buildings. Fires broke out across Paris, and people dropped where they stood. Crooked lost her head, which flew to the sky with the cobbles.

A hush went over the city. Crooked lay in the center of the destroyed alley. Marching boots came stamping. It wasn't long before the nail discovered the pestilence had taken the old name—German—but a new form, Nazi.

Beatings, rapes, brandishings of belts with crooked crosses became the order of not only night but day as well. "Vichy," "traitor," "Hitler," "*Les juifs,*" and "underground" echoed down the alley. Roux's errant kindness, Guido's crablike joy were aeons from the life of a nail.

After a while the alley became a place for the huddling of Frenchmen who would signal each other, light cigarettes, and talk in hushed tones. One conversation between two men went like this:

"Where is the ash?"

"In Rudolf's pocket."

"How many clouds are in a bush?"

"Seven."

"Did you see the diamond?"

"No. It was put in the milk."

"Give me a kettle of cod."

"Already in Hamburg."

"What heart is stolen?"

"The moon's."

"What race is won?"

"The blind."

"Can you see the way to Toulouse?"

"Through the needle's eye."

"My left knee hurts."

"So goes the bosom."

They showed each other revolvers and crushed their cigarettes. A black Mercedes came roaring into the alley. The men pivoted and ran. Shots hit their heels. They turned and fired but missed the car. Just as they were to be mowed down, the car went over Crooked hard—a loud bang—and a tire collapsed. The car veered and smashed into a wall. The men disappeared around the corner. Three SS storm troopers got out of the Mercedes and gave chase. They returned soon after and cursed their tire, and wondered what did it. Whoever did was going to pay. It was good that the nail was as dark as the night.

Storm-trooper boots and stiff steps were replaced by other boots and other steps, and in a cacophony of languages—French, English, American, Russian—the war came to an end. Paris went wild, covered with confetti and the regurgitations of wine and pâté. Crooked was kicked around the alley by brats from all over the globe shouting *Vive* this and *Vive* that.

Soon the machines of destruction gave way to the iron ball of the builders. This gigantic hunk of Crooked's kind swayed and knocked into buildings either half torn down or too old for what people kept saying was the Second Belle Epoche. It sounded nice. But Crooked had touched too much devastation. The blessing that was hers was only hers. It seemed like the alley of cobbles was the only place resistant to the frenzy of concrete spreading. It was not to be long before Crooked, too, was covered by this hard veil.

The benign doom of apartments, insurance companies, office buildings of every sort erected around Crooked, and there seemed only a token amount of wood used in the construction. Sheets of metal, a hard oil called fiberglass, I-beams, huge slabs of concrete were the order of the day. Little wood meant one thing—few nails. The fewer there were, the more Crooked longed for contact with them. But even the few stuck in the teeth of laborers shone in the sun unlike anything she'd known. They were silver, not iron, straight and thin, and had a strict round top to them. They all looked alike, and needless to say, none of them felt the breeze.

The fifties passed with toots for de Gaulle; the sixties were ushered in with Giscard; and it wasn't long before what looked to be the Lady's final war had arrived. Hordes of young people shouting about something called Vietnam streamed up and down the alley in garb that would have made Cocu proud. A lad with long hair and a bandanna sat beside the wall in the alley, resting from a march. He took a drink from a canteen (another war sign). He absently fingered Crooked and dropped her into his knapsack.

For the first time in fifty years, Crooked found herself indoors. The lad who had rescued her from the alley took her to a huge building where he showed her off to a portly fellow with tortoise-shell glasses hanging from a chain who kept saying, "The Louvre does not, the Louvre has thousands . . ." With the irreverence of youth, the new owner tried to find out her age. Suddenly, as if to prove his point about her worthlessness, the portly curator dropped his glasses on his stomach, reached into a drawer, and pulled out several iron nails from the nineteenth century.

"Zo, you zee, here is one like it, *exactement.*"

It was Straight.

"Is it too hot in here?" the curator asked the lad, seeing the youth's sweating palm.

"No. But this nail is hot all of a sudden."

"Iron retains zi heat, *oui.*"

The curator regarded his own fat palm; it, too, was moist. "*Très bizarre.* Zi AC has been on *complètement* zi whole day."

All the moisture Crooked and Straight had retained over the hard years was coming out of them. The other nails did not know; the man and the lad did not sense this reunion. As they conversed, the man in broken English and the lad in broken French, the two nails from Lourdes told each other in their way what had happened to them since separating in 1899 when the chapel was destroyed. Straight had spent time in a jar on the Tarbes woman's dresser, before being flung in anger against a wall, thrown into the garbage, finally ending up at the bottom of the Gave with sewage, which mercifully moved off him when the current quickened. Later, he was taken from a pool in the rocks by children to their home, and finally, by some local museum, sent in envelope to Paris, where he lived in a drawer in the Louvre. Nothing very exciting, about as high as a nail could go in the world, shy of being used.

Crooked related the story of how she had lost a chunk of herself in the First World War, while expressing her deep sympathy with Straight that his tip was blunted and bent. There was laughter—if you can imagine how nails laugh—Straight scraping good-bye in a drawer while Crooked dropped back into the knapsack. "My love," she spoke in a language only Straight knew. But she would never see him again.

Crooked was taken to Orly Airport where monotonous voices announced times and gates for Count Balottes' brainchildren.

A new version of English came out of the lad when he met a companion:

"Hey, man, isn't this outa sight?"

"Gosh, is that bitchin'."

"I just scarfed it from an alley in Paris."

"Do you think it's worth much?"

"Naw. But I'm going to take it home. Cheaper than postcards, eh? Hang loose."

Crooked was not hung but shaken loose from the sack in a fraction of the time it took Count Balotte to get from the Pyrenees to Paris. Frank Matter's hometown was in that land the French drooled over and mocked all at once: America.

The nail was handed over by Frank to his parents. They kept saying, "How old! How old!" as if being old were being rare. Crooked was placed in their living room in a cabinet alongside a clay jar from Mexico, a piece of rock from the Grand Canyon, a medallion of some leader named George Washington, and a speckled paperweight from Damascus. All under lock and key.

In Los Angeles, California, along a beach she was not to see, an ocean that never washed over her, underneath blossoms in which she could not lay, the nail rested. Routine followed. Mrs. Lily Matter cooks meat no diner sees slaughtered. Fish appear from no river, nails from no smith. She opens a box, and cold clouds come out. Soon what looks like ice becomes food. The Matter family—five strong—eats this ice food. During the day, machines never let quiet in: a hole Mrs. Matter throws her food into roars, a thing to open cans whines, and always the gyrating of something called a clock. It gives off a hum not unlike the hum of new lights put up in Paris. Past the living room another box talks during the day and into the night. Crooked listens to it always because she has to. And there is not much to hear. People are always laughing in the box, people who never appear. The box occasionally talks of war, but nothing seems warlike. The Matters kiss at times, talk, argue. They are very busy with their grinding things or the box, playing piano only rarely when the blue screen of the box is off.

On occasion when the Matters have other people visit, the doors to the curio cabinet are unlocked, and the guests are told about each object in it. When they come to Crooked, they make up a story. Perhaps they just don't know who she is or where she comes from.

"Magnetism," one fat man says, looking at Crooked and turning to Mr. Omar Matter one night. "Someday in the near future nails won't be seen. And neither will rods or glue or hinges or spikes or even cement. Magnetism will hold everything together."

Late at night, after the box has spoken its final words about Afghanistan or South Central Los Angeles, Lebanon or Israel, and everyone is sleeping, the crooked nail wonders about her companion, Straight. At the bottom of the Gave, watching trout swim and play wasn't a bad life. As different as they appeared, why was he the only other one like her? What was the purpose of their being brought to tremble together so many years ago? And now flung apart a second time?

Maybe the Lady lied. Maybe she was nothing but a senseless beam like this box. Crooked sits so still, feeling no movement either from the air or the rain, as one never created, purposeless. Sometimes the Matter daughter, Vivian, stares at the iron thing and thinks of giving her release with a hammer. But Vivian lacks the abandon and guile of little Michel.

She stares and goes away. She seems to want nothing. It is a terrible thing to want nothing. After 180 years, even a nail from Lourdes stops wanting.

Yet if this house falls as the chapel and the doghouse did, Crooked may find the air. She was born in the heat of day and the hand of a creator who blessed her with fire and a crook from his pained vision. She fused the separate, the lonely, those who knew neither each other nor themselves. Was it a curse to be brought to life with nothing to make one die? To be useless and deathless?

One day the youngest child, Benjamin, with anarchic pleasure sweeps aside the curios while his grandmother Matile naps. When she awakes, she finds the nail in her palm. She kisses the boy, throws her hands up at the mess, but laughs. She is old and has seen more destruction than this in her time. She takes the nail to her house in Pasadena, goes to her backyard, hammers the old, crooked shape until it is reasonably straight, and then whacks it through a tin-can lid into the branch of a fig tree.

"This lid, she keep away the birdies, honey," she explains later to Benjamin. "She bring the sun, she shine too much."

Yes, thinks Crooked, conjuring Straight, transformed into all she had loved, a little piece of metal, wood, and a dazzling light.

Honeymoon of a Thousand Hopes

Heaven is when you were first in love stretched for eternity.
—Albert Orfalea

They dove into the water, angry. They had argued, and now they were far apart, facing the open sea.

The weather had changed. The wind had torn a skirt of mist off the Pyrenees. Tamarisk along the boardwalk shook, pink flowers trembling like the straps of underthings on the line. Her first night in St. Jean de Luz the bride had touched tamarisk, pink to pink. What a strange tree—an evergreen with flower! Like their fast marriage, hoarding all the contraries together.

This last day of their honeymoon, everything stood out too well: tamarisk, linden trees, Basque tiled roofs, and the half-nude Parisian women whose shadows seemed pulled out of them by the wind and branded on the pavement. The sun was almost too strong today, thought the bridegroom. No blasting horns, no abrasive clouds or biblical thunder. A sun of judgment, nonetheless. And they were purely exposed, clothesless.

James and Iris had set off at the height of noon to swim the mile across the bay from St. Jean de Luz to Socoa, just shy of the Spanish border. While inspecting a tiny lighthouse, they had decided to switch from walking "Le Croissant," as the bay was called, to swimming its mouth.

It was at the shedlike lighthouse that James had seen death—in a red searchlight, motionless in the day. It reminded him he was out of work and married, in that order. What would he be returning to in the States? What nothing awaited him? His 110-year-old evening paper was bankrupt. Iris, ten years his junior, told him not to worry—she would shoulder the burden with her job as a clerk in a big company.

After he had proposed the long swim, his wife's eyes turned the color of the noon sea: teal. Her feet throbbed from being cut on rocks the first day of their *lune de miel*. The ones you don't see are the sharpest, she had said. And the prettiest, he had come back. I would like to be a fish and never walk again, she proclaimed, catching the carnival lights of the town square in her eyes. Now *there* was a life's goal! Reverse evolution.

Silently, Iris measured the distance from the seawall on which they stood to the center dike out in the bay, and then beyond that to the old fort of Socoa on the far shore.

"Of course," she nodded. James thought she was agreeing to something inside her own head and not his proposal the way she stretched her wrists up to the sky. Her breasts rose like burial mounds in the persimmon suit. Waves of earth. He turned away, embarrassed by her beauty.

"*D'accord,*" she repeated. She had lived in Lyons as a girl with her NATO-based father and the rest of the family. Now she was back, married for one week.

Sailboats raised their brows in water. Windsurfers and speedboats, too. The new couple studied them a while. It appeared that seacraft entered the bay near Socoa and left between the seawall of St. Jean de Luz and the center dike.

"Have to keep our eye out for boats," James croaked.

"Sure," Iris smiled. She had an off-center gap in her upper teeth, a submerged Wife of Bath. Maybe he would die off like the Wife's first four husbands. Her teal eyes flashed, and she clapped her hands together, jumped up, and bounded down the knoll from the red-eye lighthouse. She called out. She was going to rent masks.

From the minute of his challenge, James felt he had made a mistake. It was Iris, after all, who was the swimmer. For ten years she had been primed for the Olympics, the 400-meter medley. But just before the time trials for Sydney she had cracked her ankles on the cement decking of a pool after clowning with one of the high divers. Her father, who had coached her from infancy, broke down and locked himself in his room for two days.

Honeymoon of a Thousand Hopes   ✳   123

Swimming was not the same after the accident; neither was walking. Iris walked now as someone about to take a bold dance step, but never quite doing it.

James was good at floating. After nearly drowning in sprint laps on the high school swim team, he had perfected the float. Unlike track, you cannot stop to catch your breath. You swim or go down. Or you float. The coach asked if he would like to be "the manager." He thanked him and chose the student newspaper.

The bay stretched in front of them, the dike a taupe brick far out in the water. Sails were tips of picket fences. Or licks of saliva. Or teeth. And he had proposed they swim through that?

At the beach shop where Iris rented snorkels and masks, the proprietor heard them chatter in English about an impending swim. He touched James on the elbow, "Do not go beyond the deek. If you go beyond the deek, be sure you will find terrible water. Stay on this side of the deeks, all of them. Then you will be okay. *Ça va?*"

In a world of fluids, marriage was, if nothing else, a solid. But on their way to swim the bay, they fought. James flexed his muscle down the canopy of tamarisk.

"Why do you always feel your own bicep? Are you showing off?"

"No," he said, startled. "It's unconscious."

"And why are you always looking at every woman on this beach with bare breasts?"

"Because they don't do that on American public beaches. Unless it is late at night and no one's around."

"The other day at the Pile des Assietes everyone was nude, and you wouldn't let me swim nude. It amazes me that you can feel your bicep and hang your tongue out like a rope at these brown chests and then forbid me from doing it." In front of her a fat man's swimming trunk bulged with buttocks.

"It's our honeymoon."

"And?"

He burst out, "I look at trees, birds, rocks, at the sea and the starfish. My stare is about as important as scratching my head and about as meaningful."

"I have never seen a man look at trees with that look."

As they walked, the hot cobbles curled Iris's feet inward. Silence seeped out of the two. Till they reached the lighthouse.

"Why do you go into yourself like a damn sulking muskrat?" James uncorked.

Iris's face had the untested sheen of young American women raised in the suburbs, given everything to survive as one, but not so much to understand two. Suddenly, her chin bloated. She did not speak. Her new husband's job was words, or had been. She had plenty she could stab him with. But she thought: *my body.*

She had calves made solid by years of swimming, and shoulders as large as a man's bunched from the butterfly. After winning a race, she'd lean back from the pool ladder with those summer squash shoulders, laughing. They did her talking. Maybe they would again. With only one competitor who might himself go away.

A sprig of hair marooned on his sallow chest, James stalked off. He dropped over the wall onto the sand, then negotiated the seawall above the rocks. Blindly, he gathered pain toward the end of land.

Iris did not follow. Jumping on the sand, her already black-and-blue foot caught on a broken shell. The pain shot up to her teeth and forced her away from him. She found herself diving into the water a hundred yards behind the lighthouse, giving her husband a head start.

James surveyed the water. The sun was at its zenith. They were starting late. He looked back. Where was Iris? She had not followed him on the seawall. He wondered why they had allowed each other to break off with so little resolved before entering the sea. There were rudders and propellers out there—they could take off feet. Was this a ruse for Iris? Was she sunning herself topless?

A squint around the bay. No Iris. Coated with shellfish, the last rock of the jetty waited for pink flesh. Twenty summers before he would have had feet as tough as leather. And sandals. Ah, youth, and tough feet! Age gave soft feet and tough shoes. Man, made for facade even at foot level.

Sweat collected on the chest hair like spray on sea oat. His whole body felt exposed. His bathing suit was not a European black strip, a Speedo, but old-fashioned American—a multicolored covering of the thighs.

A seal's head bobbed in the dark water. Iris? He squinted. A small plane droned by pulling red letters across the blue sky: BUVEZ ORANGINA. No clouds. No sugar for *citron presse.*

On touchdown in Paris she had let him make another mistake. *"Limonade avec citron, s'il vous plait,"* he had ordered at a café. *"Citron presse?"* returned the waiter. *"Oui, ah, limonade presse."* So the waiter brought a Seven-Up with raw lemon pulp sitting at the bottom of the glass. James in his untutored French had ordered a weird combined drink, rather than two simple separate lemonades.

"We are too much in love," Iris said, stirring the extrasweet concoction, then leaning to kiss him.

James did not speak. The Eiffel Tower in the distance: was it not a wishbone?

The seal ahead pulled a V wake into deeper water. It was Iris. She had passed him. The orange dot must be her snorkel, he thought. He could not make her out exactly, but only Iris could swim this surely, breaststroking, bobbing up and down silently. The droning plane trailed off. She was headed toward the dike out in the middle of the bay, and she had not stopped to wave to him, passing. Foolishly, they had eschewed fins. They would make it, if they made it, with little more than each other.

He stopped, facing the wind. What if he didn't go? If he were to simply sit on the carpet of tiny mussels the whole afternoon? She would see him as a coward, and it would be over before it had begun. Ah, yes. She had called his macho bluff.

The seawall leeched with mussels reminded him of home, the pebblestone walkways of long, sad Los Angeles houses. But these sharps were alive. James dipped his body in the water, scraping his thighs on the rocks. The sea stung his legs, but numbed his sore feet. Treading water, he yelled ahead. Was she crazy? They may as well have chained two slabs to their necks and bid each other swim to the horizon. The center dike from water level seemed continents away.

Let her go. Let her go conquer Socoa by herself, and I will be back at the pension, leaning with a Ricard and a Voltaire grin and chide her, "But *ma cherie*? What have you accomplished? I was not there. Your feat has been wasted on the minnows!"

His mask fogged over. After clearing it, the pain forced him to beat feverishly away from the rocks out to sea.

Up close the sea was jade green and waved in front of him like a fern. Beauty or fear: which was calling the shots? The chop of the sea told him to swim and forget answers.

Iris, too, felt the sting of her cut foot evacuate as she swam. Her muscles bunched around her bones as she flexed and pulled, her blood beating strong. Anger fueled her. Since getting sick the night before on rotten mussels in soup (*soupe de poison,* she called it), her nerves had been fraying. Their stomachs were empty—they had barely managed tea and bread for breakfast. Watching anemones and starfish waver below, she blotted out James.

She did not like "going into herself." But it was her pride, her way of protecting the fire inside from a snuffing. Marriage was like that—a big wind. It had happened so fast she didn't have time to feel different, better, more understanding, all things she had thought came naturally with the vows. So quickly they had joined she did not know if she could, or ever would, trust him. Standing over the toilet wretching her guts in the middle of the night in a strange hotel in the Basque country where her school French wasn't so helpful, she expelled the funnel storm of the wedding and its richness, and was left only herself, naked, in a dark, doorless commode. The twists in her stomach ceased, but the sour smell of Iregulay wine made her swoon. She had pulled the chain, cleaned up, gone back.

Iris flipped over, and backstroked. The land dike was receding. Gulls cried out, looking down at her. She had an impulse to circle back and find her husband. But in the pit of her stomach something twisted: she did not feel like his wife.

It was as if this were a fine summer vacation with a college lover, and it was coming to an end. It terrified her, however, that she was not returning to be only herself. The gorgeous sea helped her forget, to consider James only a lover that one could say good-bye to. She turned easily in Esther Williams flip to breaststroke, pulling slower, wider, further from what probably was a malevolent James.

James stroked, more or less madly—whacking the water rather than making his hand a fin. In the States doing laps he would think about things, such as his tender affliction of the pen. Writing for him was pains-taking reassemblage of what was fractured, which was most everything. The world was a shattered mosaic, each human being holding one irre-placeable small tile. His job was to find the patterns, however remote, link them, and make the world whole, even for a moment. He'd gotten to do this all too rarely at the paper; now he might be forced to try all day. Draw sparks—fire—from trying to fit things long gone together again. That forging fire, he knew, could also burn you.

Without fins the sea was too teeming and deep for contemplation. He was lost in what he feared most, weightlessness, and dared not think or vary his stroke. His was a rhythm of fear.

Her rhythm, too, was regular, but she changed her stroke at will, now a dolphin kick, now sidestroke, fully at home. Her mind widened like a woman in love with all creation. She became receptive (at least to every-thing but him). She welcomed thought, let it pull like taffy or seaweed to the ends of her seal-like body.

The sea began to rock. Iris changed from breaststroke to Australian crawl as she entered the troubled middle water.

She liked a feel of insignificance, this merging, as if a lattice of gills pierced her skin. Her father had made her too significant too early, push-ing her as an eight-year-old swimming prodigy. She had had no time to learn of men as she gathered medal after medal, until she had met the man who covered her for the local evening paper. It would be better now to swim for pleasure alone. She pulled at the water, digging gently, embrac-ing, until startled by the whine of a motor.

It was an inboard speedboat of fishermen and their wives. The captain blasted a horn at her, waving, slowing the throttle. The wives waved. She broke her stroke and angled herself toward aft.

The men had their shirts off; one had his tied around his neck as a New Englander. The women's breasts shone with coconut oil.

"*Vous avez beaucoup courage, mademoiselle,*" shouted the captain with Basque beret and shirt bow.

She laughed, treading water.

"*Je suis mariée!*" she called, buoyant.

"*Quoi?*" he shouted, turning the boat as if she were in danger.

She threw back her head and waved to say it was no problem. The wives on board seemed indifferent and continued to take in the sun. The boat sped away. Iris continued to swim. Now the center dike grew. All she wanted to do was get there and thrust herself over the top of it.

Ropes of sun trailed in the deepening green water. She'd prefer to go down one of them with aqualung where at bottom she might find her father among the treasures, squid, and stonefish. He was always filming—underwater, above water, water, her, always her. The rays in the green sea lulled her. She awoke, set herself on the dike ahead. Not her father or husband.

Who was now far behind. Out in the bay hundreds of feet deep with no boat, raft, preserver, or, apparently, wife. A good swimmer never looks up in freestyle, but every third stroke or so James lurched for air, a bad habit from childhood. His freestyle looked like a bad version of breaststroke. For the first time he wondered if there might not be something practical about style. He was getting tired, and afraid.

Swimming with no boundaries. He had been strangely pleased at the immediate boundary of the gold wedding band, and her hand, and all who gathered 'round for the dance that became a spinning of something snug and warm. How many years wasted with thinking, thinking, thinking with Valerie? She who could never make up her mind and made him split the one hair on his chest a hundred times? Marriage was a boundary welcomed with open arms. But what an infinity Iris was putting him through! He who cringed from horizons because they were never reached and usually made someone crazed in the trying.

A windsurfer cut in front of him and broke his manic stroke. He cried out. But the fear of losing rhythm made him turn and swim in a circle until the windsurfer passed. An hour at sea, James entered the shafts of green light.

What to Iris were ropes, James took as chords of a watery piano playing in front of his eyes. He heard his breathing in the snorkel, a pipe organ.

Where was Iris?

His head shot up; the center dike was closer now than the land behind. His sweat poured ceaselessly into the water.

The sockets of his shoulders ached. He swallowed water, then blew the rest out the pipe. Float! He was the floater, after all. But the thought scared him. He did not want by overturning for a second to feel gravity's pull in the water. One false stroke without torque, and that would be it. He looked up and saw Iris's red-tipped snorkel far ahead. She was approaching the seawall in the center of the bay.

The air whipped. The sun began to slide down the sky. Windsurfers flocked near the giant slab built by Louis XIV to break the tide of the Atlantic. It was as if in uniting two enemies—Spain and France—by marrying Maria Teresa in the border town of St. Jean de Luz, Louis would do anything to shelter the union that the town itself had come to symbolize, and would break every passion before it could build up. Louis had spied her one day across a street that separated the two countries. She was beautiful in black mantilla and skin white as cream. He barely knew her, nor she him, when they married in the oak-beamed church with a miniature galleon hanging over their heads like a survivor of the fate of the Armada.

James approached the breakwater in abject awe. Surely, Iris must be here. But would she have dived off the other end already? Would she already be swimming to Socoa? To Spain? The United States?

The dike loomed like the prow of a battleship. He broke from his reverie in the shafts of green light and swam faster. A rusted, barnacled ladder of pipe dangled above the water. He grabbed the lowest rung and let the current knock him about, catching his breath. When he hoisted himself up, his foot wounds tore on the barnacles.

Fierce wind nearly threw him off the ledge. He fell on the stones and crawled away from the precipice. The stones were hot against his chest. Gull guano hard and pointed cut his entire body. His blood sprinkled the white rocks.

A long, uneven road of old slabs. How had Louis put them in place out here three hundred years ago? Not with industrial frogmen. Hauled one by one, no doubt, in wooden ships by that earliest labor union—slavery. It would have been easy to cart a few Arabs from North Africa to do the task, or blacks from farther down. The Sun King would never know that stones easing the sea into the marriage of Spain and France would one day be covered by gull excrement. And how many wars since then? Louis would not protect France from itself during 1789, neither Maria protect Spain from itself in 1936. It was such a beautiful illusion, St. Jean de Luz.

James stood up, marveling. The wind shook him like a stick. He saw no one down the stones. *Let it be known: I was here.* St. Jean de Luz shimmered in the sun far off, a roseate blurred carpet of umbrellas, cabanas, and sunstruck old pensions. He turned: the sea and its whitecaps all the way home. And Iris? He stumbled down the dike. He wanted in something of a death trap to speak final words to one most important.

From the other end of the gray dike persimmon grew.

She was sitting on the edge, facing Socoa, thinking.

"Iris!"

She didn't turn her head.

He shouted again. The wind ate his voice. He stumbled up to her and sat two stones away. She smiled, watching him recover his breath, but said nothing. She seemed to be in a trance from the sun and the strong swimming. And the sense of being in the center of beauty for a moment and not wanting to move.

"Gorgeous."

She nodded carefully.

"Are you okay?"

He was shivering. "Almost gave out in that green light. Did you see it?"

"Of course. I loved it."

"I'll bet."

They compared wounds. The wind died down.

"Why did you marry me?" she asked, turning halfway toward him and fixing him with seething eyes, cobalt as the darkening sea.

He petted the gull droppings, looking down. He waited. The wind picked up. James related a story she had not heard before, catching his breath after each sentence.

"When my father came back from the war, he wasn't so happy to be alive. Most of his friends were cut down around him on the beach at Anzio." James gestured as if the Mediterranean were right over the mountains, as if all Europe's pain were close.

"He came back from the war troubled. And fell in love with a big blonde, an ex-WAC, who took him in the backseat of an old Chevy and insisted he make love to her. But he was too shook up to do it. And she mocked him and left him.

"Then he met my mother, a virgin. She believed in him in the way they did back then—implicitly, with everything. They didn't know each other much. They married in a few months, like we did."

"I'm not a virgin."

"It doesn't matter."

"But why? Why?" She turned completely toward him. The wind doubled her tears. Her dark hair flew in the wind. "Okay, I know about your own big blonde, that Valerie, but so what? I don't want to live my life with a man only because I'm not someone else."

"You won't."

"But why didn't you marry her?"

"Because I would have killed her."

"You don't mean that."

"Well, nearly. Or she me. There were times when we were in bed she would beg me to fill her up. I mean it. And she'd push and tug as if there wasn't enough of me to do the job. And she was probably right. There isn't enough of anyone, sexually or otherwise, to do that. Her father was bad to her mother and left them all early. She wanted me to be bad to her. And it went on for years, the breakings. She thrived on them, and loved luring me back. And for a long while I must have thrived on it, too, liking to be fractured . . ."

"Stop it!" Iris put her hands over her ears, stood up in the wind, and slipped over the slabs facing the sea. "I don't want to hear about her!"

He hit the stones with his fists.

"You asked me why I married you."

"Yeah, and you're telling me about your father and Valerie with the big crack."

That stopped him. He hadn't heard her use sexual slang before. "I married you because you are beautiful."

"Oh, what are you talking about?"

"You are."

"And so is the deep blue sea. And the devil."

"Look, I can't say it exactly. I'm not talking just about physical beauty. There is something about you that says: *I last.* I think I mean you are strong."

"How do you know?"

"You brought me cookies when we first went to lunch."

"And that is strength?" Her mouth hung open.

"They were strong cookies."

They both smiled for the first time in two days. He held her hand. It was a strange, objective inspection, seeing the rills that become ridges, the lifelines that deepen in the palm, the veins that turn purple and swell after children and sinks and choler and earth.

"I married you because I had come to the edge, and there was nowhere else to go but you."

Was that the wind in his eyes, or was he crying? A spasm of disgust went up her gut—she did not want to be the object of desperation. Yet she loved him desperately, too, and in asking him she was asking herself to explain something she could not explain. She saw the wind ribboning the sea, and she listened to it. Nothing grew on the old dry stones. Yet they were building something. She wasn't sure how far down it would go, or even if it could survive, but she could almost feel something emerge from between them and sink, hard and green, into the rock itself.

They linked their bleeding feet.

"You're thinking of your father again, aren't you?"

"Yes. He said to me just before the end, 'There's no air cover, Jimmy.'"

"You don't think I think of it?" She was—hard combination to hold at once—sad and angry. She gritted her teeth. "What if our children hear about it? They will have to someday, if we have them. How do you tell a child about a blood relative taking his own—? You take me for strong, but sometimes I am afraid—"

"You're my earth cover."

"You can't, you just can't!" she shouted, standing.

The wind knocked her off balance. But she picked herself up and grabbed his head by the salty hair. "Time for a swim," she sang, the wind eating everything but "Time."

"Iris, let's rest."

"But there are too many edges here."

"Pure beauty."

"I did agree, didn't I, to swim here?"

"Yes, you did, about as stupid as me proposing it."

"Let's get to Socoa. We can cab it back to St. Jean de Luz and maybe some hot soup, a baguette, and a honeymoon of a thousand hopes."

"You're on. But together this time."

"I can't hold your hand, Jimmy."

"Nearer, Iris, nearer."

They dropped off the dike and swam quickly into the afternoon sea. The entrance to Le Croissant was not quite as wide as the exit they had just swum. Still, by the time they had reached Socoa they were winded. James crawled up on shore on his knees. Was this all prayer?

They made their way up the stony shore. From a parapet of Louis's stone fort a man was fishing. He watched the couple.

"*Vouz êtes fous ou poissons, non?*"

"*Poissons, vraiment!*" Iris chimed.

"Ah . . . you are . . . *Americains*, no? *Tous les deux*. Both. I have watching you for one hour. Because I have no feesh. And I have very good eyes. To swim to Socoa from the deek, it is crazy, no? You are crazy feesh."

The man took off his glasses. Iris asked in French how far it was to the road.

"Iris, please."

James was lifting his feet like a crane off the hot cement.

"Well, thank you very much. *Merci*."

The two shot down the walkway of the old fort, biting their lips. Though the sun had dropped to four o'clock, the stone blistered their feet. They found shade under separate ledges.

"How in creation are we going to get back to St. Jean de Luz?" James took a long breath. "We can't even get off this fort without burning our feet. No shoes to walk. It's six miles. And hey. We have no money for a taxi. It's all at the hotel."

Iris considered. "Our first case of thinking ahead."

"Yeah, we blew that one together."

They propped themselves against a cool wall inside the corridors of the old fort. Iris made out with her lips that she was thirsty, tilting an imaginary glass to them, revealing her fine neck. "Water, water, everywhere, and not a drop to drink," she recited, closing her eyes.

"That fisherman—what a phony. He must sit there all day and scan the waters for a woman. He liked you. I could tell."

"At least I wasn't naked."

"Not true. For a man with eyes like his a woman is always naked."

"Is that true?"

James closed his eyes.

"Look, Jimmy, it's getting late." Socoa, she said, had Ravel's house, the great composer, but "There's no way we're going to find his house barefoot."

Her husband was nodding off. Her lips curled wryly and showed the off-side Wife of Bath gap in her teeth. *O sovereynetee!* thought James, glancing.

"No, no. No," James smacked the stone wall. "I won't do it."

"What other way is there? We can't go by hot-air balloon."

"What about hitchhiking?"

"They don't hitchhike anymore, not even in Europe."

"True. This is the age for missiles. Do you have a missile? Then no ride for you."

"Yeah. Anyway, how would we get to the road without burning our feet off?"

"Maybe I can be a Hindu. Walk on coals."

She laughed.

"I can't do it," he said.

"You can."

"You must go slow."

"I'm not going to tread water."

"I mean it, Iris, slow and close."

"You can't dance in the water."

"This is nuts. You're going to kill me."

"We better get going before we stiffen up."

"Don't say that. I'm not a cadaver yet."

"You've got a good sense of humor. That's enough to marry someone for."

"That and twenty-five cents will get me a ticket to Catalina."

She pushed him forward and rubbed his shoulder blades.

"Ah—"

"Finished," she sprang up.

"That's the shortest back rub in history. Is this torture?"

"Can't get too comfortable. You lose the edge."

"I've got too much edge, I've already told you that."

Soon they were wading over the tailings into the water, facing what seemed to James an unreachable dike, to Iris something already close, even intimate. Truth was, she was glad it was the only option—to swim back the way they came. They were open on the dike in a hard wind surrounded by blue. *Unlike ever again.* The thought made her eyes add to the sea. She swam with sheer love and pull. *Hope you are wrong, Iris.*

The water slapped James. His ribs, pulled tight around his viscera, began to ache. He felt that between his heart and the cold sea there was nothing but skin.

The sun sharpened going down. James entered the shafts of green light again, dazzled, drained. His stroking got slower, heavier. A sail nipped the corner of his eye. A shark? A blue and red shark . . .

He jerked his head up, gulped water, and flipped over, coughing. The sky, the lid of his coffin! He floated. It terrified him, but he floated, out of breath. He went nowhere and tried to rest. Waves rocked him, but he kept his head back, arms out. James the Lesser, crucified in the bay of St. Jean de Luz. Nails driven in by a wife of one week obsessed with exercise. He imagined the news lead:

An American tourist was dredged from the bottom of the sea near the dike of Louis XIV yesterday. The wife had lost sight of him.

How fast a life is reduced and discarded in newsprint! He had done his share of these reductions. Maybe it was good that he had been driven out by the Fates. But to what end? To the book Iris insisted he finish, one he had put aside a thousand times?

He flipped over, saw his hand otherworldly through the mask. Red glows in the water. Iris undressing? He reached and reached.

Stroked slower. His head grew dizzier. The green light throbbed below, leading to the center of a watery flower, where his father called out: *Do you want to join me, Jim? I am happy now.*

What saved him wasn't Iris, though as she swam up to him he was gasping for air. No. It was the cramp. It snapped him out of his sinking like a jerked rope. She wrist-towed him for a while until he began kicking with one leg as they came up under the dike.

"I think we will be either great or terrible," he coughed.

"We've been terrible till now. There's only one way left."

Iris bent his toes back to free the cramp. Then they lay, exhausted, on the stones. The day's heat had begun to pour out of them, and they hugged the hard surface. Both felt one thing: backs beaten cold by sea wind, organs warmed by the stones. They slept. And woke in each other's arms, scraping close to protect their body heat. The wind began panting. The sea crashed, and the high wall shook. Wind swallowed their wonder cries. Gulls screeched and dipped.

After what seemed forever, the couple sat up. The sea was beaten silver, the color it takes just before sundown.

"We'll never be here again."

"We go back to St. Jean de Luz, and then home to America," she gazed out at the hardening silver, rubbing his neck, "and we become two again."

"You coulda let me go."

"No." She could not take his stare. She rubbed the stones and then her arms with both palms; the cold was already seeping into her body. "Before my mother had given birth to me, and I was the first, my father had a mistress. It was the maid. And then he had another. And another. And my mother . . . she put up with it. And the drinking. And the roaring."

"And you?"

"I was a teenager before I learned, and I sat on it for a couple years, not knowing what to say. But one day it sunk in—the world-weariness in my mother's eyes—and I blew up at him in a way I hadn't before. It was just before I fell off the platform and cracked my feet."

James was stunned. "So what did he say, your father, when you went at him?"

"He said he was sorry, and 'I want it all.' A great American hymn. My father was an only child, you know. Maybe that's where it comes from. Too many 'only children' in this country, and there's more of them every year. Less children means more only children. People born to have it all, thinking they deserve it just by being there."

"He seemed so happy at the wedding."

"He was. And he stopped his affairs, at least as far as I know. It's odd. It coincides with our meeting as much as my lowering the boom that day."

"Look, Iris." James pointed to a tanker dropping ballast out at sea. "It's wastewater, but it's beautiful."

"Anything's beautiful far off," she mused.

"You never know about a man—"

"What I am trying to say, Jimmy, is you're going to betray me."

"What?"

"Someday. You will." Her eyes were moist and blue as the coming night. "It's inevitable. You are an American. You are a man. You want more. That's one thing about women—they're as bad or good as men in all ways but one. Women don't always want more. Maybe it's a history of learning to do with less, and appreciating even a shred of respect, or food, or love. But men can have everything, and up close it's not enough."

"Iris." He held her.

She whispered, "Remember me! Remember these old stones! How warm they were when the wind was cold."

James felt the hard wash of the droppings. She had seen into him like one of those shafts of green light. There is strange exhilaration, even hope, when one is found out. It was not that he wanted to betray her. No. She had found out, without knowing herself, that he was just beginning to love her. And that it was fragile as the sea, and as wild.

"You are every—"

"Don't lie. Just remember. And remember what it costs."

She helped him down the ladder and into the sea. They swam carefully, side by side, to the far seawall at land where the lighthouse stared, red eye unblinking. Soon it would flash on and search for the imprint of souls on the night water.

She clambered up the walkway of the wall while he stood not ten feet from her, still offshore on a rock, unable to get a footing. The smallest waves punished him. His energy was out just shy of the finish. A harder wave pushed him off, another bang on the knees, fresh blood, and they were together hustling under the red eye, down under the swishing tama-risks. They returned snorkels and masks to the shopkeeper who had heard from the gendarmes that some Americans had just swum Le Croissant—back and forth yet—and whoever they were, they must be crazy because it was forbidden. The shopkeeper winked. They agreed, smiling, and closed the weathered door with its small bell.

Victory Boulevard

The detective motioned the young man to come closer and see. He squinted. There at the end of the pointer was a small hair hugging the bullet. The visitor's breath went out. A hot wind was rattling the old, cranked window. But when the young man inhaled, he inhaled air that was cold. And age. He was thirty-five, not so young after all. But now he knew it, breathed it.

"Was this the last one?"

"Yes. This was the last."

The detective stared at the hair a second too long before placing the bullet to which the hair was fused by heat and speed on the glass top of his desk in a row of four lead slugs. He went to crank the window shut, lifting the metal latch. But somehow the late summer Santa Anas were undeterred; they gave a far-off whistle and flung a mimosa in shadow, back and forth, like a woman who has lost her mind or her children.

"I'd had trouble finding that one. Couldn't quite figure where . . . And then that fellow—what was his name?"

"Walker. Jack Walker."

"Yeah. Walker. He's too eager, isn't he? Some boyfriend, I'd say. Calls up and says he's found another bullet. In the ceiling light."

The detective took a sip of his coffee. It burned him, but he didn't show it.

"Can I pour you any?" he asked softly. The visitor bit his lower lip, then shook his head. The detective looked down; a crack in the green linoleum was shaped like a divining rod. Absently, he slid his boot tip to the crack. Crow's feet spread from the officer's eyes as he made some notes, the small muscles of his face spasming.

"Officer Maglie," the visitor stammered. "I . . . Can you tell . . . Is there any way to tell if she was shooting randomly?"

Maglie got up. He went to a file draw and closed it. He reached far over the top of the file and pulled a pack of cigarettes forward with a finger.

"Crazy, isn't it? You think you'll use them less if they're out of reach. But they're never out of reach when you need them. The good things are what's out of reach." He felt himself wandering. "Smoke?" The victim turned interrogator nodded, and Maglie lit one for him.

"I've got my father's last pack."

Maglie's thick eyebrows lifted.

"Merit Ultralight. Found it in the Olds' glove compartment. He was trying to quit, too, this year. How do you quit with someone like Vivian Matter on your beat?"

Maglie acted as if this were a significant fact. He was patient with the brother, the son. Tired, having spent half the night up with the report, he took a long pull of his cigarette and picked up a pencil.

"Well, your father was here." He began drawing a rough diagram of the shop floor, placing the sister in the doorway of the storage room with an X, the father another X at the photocopy machine, the worker at the counter, the customer, and Jack Walker, too—all X's.

"But Walker told me she fired from the office, through the one-way glass. It was cracked. So he said. Or thought."

"That's impossible from the trajectories. How could she have hit the wall partition fifteen feet away at the storage-room entry?"

"Maybe she moved?" The brother was trying everything.

"Very unlikely. If she had, your father—" Maglie paused to collect his thoughts. "He would have gotten away. Mr. Matter, I've been on this police force for twenty-five years. If I had stood where your father stood—point-blank range, not ten feet from your sister—I would not have been able to react quickly enough to get away, either."

Frank Matter closed his eyes. He pressed his hands to his cheeks, then clasped them tightly under his nose.

"The best I can reconstruct it is this. He turned to run when he saw her with the pistol."

"I don't think my father would run."

"Listen to me. There were scuff marks on the floor. He apparently flipped backward. The first bullet killed him. It took five seconds. Hit him in the lower back, severed his spinal cord. There was no time to be heroic, you see? The second bullet goes into the wall partition. The third sprays off to the left into the book spines. And the fourth—"

The brother put his hand to his forehead and pressed hard, as if to hold in his own brains.

"Yes." Maglie bent his head, mocking her movement. "And it comes out the other side and flies into the ceiling light."

"So she was . . . at an angle. At herself."

"Yes. Up."

They both looked at the slug with the hair.

"So what do you think? Was she just out of her mind, spraying the damn thing all over the place?"

The detective's eyes darkened, lowered.

"My mother, you know. It's very important for her. That's how she explains it. If she explains it at all."

"How is she?"

"Barely hanging on. Drugged."

"Tell her what she needs to know to hold on. Tell her it was random. No one will ever know for sure. This isn't an exact science."

"Well?"

"The trajectories, how your father fell, all of it makes me conclude she was aiming."

"How the hell could she have been that accurate?" Matter slammed both hands on the desk. "One bullet! It was the first she'd fired in her life, I'm sure of it."

Was he sure? Probably not, Maglie thought. But what did it matter? The killer's brother stood up and paced. They were all this way, Maglie mused. None of them believe what's inside and whispering. None of them face the music. But over time the tougher might develop elaborate filters—as Maglie himself had—distractions, feints, what was once described to him as "the creative life." Those were the lucky ones. The others would die off, one way or the other let themselves go in the wake of the violence that blotted their loved one. It was on the face of murderers, that vacuousness, the light in the eyes snuffed. Others, too, who did nothing wrong, but hadn't the guile, couldn't grow the hide. He had. You had to if you were going to do any real good. Good required hide.

But this one had got to Officer Thomas Maglie. Maybe it was the expression of the father lying in his blood where he worked, the smile on his face too damn serene.

The cop got up; the brother sat. Each avoided the other's face. Maglie sighed, a sound strange for one collected, even sympathetically. He put away some papers, closed the file.

"I've got three daughters." For the first time, his voice shook, but he quickly gathered himself. "I've been thinking this summer of retiring." Matter looked up, surprised. The man was not over fifty. "I was in 'Nam. I saw it all. I've done bad stuff here, believe me, that makes 'Nam look sane. Mafia hits. Suicide pact. Even your routine mass murder by the lovers of the world. But this one—" Maglie's voice trailed off till he was mumbling to himself. "It don't compute. It's too old."

He went to the rattling window and cranked it completely open. What was blurred became too clear—the cars moving like swine called to a precipice no one could see by music no one could place. Yet it filled their fatted veins with urgency, horror.

Maglie stared out the window. There was the sign that said where they all were going: Victory. *Victory Boulevard.*

"You go down Victory east from here, and before you get to Studio City there's the store where your sister bought her gun."

Her brother jerked upward and grabbed the pane. "The same street as the police station?"

"Sure. They keep us in business. We imply each other."

"I want to blow it up."

"You don't want me to hear that, Mr. Matter," Maglie whispered, even as the stricken fellow opened the door and let it click shut with an insane slowness.

Maglie rearranged the photos of his daughters before changing into his civilian clothes to leave. For some reason, he snapped his snub-nosed, .38-caliber Smith & Wesson into a shoulder holster, concealed under his windbreaker. It was the same type of gun the girl had used. Total overkill.

No cheapie—a coupla hundred bucks. Where'd she gotten the money? He'd forgotten to ask the brother.

Outside an odd sight greeted him. There sitting cross-legged on the grass in front of the station, staring out at the traffic as if in a trance, were the brother and the older woman he had come with who had stayed outside the office during their briefing. "You don't want me to hear this," she had said. "I'll stay here." And she had sat down on the wood bench and had stayed there the whole hour.

Bizarre folk, Maglie mused, strange, dark-skinned people—maybe Italian. Iranian? L.A. was filled with them these days. He and they were alike in some ways—dark people of the vague sort of earth color that speaks of dusty homelands and olive trees (Sicily was filled with them). The kind of dark face that has no social redemption in America, no particular fiscal amenities or perks, no tax breaks or set-asides, not a hue anyone could use in court. But it was a darkness of a people who were perhaps their own worst enemy, thought Maglie, who tore each other up as if from an excess of vitality. One could say Mediterranean, that great lake of lost empire, where people love and war and usually lose at both. And have big raucous families to hide all the loss and the sun.

"Can I help you?"

The pair looked up, shielding their eyes from the glare. They were speechless.

"What's wrong?"

Matter pointed to a parked car in front of them. "I locked my keys in." Maglie noted the wire hanger twisted in the window.

"No problem." The detective's mouth wrinkled at the corner, and he went to try his hand with the hanger.

After tugging and squeezing and pulling and cursing in Italian and singing a soft lullaby to the wire hanger, Maglie let go. He went over to the mute pair and said, "I have something that burglars use to get it open. Will you wait?" A stupid question, he thought to himself. They looked nailed to the grass. They didn't answer. His own head nodded, thinking. Then he joined them, sat down with them on the grass, the green, well-trimmed lawn of law, and crossed his legs, joining them as if they were Indians at some powwow, some signing of a false treaty.

The stricken pair nodded and moved slightly. He touched the old lady on the shoulder, and she shook her head.

"The problem is the lock has no head."

They looked at him. They knew it.

"That's the way they make them today."

They were looking not at him now, but at the traffic. The Santa Anas polished all their faces, forcing their eyelids closed. And Maglie remembered as he let his thoughts loosen on the way home from 'Nam finding these little monuments to war dead in villages of France and Italy.

To the drivers caught in bumper-to-bumper traffic, the three must have presented a strange sight. A war memorial, Maglie thought.

He opened his eyes and saw the only light in his companions' eyes was a carom off the endless cars, the very light of Victory, and if the street were empty their souls would be gone. Maglie got up abruptly, shuddering as if cold, and went to the station for the Slim Jim.

All I Have in This World

We can't keep him on the respirator, Mae, after this week," Dr. Wong Lee told the woman with the shaking hands from Fullerton. "You should try—try and decide by Friday, let's say, if you want to take him off."

"Oh."

"I know this is hard for you, Mae, but if you don't decide, I will have to put a hole in Henry's windpipe. It's called a tracheotomy. Do you want that?"

"Oh, no, doctor. No. Please."

"Well, then, think about it."

"I will. But what I don't understand is: he came in here a month ago with, you said, signs of Alzheimer's—just the beginning of it, a little disorientation pretty much—and now he's almost dead. What happened?"

"It's hard to say. He's eighty-one."

"I know. You keep saying that. But I'm eighty-three, and I smoke."

"That's no good."

"But I'm not dying."

"Ho, ho," Dr. Lee smiled wanly, leaning back on the springs of his chair in the intensive care unit of the Anaheim Medical Center. Mae saw a piece of white something in the corner of Dr. Lee's eye. She wanted to remove it, or tell him to, but she just kept staring at it, waiting patiently for an explanation of her husband's swift descent.

"Well, Mae, Henry doesn't have your—toughness. He's a sweet man, but—"

"So I'm not sweet?" Mae's penciled brows arched.

"Oh, you're sweet, too, but tough-sweet, you know?"

"Like sweet-and-sour pork?"

"Ho, ho." Dr. Lee looked at her frumpy expression and decided to let her be. Eighty-three had its privileges, especially this eighty-three, this very saucy eighty-three whose husband's heart had been pummeled probably for years. Poor Henry, he thought.

Mae raised her trembling hand to the black security guard at the door of the clinic.

"Now, lookit you, Miss Mae. You walkin' pretty good."

"Oh, poo. I'm an old coot, Raleigh." It was nice, she thought, to have friends again after twenty years of retirement, and fifty-three years of Henry. In the two weeks Henry had been in the hospital, the doorman and a nurse and the taxi driver had found out her name. Or she had put it out for them like something left too long in the oven and hastily retrieved. The disdain (and secret pleasure) was hers alone.

It was March. Out in front of the hospital, Mae stood smoking her Camel Lights under a canopy of jacarandas. She watched the smoke funnel upward and disperse into the new lavender blossoms and imagined touching them. They trembled slightly. The spring rains had brought a fuzz of green along the naked earth and hillsides of Fullerton, but here in Anaheim it was flat, flat, flat, and spring's first almost imperceptible notice was the silent music of these horn-shaped, mauve flowers. They were out early this year.

She crushed her cigarette with her high-heeled shoe. Hospital visits were an event for her. She had barely been out of the house for twenty years. Wobbling with the pain of her back and pelvis, she thought: *That damn osteoporosis! That stinker beat me to it.*

The taxi arrived. Mae had never learned to drive, and when Henry's eyes clouded over ten years before, he could barely see a foot ahead. They were stuck in Fullerton like two rocks in a gully. It thrilled her, slightly, to see the gleaming red-and-black cab open for her, the driver coming up to help her at the elbow. She glanced up once more. The jacaranda horns shivered in a light wind. It was almost obscene, that tickle of memory— Henry moving his hands to her belly so long ago, then his nails lifting her panties. She glanced down and answered the driver, "Thank you, Carl. No, no better," entering the man smell of leather in the backseat. She inhaled. The cigarette nearly flew from her pack.

"You're a good driver to let me smoke, Carl."

"Mrs. Heinrich, why not? It goes out the window."

"That's the way I see it, too."

"Now get your seat belt on, Mrs. Heinrich."

"Oh, pew. Why, Carl?"

"You need to protect yourself, ma'am."

"From what? I'm ready to go."

"Is that right? Well, you win."

When did it begin, Mae mused, rolling the cab's window down slowly after some minutes fitting the male part of the seat belt into the female. My, it could be thirty years ago when my brother Omar and his family left our street in Anaheim, and Henry thought we should "move up" as Omar and Lily moved up, but not out to the Valley where they went. Better Fullerton, said Henry. It was closer and less pretentious. We were good up till then, Henry and I, filled with visits from our family, Omar's kids right down the block. Franky loved my cocoa! And Vivi—when she would run away she would run away to me! Only two doors down. It cut our not having our own. And then, boom. We were alone. In Fullerton. Down from the rest home and kitty-corner to the golf course.

Maybe it was twenty years back, when we early retired, she thought, Henry from McDonnell-Douglas and his tortured labor negotiations— funny, he never negotiated anything too well with me—and me from May Company. Mae from May, they used to say. I'd pretty much had it with those crabby women trying on one dress after another, never able to decide. My great pleasure was selling one of brother Omar's own company. That made for a two-cigarette lunch! But I got tired of the bitches and the way people flung the goods—pants over the sweater rack, scarves on the blouses. I spent half the day putting things in order after customers took a pass and left. The people who buy, I found out, make no mess. They know exactly what they want. They try on one or two things and pick. It's the ones who want it all that can never decide.

I never wanted it all. I just wanted Henry, but after we moved to Fullerton and he was retired early, Henry wanted only the cup of the eighteenth hole. Or so it seemed.

"Ever play cards, Mrs. Heinrich?"

"Oh, no, no. Well, used to play poker."

"There's a mean bridge game for seniors at St. Jude's, ma'am."

"Oh, pew. I don't know a damn thing about bridge."

"Just a thought, ma'am. Don't mean to trouble you."

"No trouble, Carl. I guess I'm a stick-in-the-mud."

"Well, it's never too late to learn."

"Yea-uh?" Mae's husky voice betrayed her disdain, arching upward, then drawing out the "uh."

Shooing off the driver's help, Mae emerged from the taxi, thanked him, tipped him well, and walked unsteadily up the three wide cement steps on the approach to her home on Puente Street. She remembered the argument Henry and she had had years before about whether to make the walkway brick with inlay of blue and white tile or plain gray concrete. Henry won that debate based on saving a few dollars. With Henry's life in the balance, everything previously dull flashed to life. "Puente," she thought. Someone once told me it meant "point" in Spanish. We've been living on the point of a lance for so long. I wanted it to mean "corner." That's certainly rounder.

Mae put her hand out to touch the tiger lilies, and a dust of pollen flecked on her knuckles. She didn't blow it off. The afternoon sun was strong now, the early morning clouds had dispersed in a breeze that left the day buffed and still. She held her hand up, as if some shadow man might accompany her into her home. Where was the breeze? It had died; on the ride from Anaheim to Fullerton, the wind had died.

A line of ants on the landing were tackling a slug, baked to a dead stop in the sun, a film trail leading back to the bed of junipers hugging the house. As always, the shades were closed. As always, the door did not open easily. Why, after all these years, Mae asked herself, hadn't she had a locksmith out? Lily would soon be there. She left the door unlocked for the first time in years. It was a good feeling.

Mail had slipped through the door slot. Mae bent slowly and took it up. Among all the come-ons for credit cards there was one personal letter postmarked from Kansas. She let the others drop, and inhaled, as a smoker does, hoping oxygen itself will excite.

It wasn't often Mae realized her home smelled. She wasn't out of the house enough to realize it, except on Sundays for mass. But she hadn't been to mass for some months. These trips to the hospital had introduced her to fresh air, air so clean it scared her. It actually made her dizzy. Entering her dim home, the tobacco odor touched her nostrils. Their bitter marriage poured over the furniture in smoke. It clung to everything: the L-shaped couch of olive plush in the living room, the dirty yellow Scotch-plaid small sofa and chairs in the den, the hallways of mist-green wall-to-wall rugs whose nap was so flattened by the years the rug felt hard to the naked foot.

The smell of the house made her want to join it. She microwaved a cup of old coffee and took her cigarette pack to the coffee table to wait for Lily. She opened the letter from Kansas.

It was a cheery note from Henry's one niece in the world, with a brochure of a senior citizens' home near her in Hays. Only one of the Heinrich brothers, four of them, had had a child. Too late, Mae thought, pitching the letter and brochure sporting a white-haired woman in a swing across the breakfast table, like a folded hand of cards.

I think it started—Henry's plunge in health, if not our terrible war— three years ago with those roofers. Mae pulled with her full lips and underbiting bulldog jaw, blowing out slowly, carefully, as if the smoke itself were her only child. She remembered that day. It was like many summer days of a hot stillness when the two of them would not venture outside all week. The heat even kept them from mass. The sunlight at the windows was a threat they shut out, pulling drapes and blinkering the wooden shades. Mae was restless more than normal that day, and when Henry said, "You didn't finish your egg," she lashed out, "Shuttup. I can do what I want to do with my egg."

"You waste food, Mae, just like a child."

"I don't care!" she called out, and went to the living room, waiting for anything to relieve her of her bitterness.

That's when those roofers rang the doorbell.

"'Scuse me, Mrs. Heinrich." A young Mexican fellow sporting a red-and-blue Anaheim Angels baseball cap had stood there, pawing with his tennis shoes as if he were about to spring. There were two others with dark T-shirts behind him. "You remember us?"

"Vaguely," Mae had said, clutching the door at the crack.

"We wuz here last year fixin' your roof. 'Member? You had some leaks from thee shingles, *si*?"

"Oh *si,* yes, *si,* I remember now."

"We promise you a yearly checkup, no?"

"No?" Mae didn't like the way the other two fellows were punching each other in the ribs in slow motion. She also began to notice the hole in the forehead of the leader, a very bad scar just above where his eyebrows ran together.

"No. Yes. We do. Can we do the checking?"

"Now?"

"*Verdad.* Sure. We do it fast, no charge, just like we said."

Mae had strained to figure out just what they had said the year before. All she could really remember was their going to the bathroom a lot. She remembered telling Henry, "These guys sure like to pee." She had two shooting their urine at once, one in the guest bath and the other in their master bath, before they flushed and went back to the roof. She had given them big glasses of cold water. It must have gone right through them, she figured.

"What's going on there?" Henry had stood in the foyer behind Mae. She turned and told him what they wanted to do.

"It's free?"

"Yeah. That's what they said."

"All right. But tell them to be quick about it."

Mae had told them to go ahead, and she began to shut the door. But the leader's hand caught in it. He didn't even scream. He just calmly pulled it back and asked if it was okay that they got a pot of boiling water to check for holes.

"Whaaat?" Mae asked, incredulous.

"Senora, we need to put the es-team through the attic. One of my boys, he go up on the roof to watch to see if the es-team comes through. That's how we check for holes."

"Henry, they want to boil a pot of water." Mae shook her head. She had already begun to smell a fish, and she was beginning to be afraid. The leader's foot was on the door's threshold.

"Water? What the hell for?"

"Oh, boy. Oh, boy. They say they're testing with steam for holes in the roof. To check their old job."

Henry's milky eyes looked down. He slowly moved his head back and forth, trying to fix the shaft of blurry light, the nimbus figure in it, trying to negotiate all that could not readily be seen, even if his sight were perfect. Since the Matters had moved, they had had few visitors. There were those Jehovah Witnesses, of course. They were easily shooed. Almost no door-to-door salesmen anymore—most of the selling was being done on computer, he heard say on television. He had almost forgotten how to deal with any human being but Mae, and she was a handful.

"Okay," Henry mumbled, retreating to the kitchen to get a pot.

"What's your name?" Mae suddenly asked the leader as he came inside.

"José, Senora Heinrich. And this guy's Jeemee. And he's Mahn-well."

"Jose and Jimmy. And Mahn-well. Well, whaddya know? You fellows sure have good memories."

"I have the bill, too." Jose pulled out a yellow paper and handed it to Mae. She got her glasses and confirmed it was a duplicate of what they had charged the year before—two hundred dollars. Everyone told her it was a good deal. Everyone being the gardener, her priest, and her sister-in-law Lily. Seeing their name "Heinrich" on the bill eased Mae some. She told Henry, and his voice softened, too: "Oh, okay. That's good."

When the water was ready, Jimmy took it out to the garage.

"Can you move your car, Mrs. Heinrich?" Jose asked.

"I don't drive."

"Could Mr. Heinrich?"

"He doesn't, either. Not anymore."

It presented a problem, Jose said. They wanted to bring their truck into the garage so they could stand on it and move the steam back and forth under the roof.

"All right, let me have the keys to your truck," said Henry, after Mae translated to his fuzzy large ear what they wanted. "You take my keys. When you back out, I want my keys back, then I'll give you yours."

It sounded ingenious, even to Mae. Maybe his powers of negotiation are still there, she thought. She didn't dwell on the powerful muscles in

Jose's arms, or the small shining scab, like nicks of battle, in Jimmy's face. Mahn-well wore sunglasses.

Soon Jimmy was up on top of the truck, holding the pot shakily with the steam rising into the rafters, while Jose talked about the Angels with Henry, how they might win the pennant this year if old Tim Salmon kept hitting, and Mahn-well yelled, "No, no, no" up on the roof.

The steamy pot was then carried inside, and, no problem, Mae and Henry escorted these good boys back into the bedroom hallway where the drop ladder led to the attic crawl space. Jimmy slowly carried it up there, while Jose asked if he could go to the bathroom, and Mae remembered that they liked to pee and let him go into the master bath. She left Henry standing at the ladder and went to have a cigarette in the kitchen.

Soon it was all over, Jose shaking the couple's hands, smiling, the scar dead-shot over his eyes pooled with sweat from the steam and the heat of the crawl space, where he had switched places with Jimmy, who also needed to pee. Mahn-well did not pee.

"It's all fine, Senor and Senora Heinrich. We just wanted to make sure. Please make sure you refer us to your neighbor, no?"

"No?"

"Yes. *Gracias.*"

"*Gracias* to you, boys. Job well done."

Two days later, buoyed for some reason—was it the nice roofers? Henry's bringing her her slippers for the first time in years?—Mae flipped the lid on the shoe box she kept in the bedroom closet to fetch the gardeners a tip. Her stash of ten thousand dollars in hundred-dollar bills was gone. It was their entire liquid savings. They called the roofers' number, but it was disconnected. The policeman who came and took their report said it was the second time in a month that an elderly couple had been scammed. Their insurance adjusters bowed their heads; unfortunately, there was no theft coverage.

"My God," Henry stared into the darkness of the living room.

"You! You caused this to happen!" Mae was on fire.

"Me? Why me?" Even when Henry raised his voice it sounded like a gentle man straining to be tough. He sat down on the olive couch and held a pillow with two hands.

"You should have—if you could see, damn it, they wouldn't have robbed us blind!"

"Hell, Mae, you can see. You didn't see them take it. What do you want from me?"

"You're the man of the house! Some man! Can't see! Can't defend me!" She shook in her slippers; her bathrobe tassels trembled. "Can't screw a screw!"

The screen of her breakfast table window vibrated. Someone had just driven up. Must be Lily, thought Mae, relieved to be rescued from the horrid memory before the worst replayed itself—her blind husband, slapped, wandering throughout the living room in sheer despair.

"Hi, Maisie!"

"Oh, Lil, I'm so glad you are here. You're all I have in this world."

Her sister-in-law was pure life hoisting herself over the threshold. She had survived a bad car crash six months before, but still drove the fifty miles from the Valley to Fullerton. A nurse without portfolio, Lily was short, buxom, smiling, eyes shined as onyx. She held Mae by the shoulders.

"Are you all right? This is hard, Mae."

"Oh, yes. Yes, it is."

"Oh, boy, it's a *jeersa* in here. Let's get the windows open." Before Mae could pour her coffee, Lily started pulling drapes, opening screens, shooing dead air as if it were a spirit. "Ah, the light! The air! You need them!"

"But it'll be cold," Mae drawled, watching Lily dart about.

"Don't worry, Mae, it's sunny out." Lily struggled with a stuck screen above the sink. "My God, when was the last time you opened up in here?"

"Oh, a long time ago."

"Thanks, Mae." Lily took her coffee cup and saucer, and seeing Mae pull from her pack suggested they go out back while it cleared inside.

"Okay. But it'll never clear."

Mae brought her cup and pack, shaking, and touched them down on the glass patio table. Beyond them in the shallow backyard up against the thin redwood fence, a one-foot Saint Francis regarded them both.

"What is this all about? Henry is dying? I thought he just went in the hospital a month ago for nerves."

"Well," Mae settled in her chair of frayed plastic straps and took out a cigarette.

"Why don't you give it up now?"

"Why? I like it just like I like you."

"Go ahead." Lily shook her head. "What does it matter what people do anymore?"

"Yea-uh."

"So?"

"What can I say? I told you he was threatening me. A month ago he yelled he wanted a divorce. Can you imagine? At eighty-one he wants a divorce!"

"Well, that's been going on for years."

"But this time he pounded—did I tell you this?"

"Maybe. Who can remember anymore?"

"He pounded on my bedroom door."

"*Your* door. You weren't sleeping together?"

"Oh, Lil, c'mon. You know we haven't slept together for twenty years."

"But different rooms?"

"Yeah. The one you'll stay in tonight with the red-dice clock's been his for a coupla years at least."

Lily sipped her coffee and stared at Saint Francis, on whose stone hand stood a tiny stone dove. She noticed the bird feeder door was open, without feed.

"When's the last time you fed the birds?"

"Yeeeaars." She drew the word out before pulling on her cigarette. "You know, Lil," she exhaled slowly, smoke the very punctuation of her life, "Henry said the oddest things in the hospital before he stopped speaking. He said he was going to get a Dodge and drive away. Now why a Dodge? He always bought Oldsmobiles. Then he'd say, 'The Cubans are coming.' Now, how is that? We have no Cubans in California. Then he'd pipe up, 'Where's the belly dancer?' I can't follow it."

"But what about this knife business?"

"Oh, that. I had a knife under my pillow. I got scared. And then he yells out, calling the police, 'She's going to kill me!' And he grabs me by the wrist and tries to pull me to the ground."

"This is a *jeersa,* you know." Lily used the Arabic again for everything from an untidy kitchen to the most pathetic, inhuman act.

"I suppose. I don't know Arabic like you, Lil."

Lily nodded. Her tribe, the Wadis, had kept Arabic in her. They had no illusions about sinking completely into American soil. Lily recalled that Mae was not Mae's original name, but rather Nazera. Her peddler mother, a mountain woman from Lebanon, had given Mae her own name, but Mae had hated it as a child. Then one day after seeing a Mae West movie in the theater, she told her brothers and sisters, "I'm Mae," and stuck out her flat chest. She was all of eleven. She powdered her brown face white as a teenager, like her sisters, and wore clinging knit tops and boosted her chest. Nazera the peddler called her *shaytan,* the devil.

Maybe it was true, Lily thought. All the money from Lebanese silk and Oriental linens had shielded the Matter family in Cleveland, where Mae's father, Omar Senior, had immigrated at the end of the nineteenth century, but not forever. The Depression hit their faces like an iron skillet. They hoarded what few pennies remained from the Avenue Gift Shop, added what the four girls were making as store clerks and factory workers, and practically slunk out to Los Angeles after the war. All four married "*Amer-Kan*" husbands. The squirreled pennies bought Nazera a little home in the Wilshire district with a gabled roof that had a floor heater, as if the whole place were suspended on blue flame. Nazera exalted; poverty made her festoon with fruit trees. But it slowly collapsed Omar Senior in a California tremor of Parkinson's, Lily reflected silently, like Mae's.

"Oh, Mae, how could it come to this? I wonder if Henry is dying from embarrassment."

Mae exhaled slowly, her forehead warping.

"Almost like yesterday I see you two dancing at the Ambassador Hotel. When was it—1948? Henry used to call you 'the hourglass.'"

"Some hourglass. More like a spyglass."

Lily laughed.

"But you know, really, Lily, I'll be honest with you. I wanted to divorce Henry twenty years ago. And you know why I didn't?"

"Why?"

"You."

"What?" Lily drew up in her seat.

"You and Junior, I mean your Omar. You two convinced me to try this, try that, put on the nightie, put on the music, light a candle. I may as well have burned the house down. Henry was a limp as a noodle."

"Oh, you're terrible!" Lily waved and laughed. "*Ya Allah,* Mae, the man is dying." Lily cut her lightness off at the knees.

"Don't tell me he's dying. I didn't do it! Cooped up here for twenty years! Married for fifty-three, half of it misery-loves-company. That's what it was—"

Mae stood up and walked with bare feet over the flagstone, shaking like her father in the tremor of the Golden State they had all fled to, seeking nothing so much as a place to hide, to salve wounds in an ocean no one ever swam in, as they were midwestern girls and no one had learned to swim. But the sun promised something to them, something long forgotten or cast aside in coming to the New World—a bit of sweetness in all the desiccation, a sweet fig, maybe, as those that Nazera tucked under her arm over the water a century ago. Could California be the Lebanon she had shucked? Could they all pass as Californians and nothing else? Could it make their own limbs and vulvae grow something sweet, like a child?

"Misery loves company! You shamed me into staying!"

"I did not!" Lily stood now, Mae retreating as if from something deadly.

"I didn't want to be with the man. I could have had twenty good years with someone else, anyone else, or even myself, rather than this, this— shaking, skinny, sick woman I am with the bark of a dog!"

"Stop, now, Mae."

"My God." Mae turned in the sparse dichondra, that weak button-shaped grass that was cool to her naked feet. "I stayed because I wanted your love, and I didn't want to break my mother's heart anymore. The other girls, Janine and Ida, ripped her up good with their divorces—all four of 'em! Goodness—good daughter Mae. 'The long-distance heart,' Omar'd say. Baloney! I hated him. I hated him for twenty years and he knew it, and if he weren't in the hospital now curled up like a dead prairie dog, that poor Kansas boy, he'd be trying to choke me or I him! Here's to your sermons on faith and love and sex!"

Mae bent and picked up the stone Saint Francis and with an unearthly yell whirled and plunged forward toward Lily.

"Now all they want me to do is kill him!"

The Saint Francis fell on the glass table and shattered it. Lily jumped up, hit by glass in the face.

"Oh God! Oh God!" Lily stumbled. She found blood on her hand and looked at Mae, who was breathing heavily, down on the dichondra. She wiped her hand on her white cotton pants and rushed over to help Mae.

"*Isma Salib al-Azim!*" Lily invoked the name of the risen Christ. She looped Mae's arm over her shoulders and carefully got her to the couch inside. Mae was breathing heavily.

"I'm all right," Mae trembled. "But my God, not you! Oh, Lil, what's wrong with me?"

Lily went and checked herself in the mirror and saw the cut on her cheek. She daubed it with water and found a Band-Aid. She told Mae not to worry, it was all out now, the poison. She cooked dinner for them both, heating up some kibbe she got from the Armenian store as at this age no one cooked it anymore, and she was right: it settled Mae. Discovering the two pine nuts inside made her murmur, "Just like Mom."

"Poor Henry," Lily whispered to herself that night, seeing the dirt marks on his bedspread that she knew was dried excrement. She stripped it off the bed, made a mental note to wash it in the morning. His alpaca sweaters—beige, bird-blue, red—were carefully folded in a neat pile on an early American maple chair, as if he were packing. Here the invading smell of tobacco was weakly fought off by Henry's English Leather aftershave lotion. On the nightstand, the red-dice clock was stuck at seven, a four and a three. It reminded her of the good times she and Omar and Henry and Mae had had in Vegas long ago, and how Henry liked craps and would call out as he threw, "Bing!" His gentle blue eyes and smile were winners, but the dice rolled boxcars in the later years, and Lily half-wondered if it was all punishment for their refusal, faced with infertility, to adopt a child. It was no consolation to think that if they were young today they could have bypassed all the rigmarole with adoption and just paid money for a squirt of someone else's semen. But that seemed a *jeersa* in itself.

Lily thought of her own mother Matile's saying in Arabic, "A couple without children is like a moldy apricot."

On Friday, Mae went to the hospital and met with Dr. Lee, who said there had been no change. Henry was suffering from an onslaught of illnesses: pneumonia contracted in the hospital from aspirated food lodged in his lung; a stroke that did not show up on the MRI but was probably at the base of his brain, stopping his speech and swallowing; very low blood pressure, "as if he himself were shutting down." Dr. Lee put his hand on Mae's shoulder.

She went alone into his isolated room in the intensive care unit. The nurses looked at her as she entered, then looked at Lily with the bandaged cheek sitting on a bench outside the room. They pursed their lips and kept up with their flip charts and medications and appointments.

"It's no life," Lily heard one of them murmur.

Henry lay with his scrawny legs bunched up toward his chest in bed, like a chick about to be born, all bones and nap. His month-long growth of beard made him appear a derelict. There was a white spot at his temple Mae had never seen before. The touch of God? She took his hand in hers.

His hand was now larger than hers for the first time in their life together because it was bloated. Henry's arms from the elbow down were filled with fluid, and the bone between his shoulder and elbow had no meat on it. Tubes ran through his nose with air, down his throat with food, into his hand with medicine, out of his rear. He was now incontinent. His eyes were closed.

"Henry," Mae spoke. His eyelids flew open, showing those sky-blue eyes. It terrified her. Then they slowly closed, like the lids of a child trying so hard to stay awake to hear the grownups talk past midnight.

His ski-jump nose, the butt of jokes over the years in a family of hooked beaks, was almost blue. It was hard for her to remember his gentle voice now, the way he had of saying "Sweetie" to her when they were good together, when their nieces and nephews were young, his handsome dark-gold German hair that he combed back from his brow as a G.I., the way he would hold his poker hand close to the maple breakfast table and snap the cards with his thumb in mock disappointment when everyone would wait to see that faint smile that would give away that Uncle Henry had a hand, a real winner, and that they should all fold before it was too late.

"I loved you," Mae kissed him on the white spot. Then she took out the knife she had kept under her pillow and cut every line going into him.

Vivi in Hell

all right, you want to know why I did it. But sit tight—no more squirming and turning away if my sentences break. You used to act like there was nothing between the phrases worth listening to. But I always knew that the spaces, the music of the spheres, is only for the most refined of tastes. You cleared your throat and turned for more wieners wrapped in bacon, or more ice (here's a platform of ice). But I had a ton in my throat. And it came out in chunks that fell on my lap and then on the rug, and I could already hear Mother say, Vivian Matter, you've done it again. Your half-thoughts are all over the rug.

Now I'm whole. This will be the whole truth. Didn't the Creator of all this say, "The truth will set you free"? Bet my death on it.

As Aristotle knew, there is a big difference between necessary and sufficient causes. None of these singly was "necessary," but together were sufficient. They had to be. It happened, didn't it?

The dirt. The dirt in my eyes at eight.

You all know dear Frank, my illustrious brother. The one with the million-dollar smile, the perfect vision twenty-twenty, the man who turns the phrases with such grace. He could capture a monarch butterfly without marring the color-dust on its wings. He could also turn his wrist.

One day Frank let fly a solid ball of dirt. A dirt clod. The whole world was dry earth when we were growing up in Anaheim. We all tried to tame it—gardens, split-rail fences, the lot. But how do you tame the earth? How do you tame a little boy with a sister coming up the street?

No harm to the air. No harm to twelve-year-old Frank, though he was whipped for it by our dear father, whose temper is part of this story, a bit part. No harm to Tommy Blaw, the bully who used to beat up Frank and was rifling a few clods himself that day from behind the dirt mound.

Harm to me. My eyes.

Have you ever gotten a gnat in your eye? Think of a thousand gnats flying into them! A thousand turning, wing-wet, buzzing insects eating up the gel of the corneas. The brain is close to the eyes. What happens to the eyes happens to the mind.

I am not talking about a dirty mind.

I saw dirt. I saw the earth in all its microscopic glory. Eye-diamonds made me ecstatic for the light that popped in my eyes, oh diamond-backed earth!

The doctor picked each crumb of it from my eyeballs with rubber tweezers. The corneas were scratched and bloody. My eyes were wound with gauze for two weeks. I walked around like a blind girl, a hostage. Then they gave me thick eyeglasses. I was the only child in third grade with glasses, and the children liked to take them off and try them on and even steal them. And they'd run around shouting, "Vivi! Vivi! Vivi can't see!"

I wanted to blot their eyes. Just like old Gloucester. But I couldn't find them to do the damage. The blind cannot gouge the blind. To really kill, you must be able to see.

I was once told that Monet painted that blurry way because he had bad eyesight, that it's part of art not to see clearly. Monet and I were meant to be. I wish I had met Monet—he would have steered me in the right direction. Not like Gerald Magnuson or Dr. Fish. Or my father, that lunatic.

How did I know it was Frank's dirt clod and not Tommy Blaw's? Because the light it brought was gorgeous, and Tommy Blaw was ugly. Because Frank was always accurate. The most accurate Matter and turner of dirt. (Little Ben came later—curse him! He almost drowned me in the pool yanking me by my hair underwater. If he had, would I be here? I wonder about that. Frank would never do such a thing, at least not as an adult. But Ben, he was a real snake. He and Frank—between the two of them, they ate up my shadow.)

So, you say, so what? You were permanently injured as a child. By a sibling. Big deal.

I recount. I do not explain. I recount what was sufficient to wield what I wielded. They were my eyes, after all. It was my glasses they took and stepped on. It was my eyeball that veered off to one corner and saw everything coming from the side and behind. I had the world coming at me all the time.

Consider: How much would your fear mount if you could actually see at all times what was coming at you from behind? And you were barely escaping it? It's bad enough dealing with what's straight ahead.

At college the fellows called me "Earth Mother." Little did they know! Dear brother made me earth mother to the retinas.

Frank ran for president of his high school class and won. I remember helping with his signs: Frank Matter, This Camel Delivers. Pictures of Frank's opponent prostrate on the desert sands, and Franky mounted on a camel, entering the oasis where a Fr. Serra High School Celt, bedecked in school colors of brown and yellow like a giant bumblebee, greets him, Pepsi upraised.

Not beer. Or marijuana. Pepsi. It was the sixties. The worst thing Frank and the rest of his little gang did was throw rotten apricots and limes at cars parked on Mulholland Drive. He wouldn't let me be a Fiend—I was a girl. And Mom wouldn't let me be a girl. What was left? To be a man, to do a man's work—that is, avenge.

Momma was a saint. And scared of the hairy cock I used to suck. Director's cock, I called it. Never got me far. Gerald Magnuson was a bum. Only part he gave me was for the voyeurs in his creepy acting classes. Imagine! Asking someone to undress in the hallway of her own apartment as an "acting" lesson! God, I was gullible.

They let you say "God" here. They let you say just about anything. That's as much freedom as a person could want. Hey, what do they say? Take an Arab, dip her in freedom, and anything can happen. *I* happen.

And I was good at it, a real earth mother, eye looking out for something coming at me from behind as I sucked. Momma. Too damn good Momma, whose teeth were shined like a toothpaste commercial.

I never in my life saw Momma frown in a photograph. We were two women in this family of men—one of us had to be honest. Men are not by nature honest. How can you be honest with that thing of theirs standing up half the time? Momma got to be the positive one. Positive, and a liar. I loved her, though she convinced me to settle for vice president of my class, saying that Sue Sellers had the presidency locked up with her perfect grades and blonde locks and ravine dimples. If you came in second, you were the veep.

"You are a dark beauty," Momma would say. What she didn't say, and what I came to know is: There's no place in pictures for a dark beauty. You've got to be a flaxen-haired, pouting-lipped blonde or Italian with bazooms the size of watermelons. I was not flat, but neither was I Mount Everest. If you've got a normal figure and you're just some kind of ethnic shade, you're nothing. You can suck from here to eternity (now there's a conceptual redundancy!)

You're a vice president. I understand Henry Clay, Alf Landon, Dick Cheney. Don't be fooled by his calm demeanor. He means more than well. He means he'd kill for it. I think he already has. I can't tell if he is president or vice president, but I don't follow elections like I used to.

The limelight, I'm talking. The heat of it. The sexual pour of pores when all the world applauds. Each wave of hand clapping goes into you like an electric current, and you're alive.

Help! Help me!

I love you, you fingered mob! My pores are high, and my skin is rippling like the flag. Help me! Take me out of here! It's too cold.

I felt that in college when I did Clytemnestra in *Agamemnon*. Greeks can be dark-skinned, you know. Bowed below my toes. What are legs for? Bowing.

I did not feel it after college.

I did not feel it when the vote came in: Sue Sellers, eighty. Vivian Matter, twenty-five.

Momma was good to me, like the Pietà.

Out, Spot, out! Not the dog, the condition. You understand this. You're here for a while, and I'm here forever, waiting for your favor. Why is my father there on the floor in front of me? I promised to tell! I won't disappoint! But surely you see it had to be? I had no choice. How does the moon avoid its eclipse? How does the grass avoid its trampling?

Franky? He was away. Frank was always away. He sent a consoling letter in perfect English—loving, supportive, funny. Said I was his vice president, and always would be.

Thank you, dear brother. But I want you to know four billion souls have unanimously voted me President! Everyone here is President! Every last soul!

It's cold. It's not hot. I'm standing on a cake of ice; so is the winged director. I think this recounting is my only way to keep from freezing.

God, I want out. Can you? Please?

Frank missed his calling—politics. I always thought he had crowd appeal, which, as everyone knows, is not the province of the true artist. Frank, in my opinion, was wasting his time writing. He didn't believe in himself enough. You have to pray to yourself like the Golden Calf to make it in the arts. I had that. I believed in myself as surely as Walt Whitman, Isadora Duncan, Larry Olivier. Gerald Magnuson tried to crush what was vital and original in me, he did. He couldn't take it—like the glare of too intense a sun on the beach when you open your eyes sunbathing and, ah! White holes! White holes in your eyes!

To quote Gerald Magnuson: "The only sin is mass murder."

Two is not mass, is it?

Even people who hear voices need a moral imperative. He was my teacher. A terrible man. Accredited. My last director before the voices talked at such cross-purposes I couldn't take direction anymore from anyone but them.

My writing was better than Frank's—honest, straight from the bowels. And I didn't humiliate myself like he did getting those incessant, droning form rejection notes, "Please forgive the necessity of this standard response to your work, but we have been overwhelmed, our budget has been, we are on vacation, you forgot the reading fee of, who are you?"

I wrote crates of crap when they locked me in there with those mad people—crates! All glistening with white American bones—straight-from-the-marrow stuff. Plath, Sexton, Berryman, and Vivian Candace Matter. Miss Rain herself! The real thing! Miss Freedom with the ball weight of an Arab. Oh, I hated it when they pointed it out and said, No parts for the likes of you.

But I didn't prostitute myself like Francisco Goya, my brother. Didn't presume. Didn't eat a peach. Yes. No. Each to each, *I* was a poet. Frank was the actor-politician, the favored brand of our times. We should have switched professions and saved each other a lot of grief. What a waste, those cattle calls, and what a waste, those tortured squeezings of love in ink. He would have made at least as good a real-life chief executive on whose watch I could have died. At least he had a goddamn heart for something other than guns and golf.

Have you noticed presidents like to go out on boats during war?

Can't believe it even here. Can't believe that that man rose up after being shot and exonerated the National Rifle Association. No, I didn't know how. But I *desired* it to the target. I was exercising the Second Amendment. The right to bear arms shall not be infringed . . .

I wish I had had that baby. The bloody mess of it. Do it, and you'll be free, they said. NOT IN MY CULTURE!

I'm surrounded by them now. They're always cocking. Why don't they just fire? It would give me relief. I mean, that's why I did it in the end, to get relief. Would you like to hear Handel's *Messiah* twenty-four hours a day?

What was I to do? Go back to Te Amo Hospital with dear Dr. Fish in his devil-red Lincoln? To beautiful downtown Torrance, the town that slept with the lights on? I know why. Te Amo Hospital, that's why! We were all sleepless in there. Even with all the dope Fish stuffed down my throat, I was awake at nights. What would you do if someone came at you with a knife in a nuthouse like that? Would you want to go back?

I know Omar wanted to send me back. I could see it in his eyes when I asked him for an advance-on-salary for the third time in a row. The disgust, the self-loathing—*Vivian Matter has come from my loins.*

It was easy to buy, that nice, warm thing as Lennon said. I loved John Lennon! Why was he shot? All good things are shot.

My father was the best man I ever knew.

He wanted to send me back to the knives.

He was suffering. Out of work five years, that original, then standing all day, copying . . .

God, where you live in warmth and comfort, I say it was mercy!

My gun was kind. How else could I have made it to this stage of pack ice with so many millions in front of me, behind me, in my ears and eyes?

Don't mistake me. I've adjusted well to fame. Look at all you out there on the edge of your seats for my whole connected speech, feeling along these veins, connoisseurs of fine capillaries. It's all of a piece now. No shards to step on and hurt yourself. This is a spectacular overview. And all I have to do to earn this peace, this wholeness that wafts over me just now, one touch of spring, quiet, no voices calling, this single moment of peace, is repeat what I've just told you.

The winged director told me it was just perfect for me. Something I always wanted in life—a long stage (though cold), a captive audience (though far). A monologue to make MacBeth's pale.

We all wish—don't we?—for that secret moment of pure desire. I assure you—it comes.

But if this prospect bores or worries you, that is because you are broken and alive. And I am completely whole, and dead.

All right. You want to know why I did it. Sit tight . . .

*

Vivian.

Vivian, stop it. You may stop now.

You can't get up. I shot you. You can't get up. Oh, no, no! What will happen if I don't repeat myself?!

You don't have to. It's over.

Is it? Is it really?

Yes.

But—but the ice. That creature there. The director with the wide, green wings?

He has left. The Lord is here.

It was so cold. It's getting warmer.

Yes.

Is hell cold?

Yes.

Is heaven warm?

Come. Take my hand.

But he won't let me. He says this is the only way I can be accepted. The only way!

No. There is another, a better, way.

But I must repeat myself! Forever!

No. Take my hand.

Oh, Dad. I am sorry!

It is nothing. Come with me. Every word will be new. Every newness will be love.

The Man Who Guarded the Bomb

Janine, Sister

Sorry. I've got to scratch this thing out with my left hand—it's the second stroke. Always wondered what it would be like to be a lefty. Here we are! They say they make better baseball pitchers, but I can tell you this, they make crummy painters. I can't paint a tree anymore, though I did a pretty good sun yesterday. So I'll do my best this way.

I know this is serious business. I hadn't any idea I was the last to see Morton. For such a talker, he was pretty much a hermit the past thirty years or so. He's disappeared? Heavens to Betsy. That just doesn't seem to fit. He actually needed people—in a peculiar way—from a distance. But he called me every day until this killer stroke throttled my throat last spring.

What season is it? I think it must be fall, but this is California. And that eucalyptus out my window there won't drop a leaf. I'm keeping an eye out for the disappearance of flies. That's a good sign the Santa Anas are blowing colder. I'd prefer to be looking out at my walnut tree at home—it turns color ever so slowly. That would be a sign of change. *C'est la vie.*

Funny how they call it a rest home. I haven't had a good night's sleep here since I came. If it isn't that bag Uretha next to me blaring the television at all hours, it's the beep-beep of someone needing their medicine, or a nurse coming in here to check my pulse at three o'clock. Seems like I wait for her from about midnight on. But it's not a bad place. I'm beginning to paint again, even if it's mostly circles. Criminy! Rome wasn't built in a day!

169

So—what did Morton tell me when he came? First, may I say he didn't look good. For one thing, his hair was blond. I know Morty likes to dye his hair. At least he has since he turned fifty. First he dyed it black because of six kids, Mort got gray the quickest. Then he dyed it burnt orange. It just didn't go with his tan complexion, and I told him so. I said, "Mort, you look like a clown." I guess he was trying to attract the ladies, but I'm afraid what he got was just the opposite. He should have known that would happen living down there off La Brea in Hollywood. Funny, I've never seen his apartment. Not that I ever wanted to. Mort is the most inhospitable person I've ever known. I can't remember one event he ever hosted for the Matter family, even when he had that nice house in the Wilshire district with his first wife, Charlotte. I take that back. He had a reception there for Cindy—that's his one child—when she married the boy next door. I don't think he could avoid that one. Too bad. The fellow turned out to be a drug addict.

But blond? I tried so hard to speak to Mort. My tongue just wouldn't move. I felt like my neck would burst. I splattered out the words, but I could tell it was gibberish. You can lead a horse to water, but if he hasn't got a mouth, how's he gonna drink? I swizzled, "Mort, you look ridiculous. You're seventy now. Curly blond hair—my God. Isn't Rosario enough for you?" Of course, I knew the answer to that. Mort has been insatiable in the sex area his whole life. It's partly the reason he quit the army, and his marriage to Charlotte, too, for that matter, but I won't get into that.

You have to realize my brother Mort can't stop himself talking. Maybe that's the way it is with hermits. They're like a clam. Maybe they store it up so long, they see a human being finally and it just flies out of them like undigested food. Years you don't see them. Morty suddenly appears on the scene, he can't control the palaver. Just gushes out of him. But I enjoyed it, being stuck dumb as I am. I can only imagine what Uretha must have thought, she with the nonstop television. Criminy!

Morty held my hand in two of his in his mortified way, and then let fly.

"Janine," he says, "I gottatellyou what I read today inthepaperabouta guy born with nolegsnofeet nonothingbutaheadandbody that'sit, Jan, nokiddin'now, whoawhoawhoa! This guy. How'shegetaround? 'Lectric-wheelchair. That's right, yeeeeah! Hegraduated—number 1 in his class.

Studies byturnin'thepageswith his nose. Yeeeeaaaah! Then he started a company. Theee: Internet!

"Youknowit'sallInternetthestocksthebondstheshoestheinsurance EVERYTHING! Goin'ontheNet,Janny. NoNetnopay. Nopaynogain. It'sallNet. Youdon'tneedarms. Youdon'tneedlegs! Youdon'tevenneedahumanbeing! Anoseatonguethat'showhedoesit. Yeeeyaaaaah!

"Now let me tell you . . . Thiscompanyhestarted usingtheNet. He pushes the keys on the computer withastrawouthismouth! He drinks the computer! Wow!

"You drinking from a straw, Jan? You could be a millionaire!!! Listentame! Listentame! Everyone turned into a spider! Ho! Criminy, we're all inna web. You can't get out. But a lotomoneyinthatWeb. That guy started a company called . . . E-Easy. E-Easy. You log on. You get E-Easy. And you make a bet. Every ten minutes it's a new game. Youbetonanything. The priceofcigarsincubaat6a.m. The number of Henry VIII's children. Make a guess and make a bet. Millions!

"Ma-kin' m-i-l-l-i-o-n-s! This guy with no limbs! Hegetsaproposalamonth to get married. Somewantscrew. Just screw, that's all. He's aWebstar, I tellya.

"So don'tworry, Janny. Yougonna make it. No one needs to walk today. Needacomputer?"

I stopped Mort on the computer. That's the last thing I need. How could I tell him I wanted a good steak? Cripes, he was tiring me out. That's the way it's been with Mort for years. He doesn't last at any family gathering for more than an hour. Mort was probably the sharpest cookie of all of us. But he popped too many fuses.

He kissed me on my head. He told me he'd seen Winny next door and that she looked worse than I did and that Winny was a sourpuss, anyway.

Then it happened. I gave out, and for some reason the bedpan wasn't there, and I felt awful as it stunk badly. That's when Mort signed off. "I'llgettanurse!" he called out, waving. "I love you. You're gonna make it. Mom's watching out for you." Our mother's been dead for thirty years.

Morty's AWOL for two weeks? Car's gone? Hmm. If Rosario, his second wife, stopped payment on the credit cards like you say, he might turn up wanting a meal.

I think something must have snapped. His first wife, Charlotte, was a nurse. She lives in rural South Carolina—a little town called Nettlesville. I remember him saying once it was the only place Sherman didn't torch marching to the sea. Or was it *from* the sea? I can't remember. A single place of peace, though. Maybe he *did* go to get the nurse.

Jeeminy Christmas! I have to get to my sunrises. I'm really doing great with them. Take one. They're free.

Kitty Jensen, Waitress

Mort is my most faithful customer. I seen him every weekday morning at nine o'clock for twenty years at this here donut shop at the corner of La Brea and Sunset. The Whole Donut, yep. He and I done got old together. Mort'd come here like he was comin' to work. But I ain't seen him for two weeks, and ya know what? I'm worried.

Mort's in his seventies, but you'd never know it. Sometimes his hair's dyed funny colors—he was a blond, and he took some flack on that one from the regulars, like Jack the retired limo driver and Ernie the father of our owner. Ernie'd owned a little bank nearby but was caught with hand in the till. These old-timers get downright honest when they hit seventy, I'm telling ya.

No question about the leader in this bunch. It's Mort. He's a born leader. Or ringleader—take your pick. If one of the help has a birthday, or it's Ernie's or Jack's, Mortie's the one to lead the "Happy Birthday" song. He'll strut up and down the aisle, getting the customers into it, raisin' a fork and knife. A real kick-in-the-pants, that Mort.

By the way, we're a full-service breakfast place here, ya know. I can get you eggs, bacon, sausage, whatever. I don't know why they call it the Whole Donut. I always thought that sorta limited our draw, but the owner is a gray-ponytailed cuckoo from the sixties who probably smoked too much grass, and he'll go into a wild dissertation about "the Whole Donut." A donut has a hole, and if you eat it you eat the donut hole, too. That means you're swallowing nothing, and we all do, and on and on. I'm not kidding you, that's the way this nut thinks. At least he pays my way so's I can help my daughter out with her daughter. She's going to a very posh school down there in Hancock Park.

Anyway, as I was saying, Mort has made a lot of people smile in this shack. Funny how I'm already thinking of him as gone. Why? I don't know. Mort was no risk taker. He's not the type to hop in the car and take off to parts unknown or run himself off a cliff, drinking. Mort was not into the suds. He was not a driver. He hated the freeways in L.A. He once whispered to me in bed that he dug my legs because they didn't have any "freeways." That was his lingo for varicose veins. (Sometime ago, believe me, mister.)

His ex-wife? I have no idea who she is or where she lives, if she's alive. His second wife, Rosie, is quiet as a mouse, a little Burmese girl—that's Burma, not China—who lived next door to Mort for a coupla years, and would cook for him. Once in a blue moon she comes in here with Mort; she works, ya know. She pretty much keeps him alive, though I know Mort's got a pension. He retired early from the army as a light colonel. Rosie'll sit here with that puffy moon face of hers and smile that's half humor and half boredom. She's probably heard Mort rip off enough of those monologues o' his to get sick, but she don't show it. One reason I never took his bait. I think he had me in mind for number 3 sometime back, and he still touches me in certain places, like the back of my upper arm, very gently. Mort has wonderful hands, soft, but strong, veined—you know the type.

Well, take that back. Only a woman knows that type of hand.

You'd think that for a fellow as hyper as Mort he'd never linger with anything. But he did lovemaking. And when he touches me even now, after payin' his check, leavin' the same quarter tip he has left me for years (it's exactly 15 percent), when he puts his hand right down here on my back, softly, and swirls it, I feel a bit of peace—for us both.

Fact is, Mort's a tortured soul. I'm one of the few to know it, as a man will let go himself in bed like nowhere else. At least that's the way it was with me and Mort. He opened up in the wee hours—and ya know? He'd talk slower in the dark. One night he got up, sat on my salmon-velveteen lounge chair, the moon coming through my blinds and cutting his gray hairy chest into stripes, just like a tiger, though his face was in the dark. I heard him weepin'.

"What's wrong, Mortie? You can tell me."

I kissed him on the collarbone a little.

"I left too soon, Kit," he murmured.

"Left what, Mort?"

"The army."

"You musta put in good time, Mortie."

"Twenty years," he says. "I saw 'Nam comin'. I was in Intelligence, ya know. And they told me, you wanna bird? [That's a colonel, see.] You wanna bird? You go to Vietnam. Then you get your bird. But I had all the figures. It was gonna be a bloodbath, pure and simple. Knew it in '61. And we'd get nowhere. They thought I was chicken. Maybe I was. I don't know. I once guarded the bomb. That ain't too chicken."

Mort felt he wasted his life. Don't we all, one way or tother? How many of us really feel we're producing on all four jets? Damn few. I put my jugs on Mort's shoulder blades, and that stopped his misery for a while.

"Damn beauty!" he growled and flipped me over.

He started foamin' at the mouth, that's how shook he got in bed. 'Course, I like a hard ride, but I was a little scared that night, 'specially after he called out, "Beauty's endless. It's a ticket to nowhere. Nowhere!" I didn't understand him. Still don't.

We stopped our little affair years ago. Now I'm not sure either one of us could fire up on one jet, much less four, though Mortie still colors his hair. There's been a badass beauty in his life somewhere, I figure, but it wasn't me, much as he was hollerin' that night. His despair was 'fore me. But I'd a thought he'd settled into his routine—dreary or not—too long to expect enough of life ta flee it. Find him. This donut ain't whole without him.

Winny, Sister

Dear, I heard Mort call, "'Bye, Win!" just after he ducked out of Jan's room. His hand was up to his ears, palm out like he was swearing in for some trial, and his head was bent. Even from my bed I could tell he didn't even attempt to look in my direction. Oooooooh, that Mort! Have you ever seen such a nervous person in your life? With Mae here now, we're all he's got left of the original Matters—Jan and me and Mae, plunked side by side in this nursing home, and he's hardly here long enough to say "Boo!" No, he hadn't come before. And by the looks of it, he's not coming again.

Personally, dear, I think he's been done in. I don't know why I think that, except Mort is a creature of habit. Dull, dull habit. Never goes out of his way for anybody, including himself. He told me he's been bleeding from his ulcer. Anyone tell you Mort had an ulcer? He's had it for years. It's the disease of people who can't communicate. We Matters may not be good at much, but we at least get it across how we're feeling, all of us but Mort, that is.

Thank you for asking, but I feel terrible, honey. Look at these hands! You'd think I was some witch. Gnarled like an old winter fig. I'm in constant pain, dear, constant. They say there's no rest for the wicked, but I never had a chance to be wicked! Honey, I got married at sixty-one! Before that, I took care of our mother, that bulldozer Nazera Matter. Nursed her through eight years of cancer—not pretty, believe me. Have you ever heard of a colostomy?

They used to say I was the smartest of the six Matter children, but I'd like to know what good it is to be smart. They never could afford for me to go to college. My dad lost his money in the Depression, like so many others. Ida was the only one of the bunch of us to get to go to college, honey. Case Western University in our hometown, Cleveland. Oooooooh! I was so mad. Ida had a birthmark right above her lip that, to use the current expression, really turned on some admission officer at Case, and she got the extra money necessary to matriculate. Honey, in plain speech, Ida Matter was a vixen. She was married twice before I even drank my first highball. Ida is dead, long dead of heart failure, before Omar was shot. (Omar was the only other boy in the family—greatly loved. Mortie was very stricken by his death, as we all were. Maybe it's a delayed reaction to the shooting. Who knows?) I'd still follow the murder line, if I were you. The plain fact of it is—Mort doesn't have enough guts for suicide, nor, in my opinion, enough patience to be melancholic.

Speaking of melancholy, you've got to try this rheumatoid arthritis out some time. Honey, I was always thin, but not like this. I am ashamed to have you see me! I must look like a skeleton. And I hate being in here. I don't even know what the place is called.

Let's call a spade a spade. They say the old folks suffer a lot from depression, and I'm afraid I do. I sit in this bed and think too much. That's what an overactive brain does to you. Don't you think I'd like to be a blooming idiot? If it kept the shadows from encroaching? The youngest of us shot for no clear reason in his own store? The rest of us wasting away with no children of our own? Did you know that? Of Janine, me, Ida, and Mae—not one of us was fertile enough to plant a biscuit! Not one child! That's why we all fawned on Frank, our nephew, and Cindy, Mort's girl. And Vivi. You know what happened to poor Vivi—just horrible. How a girl could do that is beyond me. A man I understand. But a loving daughter—no. As for Ben, by the time he came along, we were too old to fawn!

Have you talked to Frank or Ben? They'll tell you a lot about Mort. Frank idolized his uncle when he was younger. I'm not sure what he thinks about him now. Ben still does, I think.

Please. Would you be so kind as to get me the nurse? I've rung her a hundred times today, and for all I know she's halfway to Las Vegas. Honey, I can barely talk anymore. I get dry. They try and give me artificial saliva. Could you hand me that bottle over there? Thanks. That might wet my chops a little, but to be perfectly frank, I've had it. Had it with doctors and nurses. Had it with these supposedly golden years (I call them the brass years). Had it with Morton Matter. There's nothing more to say about the man but that he's been a coward. Aren't we at least called on to watch out for each other suffering? To usher each other down the last road to God? I did. And now I can't even see Jan! The best I can do is knock on our shared wall.

Who would kill Mort? I haven't a clue, dear. Maybe his ex-wife. God forgive me, I might myself, except my hands—they can't hold anything!

Gen. Bernard Roberts (U.S. Army—Retired)

Lieutenant Colonel Morton Shafik Matter? Keep your powder dry! One of the best men in this man's army. Could easily have been a colonel, a general, too. We go way back together. I mean, all the way back to our grunt days in Burma during the war. We both managed to get promoted to sergeant because men liked us and liked to follow us. Men'll do things for sergeants, good sergeants, they won't do for a captain. That's a little-known fact of army life. The stereotype, of course, is the overbearing lunkhead.

The little-known truth of the matter is that a sergeant who knows how to mete out discipline but also how to motivate and crack a joke at the right moment is the person who welds a fighting man to his army. S'pose I should say "woman," too—right, Officer? Fighting woman! I've had a few! Anyway, Mort was the kind of sergeant that showed a recruit how to clean a latrine. Not many NCOs will go that far, but Mort did. Led by example. And a wink.

He was also handsome as the devil. I think that got him into trouble once with a WAC at Holabird. That's near Fort Meade. We were in Intelligence by then. But I won't get into it.

I got a battlefield commission in Burma, but Mort could easily have gotten one for the same action. He basically gave me the nod, and by the time he went to officer candidate school after the war, I was a major.

I was Mort Matter's superior officer three times—at Los Alamos and Alamogordo, at Holabird, then Germany in the sixties. Believe me, I could have used him later at NATO. As you may know, I was chief of all Allied forces in NATO, but he had resigned by then—this was under Reagan, when we were throwing in those SSTs and pointing them at Moscow and pretty much scared the Soviet Union into collapsing. Don't buy that line that we bankrupted the Soviets and that's how we won the cold war. There's something to it, but the real gist was this: we terrified the dickens out of them. Reagan did that, all with a smile, you know. I loved the man! The Russkies tried to match us, missile for missile, but they realized, just as Hitler's generals did, that we could keep it going indefinitely and they couldn't. Slave labor has its limits; the slaves die, for one. Afghanistan didn't hurt us, either; that godforsaken place drained the Russkies worse than Vietnam drained us, I'll tell you. They were facing the whole Muslim nation. Then you think today, maybe our sending all those Stingers didn't amount to a hill o' beans. We left the place in a mess, and look what happened. Bin Laden. So we beat the Soviets with their ten thousand nuclear warheads, and we couldn't beat nineteen Arabs with a few box cutters. Amazing. Makes you rethink your profession, I'll tell you.

I'm sorry I got off on that. It happens to old generals, still fighting the old wars. Or new wars they created. Now we're suckered into Afghanistan just like the old Soviets.

Did you know my man Mort was an Arab? That's right. From an old Syrian community in Cleveland, Ohio. His dad sold linens. And isn't that something? How many Americans might shift in their sleep—maybe their ideas—if they knew that once upon a time all that stood between them and a nuclear holocaust of our own making was an Arab? Mortie was captain-of-the-guard at Los Alamos when we were experimenting with the H-bomb. Did anyone tell you about the Edward Teller incident involving Mort? No? Well, they wouldn't—it's top secret, even today. I can't tell you, but I'd like to. I wonder if Mort ever told anyone. Keep digging. You may find it.

Everything we worry about today, some nut terrorists stealing a dirty bomb in Russia where the Mafia is more powerful than the government, somebody siphoning off the hot stuff to take down a city 'cause they've been foreclosed on—you name the beef—Captain Morton Shafik Matter was the man who stood on that wall protecting us from the very misery we had created. It had to haunt him. It haunts me. There's no use for nuclear weapons today. 9/11 made that pretty obvious. Heck, now you got cold warriors like Kissinger and Sam Nunn and George Shultz and William Perry writing right there in the *Wall Street Journal* of all places: Disarm! Destroy the entire nuclear arsenal. Start unilaterally, even! They're more damn trouble than they're worth.

But we didn't know that then. We soldiered on, bought the whole balance-of-terror idea. And Captain Mort kept his arms wrapped around that enriched uranium and protected it from all harm.

Where's Mortie? Maybe his nerves gave out. Lots of things happened out there in New Mexico in the late forties and early fifties that nobody, but nobody, knows about. Why? Well, I torched the records, that's why. We didn't have shredders in those days; we did it with a lighter. And we didn't have photocopies and e-mails that make it impossible to keep anything secret. We had triplicate, with carbon paper. You ripped up three copies, and that was it—nothing about nothing.

Okay. I'll tell you this. I'm getting' too old. One day, Mort called me on the squawk box at Los Alamos and said someone was infiltrating. It was 1955. In those days, Mort was not known for his rapid speech. That came later, at the beginning of 'Nam just before he left the army. He spoke in clipped, distinct tones, and he told me, "Colonel" (I think I was a colonel then, maybe only a major—who knows? You get my age, and all the stars and eagles don't matter as much as your next meal or the smell of a good rose), "Colonel, we got a big problem here."

Sure enough, one of the Injuns in the area—that's right, an American Indian hopped up on something, if I remember correctly—had driven right through the guard stand at the Alamos front gate. My boys took out his tires right quick, but the fellow could fly on his feet, and what's worse—he had an M16 blazing. He killed two of my boys right outside the H-bomb cyclotron lab that was connected to a corrugated sheet-metal hangar. Can you imagine? There we had a howitzer mounted with a hot shell we were going to blow off in the desert—a nuke ready to go.

Ole Geronimo shot the door open. He pulled the pin on a grenade and was poised to toss it into the hangar and set off a nuclear explosion. It was pretty hairy.

Well, ole Mort spied right away what had to be done. "Won't get him head-on, Colonel," said to me. "He's holding a grenade. Think I can take him from up top." He rang off. Mort was not one to pass the buck, I'll tell you. What he did was circle around, take off his boots, and somehow scale that hangar barefoot so as not to tip off the Indian. When I arrived, I saw Mort tiptoeing, hoppin' across the tin lid, scorchin' his feet but good. Not a word came out of his mouth. Then he dropped and crawled the last few yards to the edge over the Indian, who was doing some kind of ghost dance and was about ready to send us all to kingdom come and maybe half of Santa Fe, too. People don't remember now, but the H-bomb we were testing then made the A-bomb look like a sparkler.

What amazed me was Mort had it set in seconds. He took out his .45, pointed it over the edge of the corrugated steel, and shot the poor Injun through the neck. The grenade dropped, and so did Mort. He grabbed it and flung it from home to deep center—a field of cactus and mesquite nearby—where it exploded to no harm. It was a helluva toss! The whole shebang cost him a week in the hospital with second-degree burns and cuts on his feet, and two dead soldiers. I think you could say Mort pretty much saved a couple thousand lives that day, if not more. The radiation would have been bad. Santa Fe and Albuquerque were pretty close by. We hadn't carted the thing south to the Alamogordo test site yet. Operation Teapot, I think it was called.

It's safe to say he saved the whole nuclear weapons program, as well. We'd had a scare on the Bikini atoll the year before, when the radiation from the test killed some Jap fishermen. But really in all these years of the bomb we've never had a major accident. More trouble has come from the nuclear power plants, like Three Mile Island. I gave Mortie a Distinguished Service Cross on the sly. It was all secret then. No media. The ones who heard about it, I bought 'em off with dinner (for a little signature on an affidavit). We beefed up security big-time after that one.

Now the security breaches are all electronic. I hear some Chinaman got arrested for stealing hard drives at Alamos. Why not? China's the only one testing them these days, along with North Korea. But back then, Christ. I hear about fifty thousand folk came down with thyroid cancer from radiation from all our nuclear tests in the fifties. They each got about fifty grand. A real shame. But who knew? People would come out from Albuquerque like it was a picnic to watch those blasts, and from Vegas, too. Nobody knew what effect radioactive iodine 131 could have over time. They came for the shake!

It's not easy to say why Mort's gone AWOL as an old man. Old men do such things. I think of it. My wife's got Alzheimer's, and my own mind is still good. I've still got my manhood, if you know what I mean, but where to put it at this age? Pretty frustrating. You know, Tolstoy up and left his farm in his eighties, I think, and died of a heart attack at the train station. Where was he headed? Maybe a man has just seen too much in his life and wants out. But not by suicide. Just upping and going—as if you could drive or walk yourself into the next life. You know, daring God Almighty to take you by one cursed way or another.

I do know Mort was not cold at the sight of death. When he came down from that hangar and saw the Injun's brain poured like steaming oatmeal into the dust, he started shaking like an overheated tommy gun. And another thing. You won't find this in the history books, either.

It concerns my battlefield commission. Mort and I were sergeants out on patrol in '43 along the Burma Road. We came across a depression with hands and rifle butts jutting up from it. Turned out it was half-a-dozen

Burmese men shot through and through, with their penises stuck in the mouths. The Japs had done it. You think the Holocaust was bad? You don't know what the Japs did in Burma and Manchuria. I'm telling you, it took an A-bomb to cow those people. Mort looked at me with a look I will never forget. It was as if his soul had left him. There was something completely drained out of his eyes. It's not quite the same as shell shock—there's white heat at bottom. And he took off running, yelling at me, "C'mon, Bernie, we gotta get 'em!" And we did—two crazy-ass sergeants took out a platoon of Japs with our BARs. We didn't do anything with their doodads, though. But we reduced them to a bloody mush. It was a horrible sight, and the two of us threw up till we pretty near passed out. The reason Mortie gave me the nod for the commission? He had shot a woman. It was a Burmese woman those Japs had taken prisoner to rape. He didn't see her.

I don't want any more war. I'm telling you, you get in that black zone, and you never come out. Maybe Mortie went in all the way this time. I've got to go feed my wife now and give her her shot.

Bud Plank, Friend

We all lived in a working-class neighborhood off East Euclid, in Cleveland. My father was a bricklayer. Mort and Omar's was an immigrant from Syria. He had a gift shop in the old Arcade. They had four sisters, all very striking and warm.

Mort Matter. It was *"Muttar"* in Arabic, he once told me, you know, it sounded like you were muttering something. It meant "rain." But they were pretty sunny people. Mort was a happy-go-lucky guy playing practical jokes, usually against his brother, Omar, the youngest of the six, who was favored. It seemed to me Mort took it upon himself to cut Omar down to size, though there wasn't a sweeter guy in the world than Omar Matter Jr. He didn't need cutting. He didn't have much of an ego. He was all loving kindness, my closest childhood friend. Mort, on the other hand, was out to settle things, recapture the stage, if you will.

I remember the day Mort tied Omar to his bicycle and dragged him half a block. It was all supposed to be good fun, at least that's what Omar and I understood. We were both about ten, and Mort two years older. It was no picnic. Omar had his nose bloodied by the sidewalk. He bled like a stuck pig, and when he got older, he made a point of telling people he was grateful to Mort for the "natural nose job." In his generous way he'd say, "My brother made me an American. Before that, I was an Arab." He never said how it happened, but I knew. I saw it. There was a blood streak several yards long on the pavement before I got Mort to stop.

There's something about the older brother. If a younger brother is near enough in age, he just can't resist trying to nail him. It's almost as if it's in the cards. I've seen it time and time again. My brother beat me up, too. He wasn't as creative as Mort. He just plain bludgeoned me. We're not particularly close. I don't think Omar and Mort were, either, though I think Omar wanted to be.

The Matter family had a crazy streak in them. I loved them all; they were just full of life. Mort once fried a goldfish to see if it would make a meal. I understand he married a gorgeous nurse. They divorced. I don't know why. The Matters went out to California from Cleveland after the war, and we lost track of each other pretty much. Maybe a call or letter every few years, but that's it. My understanding of it from Omar is that Mort lost his bearings after he left the army. But I haven't seen either of them in forty years. I know Omar died tragically. That a daughter would do that, well . . . It was a great blow to me. I suffer from it to this day. The other day on the ninth hole here—it's a great course, plenty of pines here in North Carolina, a good place to retire—the other day I swear I saw Omar lifting the flag when I putted. And I couldn't stop crying. I just picked up my ball and walked off the course, leaving the cart, my clubs, my partner. Everything.

If you find Mort, tell him he had a great brother.

Cindy Matter, Daughter

My poor, poor father.

He called me. I was the last person to speak with him. He said, once again, that he was sorry for everything that had happened. I told him not to worry. That that was long ago.

This was after the aunts. He'd already seen them in the rest home. He said, "Cin, I've got an important meeting. When I get back, I will call you."

That was ridiculous. My father hadn't had an important meeting since he handed his resignation thirty years ago to General Roberts. Some friend that guy was. He hogged all the glory.

What meeting? It mystifies me.

It's sad that a total of one minute in the life of a father and daughter should determine their whole relationship. In fact, I wouldn't be surprised if it colored his attitude toward the whole outside world, the world outside his little enclave there down in West Hollywood. He was never a socializer. But from that moment on, he went into a shell I've never been able to pry him out of. Has anyone? Certainly not Rosario. She's been good to Dad, I think, but she's quiet as a church mouse. She's gets in about one word to Morton's ten thousand. Have you talked to anyone who has seen the inside of his apartment? I haven't, and I'm his one child in the world.

Now it's glasses and crow's feet and a little more on the hips than I'd like. But then, when it all happened, I was seventeen and sexy. Mother of God, was I built! I'd wear the shortest shorts and tops that were tight as a drum. My bust was just that, busting out! My numbers at that time were 37-23-36. We teenage girls were conscious of these things then, and in spite of the women's movement, I have no doubt that they take the tape measures out at night and check out their ammunition today, just as then. This is America, after all—we like sex and statistics. If anything, people are more conscious of their appearance today than then. You think I'd risk cancer to make my boobs bigger? They do it every day with those implants and that silicone. But then, I was blessed by God, though I would certainly say to all who could hear me: endowment is a mixed blessing. For one thing, there's gravity. For another, there's the fact that no matter what you look like, most men get bored by sex with one woman, and not a few women feel the same way about their hubbies. If you're going to hold a man, you have to do it with a very strong spirit. I'm not sure I had it, certainly not then.

One night my cousin Frank and I—I think he was about fifteen, getting his first peach fuzz, and I was seventeen—put on some Rolling Stones and danced in the living room of our house in the Wilshire district. It was a dark place. Any way I could send some sparks into it, I would. Most of my friends were afraid to come to it. Maybe it was Dad's knight's coat-of-mail standing up by the stone fireplace. That thing was spooky.

Dad sat right in front of the armor in his armchair watching us gyrate, smoking his pipe with a steady plume that climbed to the ceiling. "I don't get NO! Sa-tis-fact-shun!" Frankie Avalon and I shouted as we danced. I think I put a hard on that poor boy that night. I'd lead him toward me and twirl him and even let him brush my red-and-white checked top and hold me in the bare small of my back. Then we put on Rachmaninoff and Beethoven's Fifth and threw our heads back and pranced around like two cranes in a mating dance. Whatever I did, shaking my fanny or lifting my vibrating hands, Frank would do. I had boyfriends coming out the wazoo, but Frank was someone special to me, and still is, sugar.

After Vivi (Ben came later), he was my only Matter cousin. And he was a teenager, like me. Maybe Dad wanted more than me. I think that's fair to say. Omar had him beat with three. I don't know if my mother shut him out of her body after finding out about his affairs. But that night, with Frank sleeping in the guest room, Dad came into my bedroom and crawled into the bed with me.

At first he didn't move, and needless to say, neither did I. I was ter-rified. I froze like a statue, and feigned sleep. I figured it was about one o'clock. The sound of the creaking door had wakened me.

I was on my back at that point and took a chance. I moved over on my side, away from him, showing him my back. Maybe that was a mistake. Maybe he'd seen too many backs in his nights with Mom. I heard not so much a growl as a whimper, the sound of a very lonely dog. He came close and put his arm around my top. I should have jerked awake right then, and we could have called it paternal affection, a little extreme perhaps, but it could have passed. But when he kissed my neck, I knew for a few seconds I was the love of his life. I froze. Then I called out, "Oh, Dad! What's wrong! What is this?" "Nothing, nothing," he said hoarsely. "It was cold in the house." And he fled the room and closed the door quietly.

Mom and he were divorced about two years later, just after my first marriage. Told her? I had to tell someone—I was terrified.

For a long time, maybe ten years, I hardly spoke to my father unless it was unavoidable at his rare family Christmas or Easter appearance. My first marriage to the boy next door, of all things, was a disaster. The fellow forced me to take cocaine. He had everything going for him. His father was a banker from an old Los Angeles family and practically handed the future on a platter to his son. He was handsome and a total mess. I left him after his second addiction treatment failed. My second husband was also a looker, a sweetie really, quiet, considerate. I left him after his affair with his secretary.

Maybe it's the years and my own failures with men. But I don't blame my father anymore. I realize I was sexy, and I think there is something horsey about men's sexual drive that seems to know no barriers when it is fanned, especially in the home, which they take to be their province. They'll jump any fence.

I'm not saying it was right—it hurt me bad for a long time. And I know others who were hurt more. It's too damn common. But this is a sex-mad society, is it not? We're all lit up five times a day—and you know the men light up quicker.

We've met, on occasion, my father and I, for lunch. We never discuss what happened. Except for that last phone conversation, when he alluded to it, to my surprise. I cried and cried. I said I forgave him, and in fact had long ago. But my God, thirty-five years and it still throbs.

I ran off to rural South Carolina to stay with my mother after the Northridge earthquake. I'd just had it with the series of disasters in Los Angeles in the nineties—fires, quakes, floods, race riots over police beatings, the police outgunned by the rioters, bizarre murders by football players and other characters who got off scot-free. The one thing in L.A. that didn't come in a flood was justice. But after six years in a sleepy southern town with the only men married, or those with no drive left or teenagers on the prowl, I have to tell you—L.A. is looking better. I'm beginning to think risk of earthquake beats a body come to a complete stop, with no other body on the horizon. I'd like to have one last go at love. I don't see it coming here in Nettlesville.

Did my father see it coming? Is that why he left? That wouldn't be a bad motive to disappear.

Frank Matter, Nephew

It's a worldfullayesmen!

That's the line I remember most of my Uncle Mort's. I was home from college, and he surprised us all by coming to the Christmas dinner at my folks'. I had a roommate home with me, and to this day he recalls that brazen indictment of Uncle Morton Matter. It's true, of course. We do have a world full of yes-men. But Uncle Mort's solution wasn't to stick in the fray and answer "No" where necessary. He became the No. I don't think there is anything admirable in someone just plain bagging all responsibilities and affinities beyond reading the paper at a donut shop.

When I was a little boy, I looked up to him. He was a highly respected army officer. He used to march me down Grandma Nazera's street to Wilshire Boulevard, giving me a baseball bat to shoulder while he called out marching orders and put me through the paces of the *Manual of Arms*. I liked it. I felt he was training me for something manly.

Then he went and promised to take me fishing. Big mistake. Every time I saw him as a boy, he'd say, "Frank, gonna take you fishin'. Yessir." It never happened. At a family gathering, he'd repeat the promise, but over the years, the dangling fish on a line I would see in my mind's eye began to disappear. By the time I was halfway through high school, it was clear Uncle Mort himself no longer believed his own promises, as he would cover his mouth after the "fishin'" and fake a laugh. I began to see that his animation about everything was a cover for an inner vacuum. When he stopped coming to family get-togethers, it didn't surprise me.

But it hurt my father, Omar. He loved Mort, his only brother. They were night and day. My father was hyperinvolved, full of sacrifice and love and, frankly, impatience for people like Uncle Mort. For all that, he was done in by his only daughter. Mort survived. He always survived.

But for us, he was already gone. It would have been a rescue if he made even the least gesture to touch our hearts after the shootings. No such luck. He slunk further away. The death of Omar, the good brother, seemed to give him just the cover he needed to conclude life was not worth a shit, other than his daily paper and donut. Deeper paroxysms of guilt? I'm not sure. I know about Cindy, my cousin. She told me what happened to her when we were young. I can understand, to an extent, Mort's humiliation at his own hungers. We all have 'em, though, thank God, I was spared that one. Still, doesn't guilt propel? Doesn't it stimulate remorse, connection, action toward the offended one? As far as I know, any distance crossed between Cindy and her father was Cindy's initiative. As far as reaching out to his sister-in-law, my broken-hearted mother, forget it.

Too harsh? My brother, Ben, thinks so. But he was too young to see the disappointment, the bewilderment, on our father's face when it was told through one of his sisters that Mort, yet again, wasn't coming for turkey. I will give him this. Uncle Mort wrote me some kind letters about my books. Mort is a good writer. Seems the Matter family had this talent—to send words out from each of their caves, like bats of longing or emergency. (I'd soften the simile to "carrier pigeons," but they don't live in caves.) In Uncle Mort's case, these were signals he didn't want answered, or answered only from afar. I haven't seen him for years.

I know Milton said in his blindness, "They also serve who only stand and wait." Both Aunt Janine and Aunt Winny always counseled me not to condemn Uncle Mort, that he was "just that way." Accept, accept, accept! I think we accept too much. I think if you have a decent heart, it's going to be broken, or shine, or fall apart, that is, if you love hard and fast and without a tremendous amount of forethought. I like plain instinct in a person. Accept, accept, accept, and the heart becomes a bog. You don't know anymore what's worth loving or hating. And that's where Mort is. If that's the bog a writer's supposed to get in to understand the world, I guess I'm lost. Maybe Mort's purer than all of us put together. That's what Ben thinks. Sorry. Don't buy it.

You've got me as to where he is. No way he'd kill himself. He doesn't drink or smoke. His teeth are as white as a model's. I remember that well! He carried toothbrushes everywhere. He was a lively soul when he was near you—an explosion of mind. And maybe that's why you hate him now—because he hoarded his liveliness away from his family, wasted it, in fact, on strangers, on those who had no claim on him.

Benjamin Matter, Nephew

Look, I work and I work and I work. I sit here in this restaurant I own and tend to the problems of the Mexicans—I pick up their children from school, I help them with immigration, I get them to the doctor. I'm thirty-nine, and I never married, like Frank, because I'm married to the burrito and all these people who hang onto me for a living. And you know what kind of profit I have in fifteen years? You don't want to know. Just look down the street there at the Taco Bell, and down the other street at the Burger King. Now you know. And don't forget those assorted Mexican mom-and-pop operations selling burritos a buck cheaper because they cheat on payroll taxes. And please—spare me the liberal crocodile tears about raising the minimum wage. You do that and poof! Good-bye to my little shack and good-bye to me and adios to the twenty-three Mexican families I keep alive. Margin? I have no margin.

You like the name? Burritomania. The kids go for it. Kind of allows them to go nuts after exams.

They say Americans like quality. Sure! I've been coughing up quality here for fifteen years. Look, there is no other way to quality but capital. I pay twice as much for nonsprayed vegetables. I'm located near a college. The kids rant and rave about the environment, but when their tap line gets low, all the ideas go out the window. Bring on Taco Bell! So when I hear you say Uncle Mort has flown the coop, more power to him!

I love the man.

My brother, Frank, thinks he's empty. I think he's full. The man is so full of emotion he can't see anyone! That's the definition of a true and sacred person. Weren't all the saints that way? Just because he doesn't pay his social dues, he's worthless? I don't buy it.

Look, the other night I had to chase one of my cooks around the block. He was running after one of the clerks with a meat cleaver! Says the guy made eyes at his Maria. When I finally tackled the jerk, I got a nice thick gash in my thigh. That's why I'm limping as you're asking me the whereabouts of the one member of my family who figured it out long ago. Just bug out!

Let's not judge. We're all in this mess together. What did my father get for all his love and devotion?

Rosario Oonjree, Second Wife

Not pretty this life, eh? Mort a-gone to I don't know. On second day he no come home, he call-ed me from the desert. That's wryt. He driving, he going somewhere where he can talk forever, maybe. No, he didn't give number. I beg him tell me where he going, why he not come back for special soup I make. He only say, "It's hot." But desert not so hot now, wryt? It winter now. Maybe he playing trick.

I met Mort in church. That true. Funny, 'cause he no go to church after he met me! I go, but he no go. He like my sweater.

I twenty years younger than Mort. Why I marry him? He handsome. Mort more handsome at 60 than much younger man. He have white teeth. He strong. He like to crack joke. He make me laugh. How many people make you laugh all time? They say laugh, you live longer. I think I live to be 110.

I don't like talk. You want more talk? Where I come from? Burma. Why? I fight for democrassy over der. You fight for democrassy, and you get one-way ticket to America. If you luckee.

Mort tell me he love Burmese people. He tow me he in Rangoon for Second War. My people kill-ed by Japanese. Mort tow me he kill-ed Burmese woman by accident. He cry. No one see Mort cry but me. He not happy all the time. Who happy all time in world?

People say Mort a-lazy. But he no lazy around me. He rub me down when I came back from work. I get hurt neck. He help my neck. He very gentle. He use lotion. No. No. I no talk about Mort in bed. That not wryt. He good person in bed. That's enough about it.

Mort have strange people in his fambily. He no visit much 'cause why? He been all over da world and see hell. He saw first H-bomb. That enough to make you wanna crawl in your covers, eh?

I live and let live. I love my Mort. He a little weird, but so what? We all a little weird in this world. I think Mort trying to find someone, something, but who or what, I no know.

I know in my bone he alive. Maybe more than me. I miss my fambily terrible. But they gone long.

Loretta Steele, Ex-model

I received a message on my voice mail from Mortie about a week ago. Shocked the hell out of me. Said he was looking out at a passing train in

Kansas, that his car was broken down and that he was broke, or, rather, couldn't remember his PIN number for that machine that coughs money out of the wall. You know, the ATM? At the time, I was on a very discreet job. I was showing a very high-ranking Japanese official the La Brea Tar Pits. That's what I do these days—I'm a VIP tour guide. Don't smile at me, Officer, and take your eyes off my luggage. Go ahead and laugh. What's a girl supposed to do who's not a girl anymore? You've got a dirty mind, I can see. I'll take a light.

I was pretty much a girl when I met Mort. I swear I haven't seen him for thirty years. He was all broken up when I refused to marry him. That was just after his divorce. Said he'd had it with women.

He sure hadn't given up on women when I met him. He was about as revved as you can get. Maybe it was the sheer boredom of the work. Mort was tending the cash register in that dress shop of his sister's—what was her name? Minnie? Winny? Okay. The store had a nifty name, "Hourglass Fashions," and it was at a nice location. I think it was at the corner of Hollywood and Highland. Anyway, I'd dropped out of Hollywood High School after my boyfriend, whose hair was longer than mine, though my legs were longer than his, told me I was meant for great things. He told me this after putting a little pipe in front of me and telling me to smoke it. It was hashish. Like an idiot, I did. And all the silly things I said afterward and the visions I had of palm trees fornicating with birds-of-paradise convinced him that we should become a road show for peace. What he failed to tell me was whose peace was he pushing, the country's or his? Like, this was the sixties. There was no logic to anything, least of all to a girl who was being raised by her aunt and uncle. My parents died in a car wreck coming over the hill to the Valley on the 405.

Well, that fellow gave me nothing but herpes, to be honest, and in fact, he was a terrible lover—much more interested in staring at himself in a mirror in a haze of dope. One of the little-known facts about marijuana is that it holds the thing down. Believe me, of this I have professional knowledge. Not that you'd turn me in, baby? I think this skirt's a little too split. Sorry my hose sounds. Just trying to keep warm. Isn't that the gentleman of you? Your very jacket to cover my legs. It is cold in here. I don't think my heater's working.

Anyway, I came back to L.A., turned in my granny dress and patchouli oil, and bumped into someone at Sorrento Beach who could not keep his camera off me. Gave me his card. Said I was born to be a model. Said something about my shin bones shining just right. Wow, was that a line! Anyway, like, I was floored. I had to get some good clothes. He handed me three crisp one hundred–dollar bills and said, "Get yourself decked out." Like, what was I to do, give it back? That's what took me to Hourglass Fashions.

Mort looked completely out of place with his cardigan sweater, white shirt and tie, and pipe. He looked more like a professor. Have you ever seen a man work a dress shop? Not me, not since. His sister helped me pick out a raft of dresses. "Oh, dear, you're going to be a star!" she squealed. Mort would comment as I modeled each item: "Nigh!" His thick dark eyebrows jumped, especially at this lilac crepe thing that showed my legs and my back. You could barely hear the *c* in "nice" when you wore something that pleased Mort. He handed me some clothes over the top of the dressing-room door, but he didn't peek in. Mort wasn't a dirty old man. He was actually shy, though I do remember him blurting out, "Toes! Nigh!" His pipe plume was like a distress signal. Mort's marriage was already crumbling.

My modeling career took off like a rocket. The Hourglass was my mainstay. Every week I'd pick out the newest item. Mort would take me for lunch next door at the Schwimmer Deli. He liked pickles. Funny the things you remember. He'd talk about everything—the cold war, the Arabs, the Israelis, the problem of water in L.A., life on Mars, the inevitably of race riots. Mort was brilliant, you know.

There was never a man I had so attentive to what I felt than Mortie. "What pores!" he called out quietly. I was tan all the time. At the beach after coming from the sea, the wind would raise my skin in little points. He kissed my big toe, said I felt more than most people because my second toe was longer than my big toe, then he zigzagged slowly, kissing my instep, and following the vein there with his mouth, then around to the Achilles tendon—touching his tongue to the underside of my calves. God, I can still feel it! I like to die in that sand. What beach was it? Corral?

Once, at my apartment, we kissed for hours. It was Mort who convinced me kissing is more sexy than sex. He painted my body with his tongue. When he finally came in, I was already shivering, then the waves—a white light of liquid rushed out of the center of me in waves and flooded my legs and arms, my chest and toes and temples. And again the surge. My innards just flooded out this hot water. Oh, Lord. Don't get too excited, Officer.

And Mort huffed, "It's like fission. But what do you feel? What is it like for a woman?"

I can count on one finger the number of men who ever asked me that.

"Me? With you? Fusion."

You'll have to excuse me. But that's what I said. I think I had read some dumb article on the nuclear test ban treaty or listened to Mort too long on the difference between the two.

You would have thought that would have turned him on forever. I certainly was the mushroom cloud, spreading. But after he gave out, he rose off me, and went to the window. That was not like Mortie. He liked to linger.

"What's wrong, Mortie?"

"I saw the first H-bomb ever detonated. And plenty after that." I remember the technical word, "detonated," as if he were trying to make sure I believed him. He told me about being in New Mexico guarding the H-bomb in the fifties. He said he was surprised to be alive, that some soldiers he knew and people who lived in the desert had already died of cancer. I'm amazed he is still alive. I said something about, "We have to have it, don't we? The Russians have it. You can't let them bully us."

"And blow the whole human race to hell," he came back. "Might have been better to let the Injun light it all up." He told me about this Indian that almost sabotaged the bomb itself in New Mexico. "Now they can't even figure out where to dump all the radioactive hot sauce. They even think they could shoot the old plutonium to the moon! Biggest hot potato in history!"

Teller? Hmm. Mortie told me never to tell. But you're cute, so I'll tell you.

One day a man in a business suit approached the cyclotron. You know, the thing they make the bomb in? And it was SOP at the time that no one could do that without wearing a white smock. So Mortie trained all guns on him.

Guess who? Edward Teller! The man who invented the goddamn thing!

I said, "Maybe you should have shot him."

Mortie smiled, grunted, and threw me on the bed.

From that point on, every time he came, he'd yell, "The Bomb!" Like he adopted my fantasy, too.

A haunted guy, I miss him. He treated me better than any man, certainly better than my two husbands. He broke down like a baby when I left him. He hadn't figured on losing his wife and his lover at the same time. Why? He was twenty years older. I did the math.

Here's the phone number he gave me. It's a pay phone in Kansas. I called it for a couple of days with no answer. Then I gave up. Thanks. The eye shadow runs. Here's my card.

Charlotte Ballard, Nurse and First Wife

Magnolias! My favorite. Why, that was so very sweet of you to notice, Captain. You're right. That's a tree both California and South Carolina have in common, one of the few things that kept me grounded all those years out West. When things were hard, I'd always take a long walk and inhale the magnolia blossoms—they have a fine, lemony smell—and the sycamores. It reminded me of home. Yes, Nettlesville is one of the only towns around Columbia that Sherman didn't destroy when he came up from Georgia. He burned that whole city to the ground, some say, because South Carolina was the first state to secede from the Union. Pure vengeance. I'm living in an antebellum home, one of the only ones left. That's why the floors sway.

Cindy loves it. She's upstairs. You say you've talked to her already? Hmm. Poor thing. Fifty-two years old and still hungry for a man. I'm not sure I'm hungry for anything but a good peach cobbler. Come to think of it, I have some cooling. Would you care to join me?

Morton Shafik Matter. That's right. Mortie's family was Syrian, the kind that peddled all over this country a century ago. I have a vague memory of seeing an old Syrian with a horse cart as a child doing our back roads, and I think my mother bought linens from him. But that was long before Mort and I met. He was a friendly, warm man who'd call you, "Ya Lady, Ya Lady! Got notions, got linens, got needles, anything, everything!" There was something lonely about him. He slept in our barn once.

I met Mort in Burma. I was his first nurse. He'd been shot just above the heart, very lucky to have made it as far as the field hospital. As I dressed his wound I thought: that's a very striking man. His face had a russet color that it never lost even as he got older, and it made him forever young, someone who seemed very alive, as if he had just come from a shower. I saw this in him even as he slept after we got the bullet out from under a rib. And I thought: I wish I were a rib of him, and he knew it, and never let me be taken out!

Forgive me. I—I can't speak so well now. I've been thinking of your visit for a week now. What would I say? Do I even want him found?

He had this . . . this *way*. When they lifted his stretcher into a medical truck bound for Rangoon and then Australia, he touched his heart like he was pledging allegiance, and took my hand with his free hand. And he looked at me with those dark amber eyes that had a pin of light far down that seemed so hard to struggle to the surface. Then he held my hand to his lips without kissing it and closed his eyes. That one gesture got me through a lot of blood.

We were married a year later at the Presidio in San Francisco when Mort was stationed at Ford Ord. We strolled one night down by the water at Carmel. We sat hip-to-hip looking out, and Mort started reciting some lines from the poet Matthew Arnold. Do you know him? They went, "The Sea of Faith / Was once, too, at the full, and round earth's shore / Lay like the folds of—:" What? I can't remember. A dress? But it ended with something that pulled me into him like iron grains to a magnet: "Ah, love, let us be true to one another! For the world, which seems to lie before us like a land of dreams . . . hath neither joy, nor love, nor light, nor certitude, nor peace, nor help for pain . . ." To a nurse, that was nothing short of a trumpet!

No need to leave the room. I just started shaking like this the past few weeks. Nothing serious. I'll gather myself up. I still have something to tell you.

He had a conscience, Mort did. When we were at Fort Holabird in Maryland, Mort did a secret study that projected U.S. deaths in Vietnam to be fifty thousand. That's about what it was in that wretched war. Mort's study went all the way to the top—to McNamara. That's a fact. But no one acted on it. It was one of the reasons I'm not a general's wife serving you tea. They told Mort: it's either Vietnam to get your bird as a full colonel or out. He said, forget it. That was the biggest mistake of his life. He should have proved them wrong from the inside. Then again he might have had his head blown off.

The dress shop in Hollywood was his downfall. He got soft in his habits and in his body, and, most of all, in his will. Why did I leave him? Young, frouncey women. Hollywood. A man without direction will go there. I know. I just lost my second one that way. You don't have to be in Hollywood for Hollywood to get you.

Why did he send me this? Yes. Turn it in the light. It's part of a rib. Is it human? God only knows where this man got this. For all I know, it may be his. What am I supposed to do? Do I have to lose my mind again?

Then here's the package. Sand. There it is. Everything but the hourglass. He wrote he was in the desert. He was coming to see me as soon as he tracked down someone who lived on a reservation. Said it was the widow of a man he'd met up with long ago. Probably someone from the war, don't you think? He wrote, "Finally, life is all amends." Here's the whole letter. Postmarked Alamogordo.